T0123200

Wilhelm

WILHELM

F. VAWTERS MCCLOUD

WILHELM

iUniverse books may be ordered through booksellers or by contacting:

iUniverse
1663 Liberty Drive
Bloomington, IN 47403
www.iuniverse.com
1-800-Authors (1-800-288-4677)

ISBN: 978-1-5320-1140-5 (sc)
ISBN: 978-1-5320-1139-9 (e)

Library of Congress Control Number: 2016919230

Print information available on the last page.

iUniverse rev. date: 01/25/2017

As righteousness leads to life,
So he who pursues *evil* pursues it to his own *death.*

—Proverbs 11:19

Contents

Lee, Myself, and I 1
Meeting Peyton 11
Bad Company Corrupts Good Character 23
Let Me Try Something New 39
I Am Wilhelm 45
Tabitha's Destiny 57
Being Seen by Maureen 65
Getting to Know Me 69
In Search Of … 75
Zoe's Bed-and-Breakfast 91
Victoria's Plan 99
When the Lie Becomes the Truth 107
House Calls 111
Prayer for Mrs. Scott 119
The Kings Suffer Violence 127
Where Do I Start? 135
Love Conquers All 145
Curiosity … Kills 153
Casey's Confession 161
Regina's Discretion 173
Constantly on My Mind 183
Will Someone Please Listen to Officer MacAleese? 193

Business as Usual 201
Nothing Is as It Seems 207
Prove Me Right 215
A Clean Heart 223
Tying All Loose Ends 227
Old Endings and New Beginnings 233
I Blame You 237
Let It Come to Pass 243
A House Divided 251
Let No Man Put Asunder 259
Love Defined 267
Visions and Dimensions 277
In the Spirit of Wilhelm 285
I Feel Free 295
I Remember: Me 303
I Remember: Lee 311

Lee, Myself, and I

The year 1912 will be gone in less than three weeks, and I am not satisfied with my year's accomplishments. In January, I became a lord under Earl Alistair's authority. I am now a celebrity and considered royal. Still, I am not content.

I have seemingly fulfilled every man's dream. Once you attain this, what is left? Silently sitting alone, my thoughts clutter the room. I have an insatiable need for something more. My twenties have left me. I am now a thirty-year-old man, and I cannot stop the years from passing. Anything that is worth being or praiseworthy is much more esteemed when it is acquired in one's youth.

Seeing a sixty-year-old in a Rolls-Royce is not as impressive as a twenty-five-year-old owning it. Who really gets excited when a fifty-year-old starts a business or obtains fame? It becomes a pathetic speech about never giving up, not how special he is. You are not revered or seen as unique; rather you're an older person who never stopped dreaming. Those observing are only happy because you accomplished something before you actually died!

These inner thoughts of mine are frowned upon by the public but wholeheartedly embraced in private. If I give this speech in front of an audience, I will be called the villain. A young heartless fool who needs to age and acquire more wisdom before I am allowed to speak in public ever again.

I want to laugh because people are such hypocrites! However, the phoniness of the majority prevents me from laughing because I am glaring at them in disgust. If that is the story they hope to tell, I wish them well. That will not be my story. That is not my happy ending, and it definitely will never be my beginning. I have a desire that I have resolved to fulfill.

I have many friends and acquaintances who will flatter me with a false reality. There is not a day that passes that I have not heard how great I am. If I get dressed and walk five feet from this hotel-room door, I will be bombarded with praise. Tonight I am finished hearing their flattery. I have silenced my ears to those who invade my space with a facade of grandeur in hopes of obtaining my favor and friendship.

Lately, my followers annoy me. I no longer see a bounty of well-wishers. I see cowards. I see a multitude of leeches and losers who never purposed to be great but only take comfort in my greatness. I then realize I can openly give this speech. These weak-minded people will probably praise me more. I can hear them supporting how honest and up-front I am. But I digress. I am not upset with the people. I am simply looking for someone to blame for the bleak future I foresee.

Clara's return to our suite interrupts my thoughts. "Why did you go get ice? You know room service will do whatever we ask," I tell her.

Clara is so happy to be here with me. Nothing can remove her smile, which seems permanent. She sets the ice on the bar counter and then immediately heads toward me. Now kneeling in front of me, she answers, "It makes me happy doing things for you."

A typical response. Closing my eyes, I give her a faint smile as I lean my head against the back of my chair.

Clara's very special to me, so I will not dismiss her. She is the sincerest person I have in my life. She goes beyond what is deemed satisfactory to display her unconditional love. However, today I have no desire for love, support, companionship—nothing that the average human longs for.

Clara rises from in front of me and then goes to lie on the bed. I watch as she patiently waits for me to finish whatever it is she perceives I am doing. If I sit in this chair a month, I am sure Clara will not disturb me. I calmly watch her occupy her time until I acknowledge her.

I then say, "Clara, what is it that you desire most? Do not answer saying it's me or this. It must be a goal of some sort. What do you want most that you have not attained?"

Clara is not outwardly beautiful, but she has beautiful features. My favorite attribute that she possesses is her long, flowing jet-black hair. She sits up, pushing her gorgeous hair from her face, exposing her large eyes, which are now fixed upon me. "Are we being philosophical tonight?" She laughs.

"Please be serious," I reply.

She lifts her eyes to the ceiling as if she is deep in thought. I wait patiently as she makes several facial expressions. Finally, she answers, "Wilhelm, truly, I'm content. Maybe I'll receive a Nobel Prize before I die."

"Why before you die? What's wrong with obtaining one now in your youth?"

"Well, surely, I won't reject one in my youth, but I haven't done anything to receive one today!"

"Why are you waiting?"

"Wilhelm, is there a point to this?"

"Yes. Do it now. Why are you waiting until later?"

Clara climbs off the bed and then comes and sits in my lap. She whispers into my ear, "You are so wonderful! Even when you're old, you will be just as magnificent and beautiful! You have nothing to worry about!"

Immediately I lift her off me and say, "Ask me what I desire most."

"What do you desire most?"

"To stay as I am today forever."

"If anyone can accomplish that, it's you, Wilhelm!"

My tour in Paris has ended. We return home a few days before the winter holidays. Clara and I are usually always together, but after our time in France, I want to be alone. I am consumed with accomplishing my goal. This is not a goal many will seek out. This isn't even a goal many, if any, have ever aimed for. Who do I ask to help me?

Despite my upbringing, I have never been into God or the devil, but I know only a supernatural being or experience can grant my request. So too, I have no will to submit to either. However, I know I must make a choice in order to receive this power.

Those who believe in God accept waiting until they die. I guess I will have to seek out the other side. I want my everlasting life now.

I purposed to have Clara as my date for New Year's Eve. There is always a star-studded extravaganza for the elite in our society. Unfortunately for her, I simply want to go alone and spend my night with someone new.

I get to the entrance of the hotel and am greeted with a million camera flashes. Although we are all celebrities, both crowd and celebrity will run to greet me. I leave the hugging and touching of the fanatics to my peers. I simply wave at the masses and then enter our private gala. Of course, Lady Helena is here lurking in the corner, ready to harass me, but as usual, I ignore her.

The night is going well. I have found an alternate date. However, I observe there is a very distinct young man present. I notice he has been watching me throughout the night. Finally, he makes his way to my party. He is related to one of the studio executives. A few people seem to be acquainted with him. He has interesting conversation. Seemingly he's quite intelligent and polished. My party is impressed with him, so they are engrossed in his conversation. Even my date is intrigued. While he has everyone occupied, I decide to get a drink. I walk over to the bar, and Lady Helena meets me.

Despite Helena's mental instability, she is flawlessly beautiful. She is everywhere I am, although we are not together. I know if we were ever in any type of relationship, she would be joined to my hip. She smothers me, and we have never officially met.

I turn around to acknowledge her, and she asks through tear-filled eyes, "Lee, who's here with you? Have you finally left Clara?"

"If I have, why does it matter? I still have not chosen you."

"Will you please make me understand what's so wrong with me?" she whimpers.

"This right here, Helena. Allow me to pursue you. If you ignore me the rest of the night, I will approach you the next time we meet."

She stands speechless, unwilling to leave me alone for one night. While she stands there subdued, I take in her beauty. She smells of lavender and jasmine. Her beautiful grayish-green eyes are magnified because of the lovely emerald gown she is wearing tonight. Helena is petite but shapely. Her body is proportioned just right for her frame. Her hair is neatly put in a bun, displaying her pleasing face. I think to myself, *What a waste.*

I am slightly tempted to take her with me tonight, but then I think of Clara. Clara despises Helena. She recently tried to have Clara removed from my life permanently. Just because I did not bring Clara, my loyalty as her friend will not be compromised for one night with Helena.

She softly answers, "I won't leave here and have you with that woman unattended."

The bartender hands me my drinks. I thank him and then respond, "And this is why I will never choose you."

She grabs my arm. I simply look down at her hand, and Helena immediately releases me. With a slight scowl, I turn and then walk away.

As I head to my date, that young man stops me before I reach her. He greets me. "Lord Wilhelm York, correct?"

"Yes, but you may call me Lee."

"I'm honored to meet you, Lee. How convenient. My name is also Lee."

I give him an inquisitive smirk and then continue walking to my date. "Lee, I wanted to talk business with you, if I may!" Lee calls out.

I turn to face him and ask, "What kind of business?"

"Well, naturally, movie business. I heard you want to go over to the States … among other things."

"Yes. Who told you that?"

"My family owns Berkshire Studios."

Berkshire is the largest production company in Britain. Ninety percent of the entertainers who are exposed in America go through Berkshire Studios.

I take my date her drink and tell her I need to talk business with Lee. She and I met here, so I am not obligated to cater to her needs. I kiss her good night and then go with Lee.

Lee and I have much in common, even in appearance. He is an attractive man. I will assume he is between twenty-seven and thirty years old. We are seemingly the same height. I examine his well-manicured hands. He is well dressed. A man after my own heart. I believe appearance is everything.

We talk business. Then approximately thirty minutes into our conversation, he compliments how well I look. He then suddenly says, "Lee, what's your most desired goal?"

I have been at this party since nine tonight. It is now nearing eleven, so I am slightly intoxicated. Hence, my courage has increased.

"Do you think you can handle my answer?" I respond.

"Try me," Lee replies in a smug tone.

"I simply want to stay as I am forever."

"What have you done to meet this goal?"

"I have been contemplating who I will have to submit to, or is there a way to obtain it without submitting to anyone?"

"I have the answer to your question. Are you interested in hearing it?"

"Of course."

"I know how you can accomplish this goal, but you must submit to something other than yourself."

"What kind of submission is required?"

"It depends solely on your choice. One requires abject submission. The other requires willful submission. One can be obtained later, but the other can be obtained today."

"I want it today."

"I knew you would choose today. Follow me."

I follow Lee to the elevator. We ride to the hotel lobby and then exit through a back door. This door leads to a pitch-black hallway.

"Lee, I cannot see you. Can you see me?" I call out.

"No, simply follow my voice and my footsteps."

His voice startles me! Although I cannot see him, Lee's voice is so loud it seems as if he has spoken directly into my ear. He has to be standing extremely close, but I cannot feel his presence. As we walk, the hall is getting darker and colder. I am now freezing. I call Lee's name, but this time he does not answer. I then extend my hand to feel my way.

I stop and am tempted to turn back, but my need for this power overrules my fear. I continue going forward. The tips of my fingers, toes, and my nose are ice cold. It feels as if I have been dunked into a pool, yet there's a very pleasing aroma saturating the air. I am not wet, but my ears sound muffled as if I am submerged. Light-headed from the sweet yet pungent scent, I feel myself getting sleepy. Now stumbling, I walk slowly, trying to prevent myself from falling. I lose the ability of my legs, which causes me to hit a wall. Still feeling as if I am underwater and drowsy, I begin groping the wall, hoping for a knob. I find one!

I open the door, and I am back at the party. Motionless, I stand perplexed. The room is so loud my ears are ringing. The light is piercing my eyes, and the music is banging my skull! I feel pressure all over my body. My skin feels too tight. I look at my watch, and it is ten minutes until midnight. I discreetly stagger to the bar and sit down. The bartender offers me a drink, but I decline.

My date spots me and begins excitedly waving. She comes to the bar and then kisses my cheek.

"I thought you had left me!" she says.

I whisper into her ear, "Please get me out of here."

Lifting my wrist to see my watch, she says, "Lee, it's less than five minutes until midnight! Please stay! I'll take care of you."

She hands me a glass of champagne as we wait to count down the new year. I hear the countdown. *Ten, nine, eight, seven, six, five, four, three, two, one … happy*

New Year! I hear the celebration in the distance. I feel submerged again, and then everything turns dark.

The smell of alcohol and bleach is strong in the air. I hear a rhythm of short high-pitched beeps. My eyelids feel sealed, but I finally get them open. I slowly pan my surroundings, and I realize I am in a hospital. I have tubes everywhere. I attempt to sit up to Clara's face. She's crying yet smiling. The nurse enters and begins removing some of the tubes and equipment from me. As she checks my vitals, the doctor enters.

"What happened?" I ask, groggy.

"Lord York, you've been in a coma for three weeks," the doctor answers.

I lie lifeless yet stunned. From lack of strength, I cannot display the intensity of my emotions. I calmly say, "Three weeks? What happened?"

"We were hoping you'd tell us."

"I remember sitting at the bar, wanting to go home. My date persuaded me to stay for the New Year's countdown. I heard people say happy new year, and that's all I can recall."

Clara painfully sighs. I am sure I can read her mind, and it's saying I should have taken her with me.

The doctor continues, "We found nothing wrong. You're in exceptional health. However, we do have a major problem. There's a mob outside that refuses to leave until they know you're well. Will you please go to the window and send them away?"

I oblige. Then a couple of days later, I am allowed to go home.

Meeting Peyton

I'm usually a homebody, but this year my friends persuaded me to attend a New Year's Eve party. Parties have never been my forte. I enjoy my solitude.

I had a great but far from average childhood. My parents were killed ten years ago, but they were ideal parents who left me an inheritance. I've never worked a regular job. However, I'll work around the clock for ministry. I'm serious and focused, and I love people.

My friends are fed up with me because they see that I'm not enjoying my youth. My girlfriend, Casey, has determined to take me to this party with a few friends, and she insisted we'd bring in the new year with a champagne toast. Surprisingly, I didn't object. Little does she know, however, I'm actually excited to finally relax and enjoy people without having to solve their problems or comfort them.

We arrive at our destination around ten at night. The party's in a penthouse. I walk in wide-eyed, and my jaw slightly drops. I'm looking around, fawning as if I'm some unfortunate soul who's been granted the opportunity of a lifetime to come here! I ask Casey how she knows these people. She laughs and says that a friend of Maurice's invited us.

Maurice is Casey's boyfriend. He's a high-paid executive at a prominent marketing firm who meets many wealthy people. His firm has been on the Forbes top hundred since 2011. Maurice is terrific, and I love Casey with him. A few more of Maurice's friends attended. Casey and Maurice have set me up with their friend Juan. Juan is nice and attractive, though not my type, but he's tolerable as a date for one night.

Everyone in our party seems fun. I'm immensely enjoying the evening. Then after a couple of glasses of wine, I need to use the restroom. Casey asks if I will bring her a margarita on my way back. I say okay and then leave. As I'm heading toward the bar, I see a very alluring man standing there. He's proper and tall. His skin looks as if he has the perfect tan. He has dark, deep eyes with dark, thick, luscious hair. He's immaculately groomed, and he's beyond beautiful. He's so beautiful I feel entranced. Once his eyes meet mine, it feels as if the room has gone silent. He just watches as I approach the bar counter. The only available space is right next to where he's standing. I smile with my eyes as I turn to the bartender and order Casey's margarita. He then leans in toward me.

"Hello," he says.

I slowly look up into his mysterious eyes and say, "Hello."

"One margarita? Are you here alone?"

"No, I'm here with my friends." I answer as I point toward my table.

He then bends closer, speaking directly into my ear. "Oh, you have a date with you?"

My heart's racing as I'm unconsciously being drawn toward him. I slowly pull myself away. "Yes," I answer.

"Lucky guy. Enjoy your night—" He pauses midsentence, waiting for me to fill in my name.

"Peyton."

"Wilhelm."

He gives an inquisitive smile then says, "Happy New Year."

Smiling, I nod and say, "You too." I return to my party.

When I get to the table, Casey asks, "Did you make every margarita! Jeez, girl. It's almost midnight!" She laughs.

I give a small smirk. She instantly sees I'm highly distracted. "Everything okay?" she discreetly asks me.

I look at Juan and then Maurice, and then I ask, "May I borrow Casey for a minute?"

They're filled with merriment, so they wave us away. Casey trips over my feet, pushing me swiftly toward an exit. She's anxious to know what's going on. I lead her to the balcony, but I keep peeking back at Wilhelm, who's intently watching. Hiding around the corner, I whisper, "I think I'm in love!"

Franticly looking around at the others near us, Casey whispers, "With Juan?"

"No! There's literally an angel at the bar! He initiated a conversation with me as if he likes me and he is gorgeous! Slowly peek around the corner, and he should be right there!"

She quickly goes to look, but I snatch her back. "Slowly, Casey!"

"Okay, freak!" she says and laughs.

She peeks and then instantly jumps back! "I think he's standing right here!" she mouths.

I'm in a state of panic. She puts up her finger, telling me to wait. "You want white or red wine?" she asks through a comical grin.

"Mineral water, please," I answer loudly.

She motions, informing me he's coming. Then she immediately walks away. Casey walks past Wilhelm, purposely not acknowledging him, and sure enough, he's right there.

"Hello, Peyton," he says.

"Hi, Wilhelm."

He whispers into my ear, "I am extremely attracted to you. May I call you? I must know if your mind is just as attractive."

I'm lost in his sexy voice and his perfect lips. My eyes keep returning to them as he speaks. "Sure." I reply, shaking myself from his trance.

Handing me his card, he says, "Please call me."

He immediately walks away as if he knew Casey was around the corner. He walks past her without acknowledging her just as she had done to him earlier.

"I heard everything! I love him too!" she excitedly whispers.

We're all giddy and laughing as we return to our dates.

It's now a minute until the new year, and I see Wilhelm approaching our table. He stops at the table next to us and counts down till midnight with his eyes fixed upon me. After I hug my table of friends, he walks over.

"Hello, Peyton. So good to see you. Happy New Year," he says as if we're old friends and hadn't spoken earlier.

He then slowly and sensually kisses my lips. It's an innocent kiss, but it's the most erotic kiss I have ever had. It captivates the entire table.

Now gazing down at me, he says, "It was good seeing you tonight. I am glad you decided to celebrate here."

He tells my party happy new year, and then he leaves. I drop my head, too embarrassed to look up. I glance at Casey, who's smiling. Maurice looks at Juan and shrugs.

"Who was that?" Juan asks.

"A new acquaintance of mine," I answer while awkwardly shaking my head, still looking at the floor.

"Hmm," Juan simply grunts. There's a moment of silence, and then we return to celebrating.

I'm finally home, and I can't get Wilhelm out of my mind. Where had he come from? Out of all those scantily dressed women, why was he so intrigued with me? Well, it's late, and I'm slightly intoxicated, so I get into bed.

The next morning Casey calls with a thousand and one questions that I cannot answer. She's mesmerized over how lovely he was!

"Peyton, he's so gorgeous he looked frightening!" she says.

"Oh my God, why would you say that? For some reason I felt very uneasy, like something wasn't right about him!"

"Why'd I say that?" She huffs. "I forgot you're the demon chaser! Trust your gut, Pate, but *please* at least call him and confirm it before you write him off! Okay?"

"Yes, ma'am!" I say and chuckle.

We get off the phone, but my antennas are up. My instincts get the best of me. I decide not to call. I shred his card.

Maurice needs help at his firm, so he offers me a position. I'm sure Casey has put the idea in his head that I need a life. I'm home or at church 90 percent of the time, so I accept the opportunity. I started as his public relations trainee, and I actually enjoy it. I get to sit in on the board meetings, and I have purchased more than a dozen new suits. Even if I know little to nothing about marketing, at least I look the part. Maurice has given me my own office overlooking the lake. It's an awesome building, and I must admit to myself that Casey was right. I needed a life!

I've been working approximately two weeks now. I have more responsibility, and I even have an assistant. Her name is Maureen. I'm preparing for our morning meeting in the conference room when Maureen scurries into my office.

"Ms. Meryl, there's someone here to see you!" she says.

Slightly agitated, I respond, "Maureen, you know I have a meeting in five minutes. Take a message and send them away."

"Peyton, I think you want to see him!" she firmly states while grabbing my arm.

I loosen her grasp, wondering why she's being melodramatic. I walk out, and Wilhelm's standing with his back toward me. His hands are in his pockets, and once I walk out, he slowly turns around.

"Peyton, I found you." He sighs.

"Hi, Wilhelm. Yes, you did! Unfortunately, I have a meeting I must be at in approximately one minute! Here's my card. Please call me!"

He immediately stops me by grabbing my arm. "May we do lunch today?"

Startled, looking down at his hand, I firmly say, "Call me."

"I will not take no as an answer," he asserts, still holding my arm.

"Okay, call me at one!" I say as I attempt to rush away.

Slightly frustrated, he says, "Please tell me where you'd like to go. I will make reservations."

"I'm not that fancy, so you'll have to make that decision. Wilhelm, I have to go!"

"One o'clock. I'll be here."

He gently releases my arm. I nod and then hurry to the conference room. I'm a couple of minutes late for my meeting, and Maurice isn't pleased.

At one o'clock sharp, Wilhelm calls. He informs me he's in the black Bentley out front. I get to the car, and there's a driver waiting to open my door. Everyone leaving the office is staring, trying to figure out what the special occasion is. I enter, and Wilhelm's sitting there, motionless. But he looks irresistible. He has on black slacks with an ox blood dress shirt, looking regal yet casual. You can tell his outfit is very expensive. It has been tailored exclusively for him.

It's the dead of winter, but we enter a lovely garden in the building. Inside is a massive greenhouse. It looks like a vision of paradise. There is a small cobblestone building hidden amid the greenery. We're greeted by the host and then led to our own private seating overlooking the frozen lake.

Once seated, I say, "Wilhelm, this is wonderful, but I'm a new employee who was late for my morning meeting. I must be back at the office by two."

He just stares. He's disappointed, I'm sure. Then he simply nods. I sincerely emphasize, "Thank you. This is extremely nice."

He looks and then nods his head again. He explains to the server. "We're short on time, so bring us out salads and wrap my food to go." A doggie bag? I'm impressed. I assumed surely takeout was way beneath his standards. He glances up. Smiling, I thank him yet again.

"Why didn't you call me?" he asks.

"I don't know? I'm new at this, so I wasn't sure what I wanted to do."

I'm too intimidated to look into his eyes as I speak. He lifts my chin with his knuckle, allowing our eyes to meet. "I want to spend more time with you. Let's go out for dinner. I need to get to know you."

I open my mouth to respond, but before I answer, he continues, "You are so beautiful. I have to have you with me."

The sweet, dizzying scent coming from his warm manicured hand relaxes me. I shyly glance up. "Okay. I get off at six," I nervously reply as I look down.

"I will pick you up from home. Say at eight?"

"Wilhelm, I'm not quite comfortable with that yet. Let's just meet after work."

Sadly, I watch too much crime TV. I fear if I move too fast, I may invite over a serial killer. Precautions are wise, but Wilhelm wasn't pleased. Still, he agrees and then returns me to the office.

After work, Wilhelm's waiting for me in the lobby. Every woman in the entire building is asking who this exceptional man is. I secretly smile as I observe their admiration.

I finally greet Wilhelm as Maurice is leaving. He sees us, so he stops, leaves the elevator, and heads our way. He's coming behind Wilhelm, so he taps his back to get Wilhelm's attention and then extends his hand. Wilhelm cuts his eyes at me and then slowly switches his focus to Maurice.

Maurice approaches us, smiling. "Hello, I'm Mr. Carlson, but you may call me Maurice. And you are?"

"Wilhelm Yoorker."

"I remember you from the New Year's party! I set Peyton up with a date, but you ran him away!"

Maurice's laughing, but Wilhelm isn't. He just stares at Maurice as he's speaking. Wilhelm forces a smile and then says, "Well, he sounds like a wise man."

Wilhelm and Maurice size each other up for a few seconds. Maurice then turns to me and asks, "Well, sis, will Casey and I see you tonight? Wilhelm, you're more than welcome to join us."

Wilhelm seems extremely irritated, so I speak for him. "Thanks, Maurice. We will! Tell Casey to save us a spot."

I kiss Maurice's cheek. He nods slightly, checking Wilhelm again. Then he walks away. We leave, and once again, Wilhelm takes me to another exclusive restaurant. It's actually located in the same building as the penthouse from New Year's Eve.

We're eating and having small conversation, and then Wilhelm asks, "Are you attracted to me?"

I'm a little taken aback, but I'm an adult, so I answer, "Yes, I find you very attractive."

"May we make love tonight?" he nonchalantly asks.

"Uh, of course not!" I state very firmly without breaking eye contact!

"How long must I wait before you feel comfortable making love?"

I find his question offensive, but I remain poised and calm. "Uh, never. I will only be making love to my husband!"

"Are you a Christian?" he asks and smirks.

Now frowning, I exclaim, "Very much so!"

At this point I'm livid, but I keep my composure. I expected him to laugh or ask foolish questions, but now he seems to be in a state of disbelief. He glowers at me through squinted eyes and then continues eating. We're silent for about twenty minutes, and then I demand, "Wilhelm, I'm ready to go. Will you please take me to my car?" He nods in agreement, and then we leave.

The building's closed, so he escorts me to my office to get my briefcase and a few other items. Once we get inside, he gently grabs my waist and turns me to face him.

He softly says, "I'm sorry. I'm really not trying to offend you."

He sounds, smells, and feels heavenly. I have no desire for him to let me go, but I know he's trying to seduce me. Deflecting his prurient stare, I gently pull away and say, "I accept your apology, but I need to get home."

"May I see you soon?" He asks.

"Yes, of course. We need to talk more. We don't know anything about one another."

He agrees, and then the next thing I see is Wilhelm standing over me! I'm lying on the lounger bed in my office. I quickly sit up. Frantic, I ask, "*What happened? Why am I lying down?*"

"Relax, Peyton. Are you all right? You just passed out."

I look at my watch, and I have lost almost fifteen minutes! "Was I out for fifteen minutes?"

He suspiciously nods yes. Now I'm really freaked out.

"Wilhelm, please leave! Security will get me safely to my car. I'll call you tomorrow!"

He walks over to me, gently kisses my cheek, and then leaves. I'm so confused! I grab my things and hurry to my car.

I get home, and after I shower, I call Casey. She immediately comes over. She wants to hear all about my date. I tell her how obnoxious he was in asking me that tactless question, but I also tell her that I still desired to see him again. Nevertheless, I have to tell her what happened.

"I'm not being wary or overly dramatic, but something isn't right, Casey!"

"Tell me. How so?"

"Once we got to the office, he apologized, but then I woke up lying on my back on the couch!"

"*What? He drugged you? How's that possible?*" she yells.

"I don't know! He claims I just passed out! Unless the chef drugged me. It seems impossible Wilhelm could have!"

"Peyton, what the hell happened? If you fainted for fifteen minutes, he should've rushed you to the hospital! You can't see him anymore! This is unacceptable!"

Casey then somberly asks, "Did he rape you?"

I shout, "No! I wasn't undressed! I was fully clothed, so that's impossible in fifteen minutes!"

Casey's adamant about me going to the doctor. She's so disgusted that I begin to regret I told her. But she was right. Watching me lying unconscious for fifteen minutes wasn't normal. Thus, I vowed to never go out with him again.

Bad Company Corrupts Good Character

I'm out with my church, passing out flyers when I spot Wilhelm in a local cafe. He's sitting at a table, watching me through the window. I quickly look away and continue the task at hand.

We're actually done for the evening, so I'm headed to my car. I see him crossing the street, but I avoid looking his way. After I close the trunk, I see Wilhelm standing next to me.

"Hello, Peyton. It's good to find you again."

"Hey, Wilhelm. I find that odd since we never attempted to call one another."

Contented, he asks, "Are you disappointed I never called?"

"Yes, I am,"

"Why didn't you call me?" he probes as he moves closer.

"Because I'm the woman." I give an exaggerated smile.

"Are you hungry? May I take you to dinner?"

"Sorry, but I'm working. I'm handing out church flyers. Then afterward, we have prayer. But you're welcome to join us!"

Giving a jaded smirk, he replies, "I will pass. But if I'm still in good standing, may I call you tonight? We need to communicate much more."

I agree. Then all I remember is him leaving. Once again, I wake up! I'm in my car, but I have lost approximately twenty minutes! Had I fainted again? I call a church member and friend Regina. I tell her to let the others know I'm going to my doctor. I assure her I feel fine, but something obviously isn't fine. Thankfully, after my checkup, all tests turn out negative. The doctor's diagnosis is that I'm probably overworked and need a vacation. I'm relieved but confused all the same.

It's eleven at night, and I've finally settled in. I'm online, looking at vacation resorts. I work for recreation and maintaining a social life, meaning I can take a vacation anytime I please. Maurice knows this. He hired Maureen, knowing she's well equipped to take my place if ever I decide working is no longer my thing.

Now lying in bed, I'm thinking of Wilhelm. I put down my tablet and decide to call him. He answers, but Wilhelm never adds anything to his greeting. He always simply says, "Hello, Peyton," and then awaits my response.

"After you left today, I fainted again," I immediately say. He doesn't comment. I continue, "I went to my doctor because this isn't normal. However, he assured me all was well and I'm probably just exhausted."

I stop speaking, and there's a moment of silence. Weird. No "Glad to hear you're fine." No "Well, yes, take it easy." Nothing!

"Well, did I call too late? You seem disinterested in talking tonight," I say.

"I'm just listening. I'm allowing you to completely tell your story. It is the reason you called me, right?"

"Well no, not exactly! I see it's not a good night." I pause, waiting for any response, but still nothing. "Oh! Okay, well, good-bye!" I hang up, regretting I ever called.

There's something wrong with this man. I feel it in my entire being. But I have acquired an attraction to him I can't shake. He immediately calls back. I don't want to answer, but that'll make me look childish. And it'll seem as if I care. However, I don't want him to think I care, so I answer.

He immediately says, "Forgive me. I am not trying to upset you. I am not good at small talk. Time is very valuable to me, so I leave the small talk to others. Once the real conversation starts, then I am more apt to engage."

Wow, Wilhelm. Is it that deep? But I do as he does and just listen. I don't respond. He continues, "I see I have ruined this call, so I will try again tomorrow. Good night."

He waits a few seconds as I sit silently. He politely ends our call.

What in the world just happened? I feel so torn right now. I want desperately to call him back, but he has made me feel so silly that I don't. Now that I've allowed Wilhelm to totally frustrate me, I try to sleep.

Unfortunately, I'm up all night. I call Maureen, letting her know I'm officially on vacation and that she's in charge until I return. This career is her dream, so she's super excited to do so.

I call Casey and let her know I'm headed to Fiji and maybe another island to rest. I'm taking a three-week vacation. Fiji, maybe Tahiti, and end in Hawaii. I actually own a home in Hawaii. Well, I inherited a home in Hawaii, so that's always my final stop.

Fiji is breathtaking. I always stay at an underwater resort at least a couple of nights. I feel submerged in much-needed solace once I get there. After dark, I power off my phone and keep it off until I get to my bungalow.

I cleared my mind a few days. Once I turn my phone back on, I see I have one lone message. It's from Wilhelm. I can't believe how excited I am just seeing his name on my voice mail. I literally have to exhale just to check his message. I listen, "Hello, Peyton. I want to see you today. Hopefully, we are still attempting to get to know one another. Please call me." I call back immediately.

"Hi, Wilhelm, I'm so sorry I'm just getting your call. I'm actually in Fiji. I took my doctor's advice and took a vacation."

"Hello, Peyton. Well, may I come visit you there?"

Is he serious? I hesitate and then stutter, "Um, sure, it's up to you! I don't own Fiji!" I let out a loud, uncomfortable laugh. Of course, he doesn't respond accordingly.

"Well, I am not visiting Fiji. I am visiting you. That's why I'm asking you."

"Wilhelm, laugh a little. I'm not really a comical person either, but you're too serious. Lighten up for me … please."

"Do I need to be funny for you to like me?"

I sigh. "No, of course not. And you're more than welcome to come hang out in Fiji with me. We can't share rooms though! Is that understood?"

"Good, and yes, of course, I will have my own room."

"Actually, meet me in Tahiti. I'm only here a few more days and—"

He cuts me off midsentence, "I can go to Tahiti too. I will see you in a few hours just text me your location. Bye, Peyton. See you soon."

I hang up and immediately call Casey. "What's going on, Peyton?"

"Wilhelm's on his way here!"

"What? Peyton are you crazy! Why is he meeting you in Fiji!"

Shaking my head, I answer, "I don't know! What's happening to me, Casey? I'm not myself! I want to say no, but I can't. I'm so leery of him, but I won't end this relationship. I like him *so* much, and I don't know why!"

"I'm coming to get you. Send your information. Bye!" Casey hangs up.

Surprisingly, Casey gets here before Wilhelm. Hugging her tightly, I say, "You're a great friend! I'm losing my mind, asking a strange man to accompany me to Fiji! Ultimately, he would've followed me to my home!"

"Never mind that. He would've taken your virginity! Don't deceive yourself! Stop acting so naive! No one comes this far and spends thousands just to *attempt* to know you!" she says, rolling her eyes.

Casey was upset and clearly disappointed in me. She sees I feel like an idiot, so she attempts to retract her words.

"But you're a wise woman. You knew you needed help, so you called. A weak person would've fulfilled their lust and then asked for forgiveness, so you're my hero! Personally, I would've called no one," she says and chuckles.

We go out and enjoy the beach, awaiting Wilhelm, but he never calls or shows up. Since Casey's here, I skip Tahiti, and we go straight to Hawaii. She stays with me overnight.

"Well, thanks for the mini trip, but I'm not on vacation. I just needed to get you home safely. I'll see you once you get back to Vermont. Love you." She leaves.

After a few days in Hawaii, I choose to call Wilhelm yet again. He answers nonchalantly with his standard greeting.

"Hey. What happened to you? You changed your mind?" I ask.

"No, I saw you and I got a bungalow. However, I realized you preferred your girlfriend's company, so I enjoyed my solitude and then returned home."

I don't know how to respond. I'm so embarrassed. "Wilhelm, I'm so sorry you felt that way. Why didn't you call and at least ask? All that money to just go back home?"

Wilhelm chuckles. "You know money isn't our problem, Peyton. Control is. I was not upset about being in Fiji. I was upset you deceived me. You made a decision to let me spend time with you. Then once you changed your mind, you called your friend instead of just explaining to me you had changed your mind. I was pretty impressed you were brave enough to invite me on vacation with you, no matter where I slept at night. Despite our not communicating, I am learning a lot about your character."

Was he attacking my character? Now offended, I asked with some sarcasm, "Well, please share what you have learned?"

"Good-bye, Peyton. Please call me once you return to Vermont, okay?"

"No! You call me since my character is being questioned!"

"Peyton, why are you so defensive? I did not say it was negative or positive, but obviously, you have concluded it is negative. Why is that? Explain your hostility."

Oh my goodness! He's so condescending! "Wilhelm, I don't know! But you're making it sound negative. Do you think what you said should've made me feel as if you were complimenting me or not? Do *not* patronize me! I know what you meant!"

"Please. Tell me what I meant?" he calmly asks.

"You meant that I lacked character or integrity to know you were coming but not inform you not to come!"

"Yes! You disagree with that?"

He tricked me. I sat silently a few seconds, thinking before I uttered a word. "You're right. I was wrong. I apologize."

"I accept your apology. I believe you have great character. Most will never just apologize. Most will explain what the other person has done wrong first. Then they might admit they were wrong. Please know that I truly appreciate who you are. But more importantly, I want to see you. Please call me once you get home. I need to see you. Talk to you soon."

He hangs up. My phone's still to my ear as I sit numb, trying to fully comprehend his motives. Wilhelm's a mind manipulator, and I know it; however, I can't figure out his method. It's tightly put together. Somehow I've been perfectly placed within his web of control.

Normally, I'm a woman in control, a woman sober and vigilant. I have never been so intrigued and needy of a man in my life. But to desire to be with someone I hardly know so desperately is very unnerving.

Happy to be back in Vermont, I stop at church before I go home. I kneel at the altar, seeking strength, wisdom, but mostly protection. My state of mind is restless. I sit in meditation for more than an hour. Then I finally head home. I take a long candlelit bath with stress-relieving music playing throughout the house. I light the fireplace and decide to sleep there in front of it for the night. Unfortunately, my restful sleeping is disturbed a little after four in the morning. I'm awakened to my cell phone vibrating. It's Wilhelm.

I wish I could make anyone understand how perfect and beautiful he is to behold. Everything about him is properly and perfectly placed—from the words he speaks to the clothes he wears. He is flawless. It's as if he has a script he follows that keeps him from faltering. Whenever I see his name on my phone, it makes me feel as if God Himself is gracing me with a visit. I know that's almost blasphemous to say, but it's the only description that fully explains how I feel around him. I feel so special because he desires me. I feel superior to all other women because Wilhelm wants me.

I breathe deeply and then answer his call. "Good morning, Wilhelm."

"Good morning, Peyton. Are you awake?"

"Well, I am now." I chuckle.

"I would like to show you something. May we meet? Say in thirty minutes?"

"Yes."

"Great. Meet me at that park next to your office. I will drive once we meet."

What can he possibly want to show me? But I'm enchanted, so I jump up, get dressed, and go meet him without hesitation. Once I'm out of my state of hypnosis, I find myself sitting at the park at five in the morning. I'm about to get into this man's car and let him take me God knows where. Because of our last conversation, I'm too ashamed to back out now, so once his SUV drives up, I man up and get inside.

I lock my seat belt and then look at Wilhelm. He gives a devious smirk, but in a comforting voice, he says, "Thanks for coming. Are you ready?"

I nod yes while looking down. He then lifts my head so that my eyes meet his. "Are you sure? I don't need you nervous."

"I'm fine. Let's go."

We're driving without conversation for about ten minutes. Then he asks, "Why do you trust me?"

"Please, Wilhelm, don't start asking creepy questions. I'm at peace. Don't stress me out while we're on the mountains alone in the middle of nowhere! It will not go well."

"How so?" he asks as he pulls over and parks along the mountain curb.

I instantly jump out of his SUV and start running, but he quickly catches me.

"Peyton, you're making me feel like a monster. Stop it! I'm taking you to a bed-and-breakfast. Very exclusive, nice and quaint. Get in the car. I will not spook you anymore, I promise."

He's turning me into a nutcase! I'm so humiliated. I must've looked like a buffoon running off into the night. Needless to say, the rest of the ride I looked out the passenger's side window, too embarrassed to breathe.

The bed-and-breakfast is amazing. It's a miniature mansion seated neatly in this quaint little city hidden in the mountains. It's all white brick encircled by a white picket fence. We enter to a cozy country atmosphere that smells of blueberry pie. Seemingly, the owners know him. They immediately seat us and treat us like royalty. I'm surprised to find so many people here. I assumed we would be alone, but it looks as if ten couples are present. The owner's daughter is the main hostess, and she's very attractive. She's also more excited to see Wilhelm than I've ever been. She can't conceal her desire for him. Although she's very professional at her craft, I know my being here with him has her frazzled.

Wilhelm and I do not interact with the others. People are speaking, but he's extremely unsociable. I smile and compliment others as they pass, attempting to disguise his unfriendliness. After a few minutes of feeling as if we're treating everyone like they're less than worthy of our presence, a couple I know appears. They called me to pray for their son a few years ago. Their name is Scott—Jonathan and Tracey Scott.

Their son was demonically possessed. Through ministering and prayers, he was delivered. They're so happy to see me, but I'm so embarrassed. How humiliating to be seen at a honeymoon hangout, unmarried, with a man I really don't know! Wilhelm discreetly but immediately goes away and talks to the hostess.

Tracey hugs me and tells me how great her son is doing. I'm embarrassed for a minute, but their testimony delights my soul. I feel as though fate allowed me to come here just to find the Scotts. We had lost contact within a few months of their son's deliverance. Reuniting with them is surely a blessing. They then tell me about a woman named Tabitha Berkley just outside of Dorset. She had witnessed a demonic attack near her home a few weeks ago. They've been encouraging her to seek my help because of how I helped their son. Finally, this date has purpose!

Wilhelm stays away during our entire conversation. Once they leave, he returns. Excited, I tell him, "Thanks so much! If you didn't know, my first job is ministry! My job at the office is for balance, or else I would be in church serving twenty-four seven!"

I go on to explain who the Scotts are, but Wilhelm stops me. "Breathe. I appreciate your excitement, but can you please return to me?" he asks.

I inhale deeply to calm my excitement. I return to my dignified self in his presence and say, "Yes. Because I can talk about God all day!"

I laugh heartily, but he simply gives a pursed smile. Encountering the Scotts leaves Wilhelm very stoic. Something is displeasing to him, and he isn't trying to conceal it. He then motions to get the hostess's attention. Her name is Zoe. Zoe immediately comes and serves us. Thankfully, we still have a pleasant breakfast. We're now headed back to the park. After thirty minutes of silence, I say, "Thanks. That was special. Now I know something about your character."

He doesn't play into my game. He simply smiles with his eyes and then focuses back on the road. Once we get to the park, he leans over to kiss me. He has been kissing me since the first time he ever saw me, so I'm not alarmed. However, he begins to passionately kiss me. I restrain him, but he simply gazes into my eyes and then starts again. I have no will to stop him, so I begin kissing him back. As we're kissing, I feel myself losing my strength. Seemingly, I'm going into a drowsy state. Everything's blurred, and it sounds as if I'm submerged in water. In my weakened state, I'm gesturing, telling Wilhelm to stop, but he continues to kiss me. He starts caressing me too.

"Wilhelm, I'm fainting again!" I struggle to say.

I black out momentarily. Then I jump up, pushing him. I'm in my seat, fighting the air as he calmly sits next to me. "Did I pass out?" I ask. He assures me that I didn't.

Franticly looking around, I realize we're snug in his SUV at the park next to my car. I get out and then tell him through the window, "Thanks again. Talk to you later."

I walk away, perplexed. I unlock my car door and then turn to face him. He's just glaring at me. I smile, get in my car, and then drive away.

The next day the Scotts' friend Tabitha calls. She's ninety-two years old, but she's a very well-cared-for woman. I call her Ms. Tabby. She's extremely wealthy. Her family is composed of royals from Britain. As we build our relationship, she begins to show me pictures of her life as a youth. Their home was literally a castle. Her home near Dorset looks like one, but her childhood home was a real one. Ms. Tabby was very beautiful in her youth, but her mother was extremely beautiful. She suffered from affluenza. She was royalty, but her sense of normalcy was nonexistent. Thus, she became mentally unstable. Her mother had fallen in love with a man who never loved her. She became obsessed and eventually was institutionalized.

Ms. Tabby's history is very interesting. Her life is one to be envied, but her recent experience isn't. She now starts telling me about what she witnessed near her home.

Ms. Tabby would often go out by the lake at night to relax. Young couples frequented her beach as a romantic rendezvous. However, on this particular night, an attractive couple caught her eye, but what she saw traumatized her for life. She actually witnessed a demon or something kill a living human. The man didn't look hideous. She says he was attractive. However, he basically ripped the pretty young lady apart. But whatever he did next, Ms. Tabby didn't stay around to witness. She fled for her life.

Ms. Tabby is very sane. Her age hasn't deterred her mobility in any capacity. However, it was still hard for me to wholeheartedly embrace this story only because it sounded like something straight from a nightmare. Nonetheless, I'm consumed with Ms. Tabby's story. After a week at least a half dozen people from her neighborhood share their own stories about this mysterious being. The people never witnessed a person. They simply felt an eeriness near the lake certain nights. Several others just sensed pure evil in the atmosphere. I listened to story after story. Then I decided to walk her property with a few ministers I knew. After a few visits, we discerned this area definitely harnessed some type of evil.

I take a hiatus from the office so my ministering team and I can go to this community daily. We've been going there for nearly two weeks. I've been so consumed with Ms. Tabby that I've neglected everyone. Then one night as I'm driving to Ms. Tabby's, Casey calls. I haven't spoken to her in more than a week. I answer and put her on speaker.

Annoyed, she asks, "So you quit your job at the office? Peyton, you were doing so well! They love and need you there! What's going on? How's your love life?"

I let out a hearty sigh. "Casey, I know! But everyone who knows me knows ministry is my first love! So the office and definitely Wilhelm, who hasn't called me in weeks, are secondary!"

"And why is that?"

"I told you about the bed-and-breakfast, but I didn't tell you about Zoe!"

"Okay, who's Zoe?" she says and huffs.

"She's the pretty owner of the bed-and-breakfast who was devastated when she saw me with Wilhelm! In fact, I think I've figured out his MO! He's a womanizer. He seduces women, and we become obsessed with him! He then puts you away and only chooses you when he wants you!"

Unmoved, she asks, "How did you come to this conclusion?"

"Because he actually asked to sleep with me our first time out! Remember? And he just wanted to be alone, kissing! He knows he's dangerously handsome, and he uses it to his advantage. Fate led the Scotts there to get me far away from him, and I'm thankful! They were my way of escape!"

"Okay," Casey responds.

"Okay, I have to focus. Love you. Bye."

We get off the phone, but I know Casey is disappointed. Nevertheless, I'm not concerned about pleasing her right now. Love and fun are nothing compared to this task, and anyone who doesn't understand that isn't for me, period. I'm at peace, and I'm more than sure I'm a lost memory in Wilhelm's mind by now.

Let Me Try Something New

After that debacle involving this fanatical couple, I decide the pretty lady at the bed-and-breakfast might set me free. Peyton has not called. I have never wanted for anything, let alone any woman. It was a humbling feeling that I despised.

Zoe has called and invited me to some concert. Concerts are not for me. I tell her I have a box at the opera in New York and ask if she would prefer to go there instead. Naturally, she is ecstatic. We take my jet there and her finite, underprivileged mind is blown. I plan an entire day for her in New York. I give her the royal treatment. We have adjoined suites. She assumes I am being a gentleman, but I have no desire to be intimate with her. I send her to a tailor, and they groom and pamper her properly for tonight's events.

We had breakfast in my suite and lunch at an exclusive restaurant, and we had dinner amongst the movie stars, then we went to the opera. She was astonished. I just watched her. She had never experienced anything like this in her life. There was no convincing her I was not in love with her. However, her appreciation for me began to grieve me. It made me angry at Peyton. I pondered what this woman's problem was.

I guess this is my season to reap what I have sown in countless women's lives. Losing my desire for companionship just to one day need it desperately is so frustrating. Witnessing the person you want so badly act as if she could care less if you live or die is just unnatural cruelty. Maybe Peyton had sold her soul, and I did not know. I shake myself and return my thoughts to Zoe.

During the opera performance, I notice Zoe is getting restless. She wants me to kiss and touch her desperately, but I am so uninterested in her.

I whisper into her ear, "Are you ready to get out of here?"

She replies, "Yes!"

Once we're inside the car, I move to my corner and close my eyes. I feel her moving closer. Then suddenly, I feel her lips kiss mine. I open my eyes and blatantly stare at her. She kisses my neck. I am expressionless. I know she's embarrassed, but I show no mercy. I continue to grimace until she moves back into her corner of the car. Once she's in place, I close my eyes and think of Peyton.

We get to the room, and before she enters my suite, I stop her and say, "I should have told you I am a Christian, so I do not have sex."

I lie, hoping it will stop her annoying petting. I need to know what she knows about me without the unwanted advances. Now that rules are in place, I invite her into my suite.

"So what have you heard about me?" I ask.

"Well, definitely not that you're a Christian," she answers, perturbed.

"Does that bother you?"

"I won't say it bothers me, but I surely choose not to be preached to!"

I give a faint smile as I watch her. She is feigning to be ravished. I continue, "Well, tell me what you have heard."

"I heard you were the ultimate heartbreaker and demented mind controller!" She pouts.

"And you desired to be involved with me?"

Her mannerisms reveal she feels *judged* simply because I lied and said I was righteous. In a catty tone, she replies, "Well, I'm sure you weren't so proper before you were converted!"

Surely, I had judged correctly. I begin to laugh. This woman is so simple it's embarrassing. She was so disgraced by my laughter she jumped up and hurried to the door. I call out, "Zoe! Please come here."

I meet her as she heads my way. I kiss her. Then I begin whispering into her ear. "Earl Alistair was born in 1839. He was only forty-three years my senior. Can I possibly be the Wilhelm you seek?"

She responds between her kisses to my face. "Yes, that's only … ninety years … or so."

"Zoe, that is 175 years ago," I say as I slowly push her off me.

"So?"

Agitated, I ask, "How old do you think I am?"

Nervous, she answers, "Twenty-five?"

"So my father is 150 years my senior?" I frown.

She stands there in a mindless gaze. This Zoe is clueless. I just blatantly let her know this is her last day alive.

Now sober with a confused expression, she says, "Huh?"

"I will answer every question you have. That way you will die knowing all truths concerning Wilhelm York."

I lead her to my bedroom. I lie on my back at the foot of the bed with my feet touching the floor. She is standing in the room doorway as I tap the bed.

"Relax. Come join me." I tease her.

She walks over slowly, frightened and sobbing. I sit up and yell in her face, "Stop crying!"

I watch momentarily as she heaves like a baby after a hard cry. I then give her a lecture. "Zoe, why would you travel out of state in a private jet with a total stranger? Why would you allow a strange man to spend tens of thousands on you and think you deserved this? Did you think I wanted you that badly? Please answer me."

She desperately attempts to answer, but instead she begins screaming uncontrollably. I snap her neck and let her fall lifeless to the bed. I lay her in this very nice marble shower. I must admit that the architectural design and the carefully crafted details are phenomenal. After admiring the craftsmanship, I decide to move her to her own suite, sever her veins, and leave her in her own shower.

I keep her cell phone throughout the night for my amusement. Some loser she was dating called back to back. He then texts, "Please call me I love you! Please don't do this!"

I then decide to scroll through more of her texts, and I see Tracey Scott's name.

Tracey: Hey Zoe! Hope all is well. Just wanted to know if you knew my friend Peyton's boyfriend?"
Zoe: Not particularly why?
Tracey: Peyton just started dating him and asked me if I knew anything about him. I don't, but I told her I'd ask you.
Zoe: What does she want to know?
Tracey: Married? Baby mamas? Gay? Saved! Lol!
Zoe: I know he's extremely wealthy and somewhat of a player, but very charming.
Tracey: Well, that's not good! Lol! Well, thanks anyway. If you hear anything, let me know. God bless!

Since Tracey Scott is Peyton's spy, I think maybe I need to introduce myself.

I sleep soundly and head back to Vermont in the morning. The police call and ask me a few questions.

I simply explain, "Zoe was an obsessed admirer whose bed-and-breakfast my family has frequented for generations. I tried to show her kindness by taking her out, but she was distraught once she learned I was celibate. She basically lost it, so I sent her to her own room. I paid for everything, even her first-class ticket back home. After she became uncontrollable the night before, I had vowed to never be alone with this lunatic again."

They assured me it was suicide. After she slit her wrists, she fell in the marble shower and snapped her neck. She was fully clothed, so the heels surely caused her to slip on the wet pavement. They just thought I should know. I pretend I am devastated. They give their condolences. We end our call.

I Am Wilhelm

Late 1922, the few people I interacted with really began to concern themselves with why I was not aging. I had already been out of the public eye for nearly ten years, but an unfavorable event vehemently resurrected the people's interest in my whereabouts. It is then I decided to become a missing person. I hid for twenty-five years. Then I reemerged in the states. However, this year I recently found a very quiet town in Vermont a few miles from Dorset.

My appetite is modest. Well, I am at peace at how I feed. Life was well, and I was content … until I saw Peyton. She was absolutely beautiful to me. She seemed to possess a glow upon her face. I hoped she was not an angel, but unfortunately she was the closest thing to one in a human body.

An elderly woman recently recognized me. She was a fan of mine from her youth in the 1920s. Her grandmother would show her my work, so as a child, this old woman admired me. She began to follow me, hoping to approach me and say how much I reminded her of … myself. However, the night she followed my date and me, she witnessed me kill her. Because this woman is in her eighties, maybe even her nineties, I know that most won't believe her story. But the small town she lives in believes her because they know she is not senile.

Peyton is actually a minister or something. She is a woman of faith who has been coming here for weeks, praying with the people to comfort them. Because of my state of being, companionship and physical satisfaction has not been a desire I have had in at least sixty years. But once I saw Peyton, I desired her. I had secretly watched Peyton long before I ever approached her. Therefore, tonight I have decided I need her.

I walk right into the midst of their prayer meeting, and the people go ballistic. They are gathering at the bridge, so I follow. Although Peyton does not reside here, she seems to hate me most. In her eyes I am some vile demon, and God has sent her here to destroy me. Unfortunately for her, I have no fear.

They have lured me to the bridge to shoot me, throw a gasoline concoction on me, and then burn me. The men have formed a circle around me, so I pretend to submit by kneeling for them. Just as I go to attack, I see Peyton approaching, so I remain still. She and the town women walk my way with their potion in hand. My head's hanging down. I refuse to look directly into her eyes as she stands next to me. I smell her sweet scent of purity, her undefiled soul, and her perfume.

She responds, "I'm not only good. I smell good too."

Had she known it was me? I'm a little confused, but I remain focused on the crowd. I will not thwart my own plan. I use my dark gift to convince all the women to attack me from behind, yet I have Peyton attack me from the front. She is my shield to prevent the men from shooting me. Everyone is paralyzed from fright, but then someone yells, "Run!" He breaks everyone's concentration, and Peyton realizes she is alone, so I attack her.

I blind the people with a black haze so I can take her virginity and make her unconscious. Once she is out, I take her to my home. I just sit motionless, waiting for Peyton to awaken. She wakes up sobbing and in pain. I say nothing, but I watch her until the fear of me overwhelms her.

"If I'm going to turn into a demon, kill me!" she cries out.

"A demon?" I ask, confused.

I must decide if I want her eternally. As I contemplate this choice, I watch as she agonizes, wails, and prays. She's actually in a state of madness.

I pull her to my face and say, "I'm sorry I am not moved by your tears. I have no feelings, but for some reason, I feel for you. I have watched you for months. I would have waited until the desire ceased, but your town meeting was such a perfect opportunity for me to act that I could no longer resist."

I made love to her and tormented her for a couple of days. I bathed her, fed her, and did everything I thought she needed. However, she is a mute in my presence. I ask questions, but since she refuses to answer, I do whatever I please.

The next morning I check the news to see if anyone is looking for her. I find nothing. Legally, it is too soon for anyone to report her officially missing. The system is always on my side. I did not want to take her out in public, but she was not well. Although I did everything to nourish her, she was dying. I decide I want her alive just a little longer, so I know I need a doctor.

"I do not want you dead yet," I softly say into her ear.

She finally speaks, whimpering, "Please don't let me die! I will be dead soon if you don't help me."

"I definitely don't want that, so what do we do? If I take you to the hospital, you must behave, or a lot of people will die."

She agrees to my terms. I take her to the hospital, and surprisingly, she says nothing. She gets her treatment and goes to sleep. The staff checks to see if she'd been rape and performs their other medical rituals. Everyone finally leaves the room. I pretend I left something behind to remind her to keep quiet, but she is gone. I ask the nurse where they moved her.

She answers, "We didn't move her!"

I patiently wait as the nurse pages the doctor and security. Nonetheless, I am a man of my word. I massacre the entire floor, and then I go home.

I am a wanted phantom. No one knows I was there except Peyton. My anonymity is good, but losing her has me home distraught. I am watching the news, awaiting her appearance. I even visit Tabitha's town, which now resembles a desolate ghost town. The only lit home is Tabitha's.

I return home, forced to wait. As I brood over this situation, I soon realize losing Peyton has revived an unwanted emotion—desperation.

I am not human. I dare not say I am a devil, but I really do not know where I stand as a being. I am alive yet dead. I am human yet demonically possessed. I have chosen to ignore my demons, but today they are relevant. I hate I do not have this woman, so I begin to ask for help. I certainly cannot ask God, but I am certain I know He is more real than even Peyton knows.

I asked for this possession—to remain young, rich, and powerful. Everyone like me has desired to be this wicked being. We do not go around changing people because we frankly don't possess the power to do so. And if per chance we do successfully convert someone, he or she may choose not to be ours and destroy us. We talk as if we have the power, but we do not. We were granted wealth and eternal life, but we are slaves to something sinister and far greater than ourselves.

We are so arrogant and blinded by the power and constant praise from others that we convince ourselves we are God! And this God people blindly praise is really us! My wealth keeps me in that circle of debauchery and wickedness. I see the people and the demons with chains around their necks, leading them like dogs on leashes, yet they swear they are in control.

I know wickedness very well, and their hearts are so wicked I would never warn them of their fate. In fact, it is my comfort and my peace knowing many of us will perish together.

I watch the news all day just to see where they are in catching me. Then behold, my Peyton appears with a precise sketch of me! I have to laugh because clearly, someone just drew a picture of an old photo. A photo she obtained, I am positive, from that old woman who surely thinks she knows my name. However, years ago most called me Lee York. I now go by the name Wilhelm Yoorker. So Peyton was wise not to add a name.

Despite her ignorance, I am still enraptured by her television appearance. I just want to be near her so badly at that moment. While she is at the station, I call and request to speak with her.

This world's media is certainly twisted. They are ecstatic to receive my call. Anything for ratings! Clearly, they see Peyton as a joke, a sport to entertain the senses of the masses on her behalf. So of course, the station leaves her on air to speak with me.

"Hello, Peyton." She says nothing but peers through the camera as if she sees me. I continue, "I will turn myself in to you only."

She looks back to ask what to do. Then she agrees. She asks where, and I simply reply, "Wherever you want." Of course, people are so predictable. She chooses the county jail. I oblige and then head to their hoosegow.

First, I go home and get very dapper. The women will find me irresistible, and the men will envy yet want to be me. All will try to accommodate my every demand, although I am being accused of murdering men, women, and children coldheartedly.

I walk in, and an officer goes to cuff me. I assure him that I will not run, that I want to be there. Of course, he grants my request and leads me into a private holding room without cameras. I sit. Then in comes the woman who has unknowingly tricked me out of my safe haven. I look at no one but Peyton.

I can tell she is extremely uneasy. Smiling, I say, "I am happy to see you again."

She just glares at me in disgust. She then begins asking these scripted questions. It's absurd, but it's clearly what the media wants.

"Are you a vampire?" she asks.

"No."

"Are you a demon?"

"No."

"How were you able to kill all those people alone?" she asks, frustrated.

"I didn't."

"You didn't what?"

"I did not kill all those people."

She aggressively balls up the sheet of questions and then tosses it behind her shoulder. Obviously agitated, she asks, "Well, are you denying raping me?"

Now glaring her way, I brashly reply, "Yes, of course!"

Showing her wounds, she shouts, "Are you denying doing this to me?"

"No," I calmly answer.

It stuns her and the crowd that I answered negatively this time. Frenzied and moving away, she asks, "Why did you agree to do this interview?"

"Because I've missed you."

She turns, telling the police that she is done, that she cannot do this. I call out, "Peyton, I promise I will answer all your questions! But I want it done privately, not like this. May I please have some privacy?"

"No! Are you crazy—"

Midsentence, her spokesperson or whomever stops her and whispers into her ear, and then Peyton reluctantly says, "Fine." They escort her out of my presence.

I am sitting alone now, but I can see her fighting with these people. I see my lawyer enter as well, so I acknowledge him. She is trying desperately to explain that I can get out and that they need to put me in chains or something. They attempt to comfort her, but to no avail. However, they send her back to me, unrestrained. Once again, my plan has succeeded. As soon as she enters the room, I seize her, and we are gone.

She awakens in my home once again. She instantly begins to weep. However, this time, alone in my presence, she speaks. She despondently asks, "Why me?"

"Because you are special."

Through tears, she calmly replies, "I will never submit to the devil!"

"I am not the devil. I am Wilhelm."

"That's not even your real name!"

Laughing, I ask, "It's not? Well, tell me what it is then."

She just shakes her head and then moves into the corner, hugging herself. I begin walking toward her, but she begins to pray loudly. Now prayer is very disturbing. I see nothing. I feel no fear of it. Still, it just makes me uncomfortable approaching her. I guess it warns me that if I ignore it, there may be severe consequences. I stand back as she prays, and she prays for more than an hour. She finally stops, and I instantly attack her. If I wait a nanosecond, I know she will begin to pray again.

This time around I refuse to feed on her because I do not want her to die. However, I bring in my victims and make her watch me murder them. The people cry for her to help them.

I taunt, "She's a woman of God! Let's see if her prayers can save you!" Of course, they never do. After four kills, I ask, "Why do you keep praying to a God that does not answer you? I will give you whatever you desire."

Disgusted, she says, "You were able to lure those people because they rejected God just as you rejected God, so their fate was death. However, I'm here alive! Seemingly, I'm the one person you have no desire to kill, yet I fear God! So He surely answers my prayers!"

"Well, haven't you prayed my death yet?" I ask.

"You're already dead, so that prayer was answered decades ago."

For some reason, that bothered me. I wanted youth and wealth, but I forgot to say I wanted to be alive, actually living forever. I wanted Peyton because she was alive physically and spiritually. I only exist as a spirit. It is a malevolent, malicious spirit that sustains me. Peyton was life for me. I wanted her and to be her. I needed her here because seemingly as of late, this existence was so meaningless. I actually desired death. But I feared death because I knew my end. I stand speechless. I'm thinking of a way to coerce her into accepting me. Unfortunately for her, I respond physically.

She has been with me for days, and I have purposed this time she will not escape. She is getting to know me whether she wants to or not. Several more nights have passed, and I am planning our departure from Vermont. Oddly, Peyton seems peaceful as she watches me.

She asks, "Wilhelm, are you dead or alive?"

"I am both."

"How's that possible?"

"I am not alone in here. I am possessed."

"Can your demon be cast out?"

"Yes, but then I would die and be damned."

Feeling empowered, she asks, "Who told you that? A demon?" I simply nod. "Demons are liars. They won't speak truth. Nor do they know the truth!"

"Peyton, I cannot be saved. I hate your God."

My arrogant response causes her boldness to diminish. She timidly asks, "Why?"

"Why not?"

Looking through me, she pauses and then says with confidence, "Well, I think our encounter has purpose. In fact, I know it does."

Peyton swears she has said something deeply profound. I laugh inside at her ignorance. I pretend as if I do not comprehend her. I endure this positive Christian jargon she's spewing by simply listening.

"Peyton, I did not want to hear your fluffy, feel-good rhetoric then, and I definitely have no need for it now."

I have had Peyton for more than a month now. We own an estate off the pacific coast in Washington. The past few days, she looks lifeless. She tells me she needs the sun. Even though I am hesitant, I take her out to our beach. I take her around six in the evening, giving us an hour or so before the sun sets.

Peyton is lying on her stomach, watching the people. I know she wants to get help. I lie next to her and whisper, "Please do not do that. I am not here to hurt you. What is so wrong with being with me?"

Of course, she does not respond as I gently grab her arm and lift her to sit. We now sit facing each other.

Emotionless, she stares back deep in thought. She then leans in toward me and actually starts kissing me. Shocked, I slightly pull away. I stop to discern her motive. I look deep into her eyes as she begins crying. Crying? That's confusing. Crying is an emotion I have lost and obviously no longer comprehend.

She then pulls me close and begins kissing me intimately. She looks at me in adoration between every kiss. I am so vulnerable. Is she in love with me? Am I experiencing the emotion love with her in my supposedly soulless state? Whatever it was, it made me feel alive. I felt human again. A man in love with his woman.

After months together I learned about Peyton. She is from an upper-middle-class family. Her father was a pastor at a modest church in Montpelier. Her parents were killed in a jet crash when she was nineteen.

Peyton is twenty-eight years old. She is an only child. Her parents were missionaries for decades, traveling all over the world. Her father had the gift of casting out demons, and she was following in his footsteps. This is how she became well known to the locals when it came to religious matters.

The woman who saw me in our town is Tabitha Berkley. She is a very wealthy woman whose family I actually knew from Britain. Tabitha's grandmother was a small-time actress that played as an extra in several of my productions from the early 1900s. Her name was Baroness Helena Berkley, or as we prefer in Britain, Lady Berkley. She stalked me for years.

Because of Helena's obsession, she introduced my work to not only her daughter, Constance Berkley, but

Tabitha as well. Constance died while birthing Tabitha in the insane asylum. Immediately after her death, Helena began to indoctrinate Tabitha with the gospel of Lee Wilhelm York. Three generations of Berkley woman were cursed to serve me.

Helena stalked me, but Constance actually spent time with me. Because I had no needed desire for women, Constance could not comprehend that I did not want her. I never killed her because her crazed obsession amused me. I took pleasure in taunting her and her mother at the same time. I caused a bitter rivalry in that home. And once she was put away, I laughed heartily. Her torment was my amusement, and her death was her own mother's satisfaction.

Tabitha told Peyton, she and Helena would watch my work from dusk till dawn. She was devastated once I was pronounced dead, but she never gave up hope searching for me. After seventy years of nothing about me, she was overjoyed to see a face so identical to her long lost obsession. I had no knowledge she had followed me before. The day she witnessed me kill my date was Tabitha's birthday. Tabitha had purposed to approach me as her own personal gift. Once she discovered I was a monster, she sought Peyton. She simply told Peyton I was missing, not dead. She kept the dark details to herself.

Initially, Peyton was simply entertained by the far-fetched story this little elderly woman had imagined. But once she visited our town, she instinctively knew there was evil. Peyton was excited to deliver me. She felt as if she were finally walking into her destiny.

Tabitha's Destiny

If anyone can proclaim they were born with a silver spoon in their mouth, it would be me. In fact, I would correct you and say, "This spoon is platinum." My family had an abundance of wealth, but we overwhelmingly lacked love and morality.

I was raised by my grandmother, Lady Helena Berkley. She was the star of the family. Helena this, Helena that! The Berkley family sat around the table, praising our beloved Helena. That's what she told me. However, the truth is that once my beautiful mother, Mistress Constance Berkley, was born, Helena envied and then hated her most. This was due to an actor turned lord named Lee York.

Immediately after Helena's death, I started going out regularly. I was twenty years old. The first place I visited was Lord York's estate. His home was phenomenal. The Alistairs refused to sell it to anyone, but it remained well kept via Earl Alistair's dying wishes. There were no photos of Lord York anywhere. The only family photo in the entire estate was a grand painting of Bishop Stratford York and Lady Kate York, his parents. The workers didn't bother me or any of the visitors. They simply let us enjoy his home at our leisure.

I finally made it to Lord York's bedroom, and it was astounding. The entire house smelled as if incense or something was burning, but his room was very potent. I stood in the doorway of this beautiful royal blue room awestruck. I then walked to the foot of his massive bed, which sat between four huge mahogany pillars, unable to move.

Suddenly, someone said, "Regal, isn't it?"

Startled, I quickly turn around to behold a darling middle-aged woman.

"Sorry, I didn't mean to scare you, but I heard the lovely Miss Tabitha Berkley was here, so I had to introduce myself. I'm Tilly Jordan."

The infamous Tilly Jordan. She was once Lord York's most trusted servant who revealed that he was now possessed by a demon. I quickly reply, "I'm honored to meet you, Tilly."

"This estate closes in ten minutes. Would you like to go have tea with me?" she asks. I accept her invitation, and then we leave.

We're at a very quaint cafe on the far side of town. After we're served, I ask, "So how'd you find out Lord York had left God?"

Tilly then takes me back to December 23, 1912. She starts, "Wilhelm was a perfect gentleman. Everyone loved working for him. Every woman worker wanted him, but no one would dare disrespect him by being forward or overbearing. They'd often tease I was his favorite, and I was. But it was more less a student-mentor relationship. Never were we romantically connected, but our relationship blossomed into so much more."

She explains Lord York received this title because he was beloved by Earl Alistair. She didn't know what Lord York had done specifically to receive this title. Nevertheless, it was a legitimate office bestowed upon him.

Tilly and I remained friends for decades. The closer we became, the more she revealed about my grandmother and her obsession for Lord York.

Helena desired him more than anything. She wouldn't attend any function or event, whether a funeral or a wedding, if he were not present. When Helena fell in love with Lord York, he was a mortal man. His family was wealthy yet low in rank among the nobility but still a respected upper-middle-class family. Lord York's beauty as a young boy got him into many places where his family's status could've never taken him. By the time he turned nineteen, he was the lead male of almost every production in Britain. And before he received a title, the masses simply knew him as Lee.

Once Helena found out Lee was an actor, she purchased her way into his productions. He never requested her as a leading lady. Thus, she was always some extra lurking on the set. She wasn't good as an actress, so that halted her plans as well. News began to spread that Lee had planned to take his career permanently to the States, but he was given this lordship. He then decided to stay in our country a little longer. Knowing this information, Helena immediately began thinking of craftier ways to trap Lee. Helena conceived a child by someone other than Lee. In her scheme, that was supposed to make him jealous.

"I wasn't close enough to Helena to discern all her wiles, but seemingly, Wilhelm knew her through and through," Tilly says.

"How do you think he knew?" I ask.

"Before he left God, it was his gift. He had discernment like no other I ever encountered. However, the gifts of God come without repentance. I'm sure even now he still has that gift. Unfortunately, he can see what we desire he'd never see in us." Tilly answers.

Tilly then revealed to me Helena's scheme was marriage. She married a baron who worshipped her. She used him to boast to Lee of how phenomenal she was as a wife. Helena didn't respect marriage, but Lee had been raised contrary. Although Lee was very promiscuous and went from woman to woman often, he still refused to be with her. He despised her obsessive need for him. Moreover, he respected the institution of marriage. His conviction caused him to despise her antics even more.

Helena's plan failed, and once she was pregnant, abortion wasn't an option. This wasn't because she was a woman with motherly love but because of a curse. Helena honored the curse and believed having a baby and offering it as a sacrifice was her last option to obtain Lee as her own. Helena was deceived into not killing Constance at childbirth because she was told her child would be her link to Lee. Constance was Helena's link but definitely not how she desired.

Unfortunately for Helena, Lee had a need for something, but it was no longer women. He would periodically pick and choose certain women once or twice a year to fulfill natural desires, but being with women had almost abandoned him.

Helena was three years Lee's junior. However, Lee stopped aging at age thirty. Although he had lived at least thirty years, the exchange he made kept him looking an age you were unable to determine. If he said he was twenty, you'd believe him. If he said he was twenty-five, you'd believe him. However, if he said he was thirty, you would think, *Oh my, I wouldn't have thought he was that old*!

Constance was born in 1904. Lee was twenty-two years old when she was born. Constance believed he was only twenty. No matter what she heard, he was twenty. Tilly said she didn't know if Lee had told her he was twenty or if she had heard he was twenty, but that age was burned in her consciousness. It was the only age she ever accepted.

Lee rarely heard of rumors inquiring about his unchanging youth. It was Helena and Constance openly warring for him that ignited them. The people were perplexed, trying to comprehend how he was now youthful enough for the daughter yet younger than the mother. Lee blamed Helena for the constant attention to his unique condition. As a result, he hatched this diabolical plan, hoping to destroy both Helena and Constance.

Despite Lee's disdain for Constance, she was every other man's dream. Constance couldn't comprehend why out of every man the one she desired despised her. She knew Lee despised her, but Helena didn't know. As Helena's punishment, he went over to Berkley's estates and requested Constance. Lee courting Helena's daughter was a fate worse than an eternity of torment. Every night he came to take Constance out, Helena cried and cursed God. She sought every witch and supporter of dark magic to kill Constance.

Lee played this game for a couple of years. The night Constance lost her sanity is a night she was out with Lee. There are many stories about what may have happened, but only Lee York knows exactly what happened.

One story is he pretended they were going to run off and get married, and then he told her he'd changed his mind, so she snapped. Another story is he told her it was his last night with her, so she snapped. Still another story says that he tricked her into sleeping with my father, thinking it was him. He then put lights on, and once she saw it was my father, she snapped. However, the one I believe is true—because it almost made me snap—is one day he was no longer around, so she snapped.

Constance was the last person to see Lee before he disappeared. How my mother met my father is a greater mystery. Tilly was even ignorant to their courtship.

Lee was gone approximately six months, and then four months later I was born. This started another slew of rumors, yet my dad vehemently attested that he was the man who had gotten her pregnant. He spoke at the open square how he loved Mistress Constance and how Lord York asked him to make sure she didn't leave this earth without a child! He asserted that was always her one request when Lee would talk with her. Of course, Constance desired Lee's child, but somehow Lee convinced my gullible father that impregnating my mother was a kindness. A kindness bestowed upon them both from their beloved Lord York.

I guess my mother couldn't mentally endure losing Lee and having another man's child. As a result, she went completely insane with no chance of ever regaining her sanity.

After Helena had been dead for years, the chatter of her treachery began to surface. I heard Helena taunted my mother by wearing a pillow under her dress at the asylum. She would say, "You're having sir nobody's baby, and I'm having Lee's son. We are naming him Lord Stratford Lee the second." Her taunts made my mother wail so loud you could hear her throughout the town.

Helena told me story after story about what a terrible child my mother was. The reality is Helena was beyond obsessed with Lee. For as long as I can remember, we watched, talked, lived, prayed, and breathed Lord York. She made me into a recluse. We never left our estate. The new world was considered nothing. All I knew about art was Lee York. All I knew about royalty was our family tree and Lord York. Once Helena died, I was thrust out into the world, but I was consumed with finding Lee York! Nothing else mattered.

My life's been productive. I graduated from college. I've had companionship. But whether a curse or a learned, unwavering obsession, I never desired children or marriage. I only desired Lee.

I heard through British folklore that our beloved Lord York never ages and he's still seeking his one true love. I didn't know if it was true, but it was the truth I desired.

Helena's curse was fulfilled. Constance was dead. And my sacrifice was fulfilled. I found Lee.

Peyton is a lovely girl. I heard through the Scotts some eerily attractive man had accompanied her to the bed-and-breakfast. I instinctively knew it was him. I needed her to lead my love back to me. He possessed the power of eternal youth. Therefore, my age never deterred me from seeking him. I believe once he finds me, he'll restore my youth. He'll then make me his eternally!

Being Seen by Maureen

Peyton was not pleased with our first date. I did not plan on taking her home tonight. I was certain she would desire we make love. Then we would progress from there. Once we're in her office, she seems slightly agitated and eager for me to leave. I'm unwilling to just go my way. I suppress her with demonic powers. Then she falls unconscious. She is not possessed or oppressed. I am inhibiting her life, which is slowly suffocating her, as I decide what to do.

I lay her on the couch in her office. Her scent is so natural and tantalizing that I begin to sniff her in her comatose state. I observe her lifeless body and begin to get lost in her beauty. I gently kiss her lips, which taste like candy. I lick my own lips to remove her sweet gloss off my mouth. I momentarily admire her as she remains unconscious. I then kiss her again.

I assumed my desire to devour her would be aroused, but it was not. I only desired she'd want me in the same way. My emotions are confusing me. I could have tried to possess her and make her submit to me against her will, but I did not desire her that way. I am overpowered by a need that will only be fulfilled if she willingly chooses me.

I walk over to her desk and sit and stare at her motionless body. I know I need to wake her soon, or she probably will be dead shortly. I sit, pondering what to do. I begin to look through her drawers, not expecting to find anything. I am simply occupying my time. There is a picture of a middle-aged couple on her desk. I assume they are her parents. They are attractive people. Her mother is beautiful, but Peyton looks more like her father. I remove the picture from the frame. The back confirms that they're her parents. I look at them and frown. They made her this counterfeit angel.

I return the picture to its frame and then go to Peyton. Lifting her head, I close my eyes and gently kiss her face. I then decide I want her to come with me. As I prepare to take her, I open my eyes to a woman peeking through Peyton's office window, watching us. I gently lay Peyton down and go to greet her. She turns and begins walking quickly down the hall.

"Excuse me!" I shout. She stops briefly and then keeps walking. "Please! I need some help!"

The young lady finally stops and then slowly heads back toward me. She's now standing in front of me.

I say, "Hello. My name is Will. What's yours?"

She hesitates and then responds, "Hello. My name is Maureen."

"Hello, Maureen. Do you know Peyton?"

Shaking her head, she answers, "No, I'm a temp worker. I'm simply looking for someone who can help me."

I sense she is extremely nervous. I never lose eye contact as I examine her body language.

"Peyton had too much to drink at dinner, so she is resting for a minute. I am just about to wake her. Where will you be? I will have her come help you?"

"Thanks, but I think I figured it out!" Maureen replies.

"Please, will you assist me in waking Peyton?" I keep my eyes fixed on her.

Maureen stands earnestly thinking of a way to avoid returning to Peyton's office. As we stand in the middle of the room staring at each other, another female coworker comes over.

"Excuse me, Maureen. I need your help immediately!" she says.

"Help from a temp?" I ask, my eyes still fixed upon Maureen.

"Pardon me? I'm not a temp!" the woman responds.

"No, pardon me. Thank you for your help, Maureen. I would appreciate your discretion." I give a daunting smirk. Maureen nods. Then I return to Peyton.

Peyton has been unconscious way too long. I immediately bring her back. She awakes instantly. I am still standing over her. She wakes up hysterical. I cannot lie to her. Clearly, she was unconscious. I have no clever response, so I just watch as she franticly gathers her belongings. She asks me to leave and calls security, and then she calls Maureen.

"You are looking for the temp, Maureen?" I ask.

Peyton is so upset she is fidgeting and rumbling through her briefcase.

"What? I need my assistant!" she says through her scowl.

She picks up her desk phone and pages Maureen. She hangs up and promises she will call, but she begs me to please leave now. Although I am contemplating taking her against her will, I calmly leave, closing her door behind me.

I see Maureen approaching. I'm headed her way toward the elevators. I happen to read the nameplate at the desk directly outside Peyton's office, and it reads, "Maureen Reagan."

I ask, "Ms. Reagan, why would you lie to me?"

She tried to pass without acknowledging me. My words startle her. She abruptly stops.

She responds, "I don't know you. A woman has to protect herself."

"Do I look dangerous?" I smile.

Smiling, she answers, "No, but looks can be deceiving."

"So very true. Well, Ms. Reagan, I am sure we will meet again."

She goes to smile, but I suppose my glaring makes her uneasy. She becomes tense as she shakes my extended hand. She watches me as I walk to the elevator. I get inside, and she is still watching. I stand glaring at her. As the doors close, I wave good-bye.

Getting to Know Me

Going to the beach became our routine. I purchased our home in Washington, hoping that would make Peyton forget who I was in Vermont. We were a real couple for half a year. Then one day Peyton disappeared. She always walked the shore, collecting seashells off the beach. She'd use them to create little trinkets, journals, or jewelry. I stood up to tell her, "Let's go home," but she was nowhere to be found.

All night I called her cell phone repeatedly. She never answered. I cannot call the police, so I am forced to wait. After a week of not hearing from her, my heart is shattered. Her cell phone is now disconnected. What? I am now confused, depressed, but mostly angry.

I am feeding more to kill. Then after two weeks, I hear her voice. I go to the television, and there she is, beautiful, well taken care of, and exploiting me! Her first words are, "By the grace of God—" That's all I needed to hear, and my love turned to pure hatred. I vowed I would find her, torment her, and kill her luridly.

She continues, "I couldn't understand why God allowed this to happen to me, but as time passed, I saw clearly why I was chosen. I know all his weaknesses, and I alone know how to destroy it!"

Wow! I was an *it*. I wasn't even a man to her. I had so many tormenting nights, dreaming and envisioning all the time we spent together. I told her a century of stories. She laughed and initiated intimacy almost every day, yet I was the wicked one? What type of heartless being could pull this off without training? The pain in my newfound heart is excruciating. I am ready to end it as long as I am granted my last request to destroy her first.

In the past I was pretty brutal. Now I am the worst thing you ever want to encounter. My victims are unrecognizable once I kill them.

Peyton's story is relevant for a few weeks, but after a few months, I cannot find her story so easily. It is now time to act. Finding her was fairly easy. I simply befriended the ghost magazines, papers, and paranormal stations that relentlessly interviewed her through hired help.

The night I decide to confront Peyton is on a yacht. She is now a celebrity in the paranormal community. She is often invited to some ritzy event, but tonight is my night. I am dressed to perfection to greet her. I do not let her know I am there until the yacht docks. I watch her dance and laugh. She looks glorious. I am intoxicated by her smell, her voice, her joy. I actually shed a tear. Who knew I could cry? Seeing her this happy because she is free stabs at my renewed heart. I watch her walk alone to the balcony overlooking the ocean. I wait until she closes her eyes, taking in the breeze. Then I whisper into her ear, "I found you." She instantly is in pure terror and rightfully so.

I continue, "I surely despised your interviews. You successfully deceived me because I truly thought you wanted me."

As she goes to speak, her so-called man joins us. His name is Simon. He kisses her and then extends his hand to me for a shake. Peyton instantly snatches his hand back.

"Simon, I will be downstairs shortly!" she says, nervously glancing at me.

"No need," I interrupt as I extend my hand and introduce myself. "I am Will Yoorker. Nice to meet you, Simon."

Faintly smiling, he shakes my hand and then turns to Peyton to ask if she's all right. Peyton just stares wide-eyed.

Staring back, I say, "Talk to you soon." I give an artificial smile, and then I leave.

She looks tormented. I am pleased. I am not content or satisfied, but I'm glad this process has started. I go to the cliff that evening, just staring out into the vastness of the ocean. I must have stood there for days, hoping, wishing, but then finally, I accept that she hates me.

Our last cordial encounter is at the mall. She is looking through suits. I am watching her from a distance. She must have sensed my presence because she begins to look, around and her eyes find mine, which are piercing through her soul. I approach her, and she immediately tenses up and begins panning the room for potential help.

"Peyton, we need to talk."

She briefly closes her eyes and begins to shake her head. As I am moving toward her, she is moving backward, so I stop.

"I am not here to abduct you. I just really miss us. I hope that we can be together somehow."

She looks up at me as if she cannot believe I have said this. I am standing still, but she continues to slowly back away. Stopping momentarily behind a rack of clothes, she sharply says, "Wilhelm, I'm not going anywhere alone with you."

"We can stay here if you like. It does not matter to me," I explain as I move toward her.

Moving away, she says, "And do what? Display our relationship in the open? What are you talking about?"

"Well, we can go to a discreet location—"

She interrupts, yelling under her breath, "I'm not going anywhere alone with you, Wilhelm!"

She franticly begins looking around, searching for a way of escape. I raise my hands, motioning for her to relax.

"Peyton, please help me. I want you to cast my demon out. I am willing to take that chance. Save me." I start begging.

She instantly becomes perturbed. She then looks through me with those magnifying eyes that appear to see every inch of your motives and being. "You can't be saved," she replies.

I reach out to grab her, but she escapes my slight lunge and screams, "Fire! Please help me!"

I teleport to a hidden corner. I watch as she is surrounded by security, employees, and a host of people. I stand in the shadows, watching intently, wishing so badly she would have come with me for one last time.

Peyton was right. I had no desire to be saved, but I did desire we try to spend time together. I was really trying to be human for her, but to no avail. I was now ready to end this madness. The little heart I found when we were together was altogether stone. It may have become diamond. It was the hardest element ever created sitting inside my chest.

She actually moved into church after that encounter, praying without ceasing with her people of God. The church remained filled. I could easily come in and pretend to pray with the crowd. She cried and moaned on the altar, and then around two in the morning, she headed to the back to sleep. I sat in the corridor, waiting to take her, but then I was constrained and reminded church was not the wisest place to act. I'm getting angrier and angrier! Inside I'm screaming, *Think, Will! Think!* I then decide to visit Tabitha.

I get to Tabitha's. She is elated to see me. I want to appear saddened or anxious, but the only emotion I can conjure up is hatred.

"Ms. Berkley, I need a favor," I say.

"You are perfect!" she says, gushing. I do not respond. "Whatever you need, Lee."

I sharply correct her and say, "I am Wilhelm! I need you to call Peyton. I will do the rest."

Tabitha adheres to my request without questioning. She calls, and Peyton answers, startled.

"Ms. Tabby? It's 2:00a.m. Are you okay?"

I immediately take the phone. "Hello, Peyton. We need you to come over to Ms. Berkley's, or she will die. And her death will be on your hands."

As I am speaking, I am looking directly into Tabitha's eyes. Her face turns ghastly. Her eyes have widened as far as they can go. Peyton is thinking of a rebuttal. I wait silently a few seconds. Then I tell her, "You have two hours, but please come sooner. I am extremely anxious to see you."

I stand in the foyer awaiting her arrival. My promise of a brutal death to Tabitha convinces her to leave me undisturbed. Peyton finally arrives. She must have wept the entire way here. Her eyes are squinty, no makeup, her hair pulled back. She looks extremely exhausted. Still, she is the most beautiful woman I have ever seen at that moment. I grab her hand as she stares at Tabitha. Tabitha then falls to her knees and asks Peyton to forgive her.

Tabitha started this debacle, but it was all an affront. She never feared me or wanted me destroyed. She simply wanted to have me, but Peyton and I are paying the price. Neither Peyton nor I respond. Then we leave.

In Search Of …

Wilhelm has zoned out on the beach. Finally, he has let his guard down. Quickly, I go to the beach store. The owner's name is Victoria. Victoria's watching me creep out her back door. She's helping other customers, but her focus is on me. I smile and give her a thumbs-up to comfort her. She nods, smiling, and then she returns her focus to her customers.

I sneak out the back, sprint to the parking lot, and search for open cars. I prayed there would be keys in a glove compartment like on television, but that would be a miracle within this miracle. I find the SUV hatch filled with clothes and bags as if someone is living in their car. I hide inside. I know running down the road will surely get me found by Wilhelm. I hid in this heap for centuries, it seemed, but approximately ten minutes later, five college students enter. They're headed to the local Ocean's View Grill.

Once they get to their desired location, I exit their vehicle, go to the office building across the street, and call a cab. I take the cab to the nearest bus route that will take me to the airport. I only have forty dollars in my possession. I need money, so I stop at a convenient store and call Casey. She instantly starts crying.

"Oh my God, Peyton! Where are you? I've been losing my mind! Maurice, Peyton's on the phone! Oh, thank God! Hallelujah!"

"Hallelujah, but please listen. My time is limited!"

"What? Why? What's happening?"

"I'm running for my life! I'm in Washington state. Please purchase me a flight back to Vermont! The first plane leaves in four hours. Please wire me money. I need to purchase a cell phone and clothing to disguise myself!"

"I don't understand—"

"*Casey, please!* I'll tell you everything once I'm safe! Just please hurry and do as I've asked!"

She gets my information and wires me money within the hour. I get a short wig and colored contacts. I purchase a cell phone under Casey's name. Then I prepare to go home.

I'm waiting in the airport so stressed I feel as though I'm on the verge of a panic attack. I feel myself slightly hyperventilating. Instantly, I begin to pray and think of where I can go in Vermont without putting anyone at risk. I know by now Wilhelm is in full recovery mode.

I'm watching the people live their *normal lives*. Do they even realize how blessed and fortunate they are? Sadly, most aren't thankful. Most see nothing good in this day. Instantly, I begin to count my blessings. It's truly a miracle I'm free. It was the wisdom of God that even gave me the strength to stay calm and focused enough to endure Wilhelm until he trusted me.

Finally, my plane is ready to board. Once I get to Vermont, I get a hotel room. Casey is begging me to come to her home. I tell her to meet me at the church. I don't want to lead him straight to her front door!

Maurice, Casey, and Regina meet me there. We just hug, cry, and pray.

"The police told the pastor you were in a psychiatric hospital! Wilhelm's lawyer submitted paperwork and everything! What's going on?" Casey frantically asks.

"That's a lie. I'm glad it's just us three because what I'm about to share will make me seem insane, but I'm not!"

I begin to share my horror stories. They are flabbergasted. They all weep as I tell my terrifying ordeal.

Maurice responds, "I know it sounds crazy, but you need to come out of hiding immediately! Now you need the public, security, paparazzi, just whoever watching you! The public attention will keep him at bay."

As much as I dread Wilhelm knowing where I am, Maurice is right. I wanted to wait another day, but time was limited. I go to the police. They suggest I remain missing a week or two to coerce him into turning himself in. I thought the police were giving me sound advice. However, their real reasoning for that suggestion had little to do with convincing Wilhelm to surrender. Police are trained to be logical. Demon chasing isn't a part of their duty or logic. Because of their lack of concern, I needed security.

Upon my return, I was pampered and comforted by all involved. My church hired me security. My two-week, round-the-clock protection was heavenly. Then the dreaded day came. The media people interviewing me dolled me up like I was a mega superstar. The hair, the makeup, clothes, jewelry—they just wanted me to shine as I exposed that the supernatural world was real. I was a nervous wreck, but as the cameras rolled, I began to feel empowered. This was my ordained platform. I talked about the power of God and the truth of the devil so boldly. I may never get this chance again.

"Ms. Meryl, it's documented that you have been under psychological care since your disappearance," the interviewer says.

"No, I've been hidden in a secluded area off the West Coast."

"Do you know where you were?"

"Honestly, no. Most times it felt as if I were in a different dimension."

"Did he ever say his name? Perhaps he's the spirit of someone known."

"The name he's given is irrelevant. It's only a cover-up. Demons have names. That's the name I need to know, even the world. That way, if ever it appears again, it can be called out and cast back into hell where it belongs."

"So he wasn't a man but a ghost? You weren't with a physical being?"

I look out into Regina's devastated eyes, Maurice's confused eyes, and Casey's skeptical eyes. I take a deep breath and then answer, "The spiritual world is more real than this physical world. Even if it's not physically visible to the masses, the person who comes in contact with that world experiences a real world that seems tangible. However, who or what he is isn't the story I want to expose. The story I'm compelled to tell is of good and evil—the story of God … and His and the saints of God's enemy, the devil. If you never believed or thought this battle was real, I am here to tell the world it's very real. I've seen into the pits of hell. If you don't desire to go, believe serving Jesus Christ is your only way out of an eternity of torment."

The interviewer lets me preach on salvation for approximately ten minutes before she leads me back to a paranormal story. I vaguely entertain her questions, and then the interview ends.

After my initial interview, I had no rest. For at least three months, I had interviews, photo shoots, or media broadcasts of some sort that I was asked to attend. After a couple of interviews, the *normal* world was done hearing about this story. The paranormal world was too, but people never tired of hearing about Wilhelm. They never stopped treating me like a celebrity. And the studio invitations were escalating.

I thought my nightmare was over because it took Wilhelm approximately six months to approach me. He revealed he had found me seemingly as soon as I came out of hiding. Wilhelm was wise. He did nothing rashly. Everything he did was plotted, planned, and successfully completed. The day Wilhelm returned to me, the paranormal television network was celebrating because their viewing public was escalating. I was invited because my interviews were amongst the top-ten shows on their network. I captured a Christian audience for them. This celebration took place in California on a yacht. I actually had a date when Wilhelm found me, and he was extremely annoying. After a few hours, I wanted to be rid of him.

The yacht had to take us back to the mainland, so I decided to go to the upper deck. I needed the ocean breeze to relax my mind. I close my eyes, and before I exhale, I hear Wilhelm's voice. Immediately, I'm relieved. I open my eyes to behold his beautiful face. How can someone this evil be so unimaginably beautiful? I fear seeing him, but the sound of his voice is so comforting and his tone alluring. His spell is certainly being cast.

I often say Wilhelm has me entranced, but not literally. I'm not in a controlled state of mind. I willingly want Wilhelm. My heightened fear is slowly dwindling the longer I stare into his almost weepy eyes. He looks so sad and wanting. I just watch as he stands in my personal space, gazing down at me.

I watch longingly as he examines me as if I'm an intricate painting. After he takes a thorough view of my face and hair, he lightly bites his bottom lip very sensuously. He then moves my hanging hair to one side of my neck. He slightly leans in to smell me. It's not creepy or awkward but erotic. He then whispers, "You always smell so good."

I stand overwhelmed at how much I desire him in this moment. Wilhelm slowly walks behind me. He leans in to whisper into my bare ear. He begins to breathe deeply. He isn't touching me, but his closeness is so seductive and arousing that I shiver. The chill goes down my spine. He continues breathing a few seconds more before he speaks. He explains how I deceived him into believing I wanted him. Then he pleads, "Don't you want me?"

He rises and returns to facing me. His expression displays a needful yearning. I am defenseless. I stand in awe of his gentleness and neediness. He's vulnerable and endearing. I wanted to have him right here on the deck of this yacht. Wilhelm's staring, awaiting my answer, and my mouth has slightly dropped open from desire. I go to tell him yes, and then instantly, Simon awakens me from my hypnotic state of mind by hugging my waist. He extends his hand to shake Wilhelm's. Instantaneously, I have a vision of Wilhelm stretching out his hand and ripping off Simon's head. I jerk Simon away immediately. I'm sure he thinks I've gone mad!

However, seeing my desire and the ignorance of Simon to his identity, allows Wilhelm to stay poised. He realizes he's able to hatch a newer and better scheme than abducting me like a criminal.

Wilhelm shakes Simon's hand and politely introduces himself. Then he just leaves. Watching Wilhelm walk away was torturous! I can't even find the words to reveal his identity to Simon. Simon touches me again, waking me from my entranced state. My mouth was still hanging open, and I drooled. I discreetly wipe my mouth with the back of my hand. I fix my hair and then turn my head away from Simon. I desperately want to go with Wilhelm. I can't even look Simon in his eyes. I'm tormented when I think of kissing his sweet lips and my ardent need to be near him. I try to hold back my tears, but I feel them streaming down my face. I remain facing opposite Simon. I ask him to please leave me to myself for a few more minutes. Simon respects my wishes and quietly leaves.

I get home and decide I'm tired of the freak celebrity life. I begin rejecting the nonstop invitations. I want to return to the office. I just want to feel normal again.

I'm at the mall, looking for new suits. I'm hoping to start the week off at work. As I'm shopping, I can feel Wilhelm's presence. I try to ignore it, but it's so prevalent I begin to pan my surroundings. I find him lurking in the corner. Once our eyes meet, he immediately starts heading my way. I want to run, but I know he'll catch me. Then I'll be back at square one. I remain calm outside, but on the inside I'm screaming. I refuse to stay near him as I had on the yacht. Surely, this time I'd be persuaded to leave with him.

Although fearful, a sigh of relief comes over me. After analyzing my contentment in seeing him, he attempts to get next to me, but I steadily move away.

"Please stop moving. We need to talk," he says.

"Was that you on the phone last night?" I ask.

"Yes."

"Well, explain yourself."

"Pardon me? What am I explaining?"

Casey wasn't feeling my interviews or my supposed hate for Wilhelm. She and I had gotten into a terrible argument the other night. We didn't yell or anything, but I knew she purposely wanted to get a reaction out of me by making mention of a woman she suddenly met who may have been with Wilhelm.

I immediately ask, "Is it true what Casey has said?"

"How would Casey know anything about my life? You're the only one who knows me, Peyton. Have I ever had a girlfriend?"

"No."

He moves closer, but I step away again. He asks if we can go somewhere alone, but I adamantly refuse. He then talks about how he's willing to change, but I'm only interested in this girlfriend.

"Wilhelm, Casey says she's a lawyer."

Looking into my eyes, which I'm sure are filled with pain, he replies, "She was my Simon. Wasn't he your boyfriend? Weren't you intimate with him in my absence?"

I stand speechless. He continues, "Answer me! Why do you feel justified in having an intimate relationship, yet seemingly, you feel wronged and at liberty to question who I may have been with? Today, let's start anew. No more master-and-slave mentality. Let's be mates."

"I thought you were devoid of affection and had no need for intimacy until we met."

"What's your point?" he says and shrugs.

I can't believe his words. I don't know how to even feel. Unfortunately, I feel devastated and betrayed. Then I want to be far away from this devil. I begin searching for safety. He then calls out, "Peyton! Free me from this demon. Cast him out!" He then manically whispers, "Save me."

Disgusted, I say, "Devil, you can't be saved!" I yell and then run for safety.

Again, he quietly goes away. I try to explain my dilemma to the security, but I just stop. I simply ask they get me safely to my car.

It's now apparent he's coming to get me. I resolve to live in church. I tell Casey and Regina of my choice. They begin to tell every member they know. I am overwhelmed with support.

Casey stays with me the first night at the church. Alone in my office, she says, "I know you don't want to relive that nightmare, but can you share with me what happened? I get the interviews, the demonic parts, and all that, but what is it he wants so desperately from you?"

With a blank stare, I sit unable to speak for about ten minutes. Casey sits patiently waiting for me to muster up the courage to talk. Tears begin to flow, but I answer, "Love."

"Did he actually say that?" she asks, confused.

"No, and he never said he loved me either. Still, that is what he lacked, never experienced. His parents, women, many people loved him, but he never loved anyone but himself. That isn't love. It's self-worship and pride."

Casey stares. I ask, "Casey, what do you want me to say?"

She huffs and says, "Peyton, what were you doing with him all this time?"

I simply stare at her emotionless. Never will I verbally reveal the things I had to endure with anyone. I didn't have the courage to speak the words. She inquisitively glares as I shake my head no. She quietly leaves. I cry myself to sleep.

Casey came to the church to pray with me, but my silence bothered her. Regina revealed to me that Casey thought maybe I was possessed. Casey couldn't comprehend why I refused to talk about it. She concluded I was protecting Wilhelm. That he needed love was the most asinine response I could have given in her mind.

That answer defied logic, which proved I was obviously in love with evil. She was so wrong. Still, her untrue cancer spread throughout the church.

The members who didn't personally know me never wavered in prayer for me. However, those who knew me were now divided. Regina's team respected my wishes to keep my secrets. However, Casey's team was fully persuaded I needed my own exorcism. Nevertheless, the truth is that I'm somewhere in the middle.

I wasn't possessed by a demon, but I did feel oppressed when I thought of this romantic relationship I shared with Wilhelm for half a year. It often left me feeling as if I were going insane. Regina's undying faith in me kept me balanced. Whenever I asked myself how I could be with him and not be infected, she always reminded me of my holiness.

She'd say, "It's the stronger man who keeps this evil spirit out!"

Whenever I heard those words, I'd feel strong, but my constant thinking of him kept me on the verge of insanity.

I hate that I love looking at Wilhelm. I love his voice. I admire his wisdom, and I'm intrigued by his very existence. Whenever we were out together, I felt like royalty. People treated him like he was a king. But when we were alone, I often felt like I was in the pit of hell. He acted for the public, but he revealed who he truly was in private. That part of Wilhelm was who I didn't want to see. He asked so many questions. The conversation I remember most was about love, but he never dared to say the word. It was as if he were selling out to God if he even mentioned the word.

We were sitting in our home's library, no lights, just the fireplace. I was sitting on the floor next to it. He was sitting in a chair hidden in the corner. The rest of the room was pitch black. Periodically, I could see his face through the darkness. He just sat watching me.

"So why aren't you married?" Wilhelm asks.

I pause and then modestly answer, "I didn't find the one I love."

"Don't you want children?"

"Sure, every woman wants children eventually. At least I think so."

"You are so committed to your God, so why didn't you ask Him for a husband and children?"

"He knows," I reply.

Wilhelm scoots to the edge of his chair. Through a piercing glare, he says, "He knows what?"

"H-He knows all my desires," I stutter.

"So you desired to be here with me?"

How do I answer this? I softly respond, "What are you asking?"

"I can be your husband. Do you think I could be a good husband?"

"Yes," flows effortlessly yet insincerely from my mouth.

"How so?"

I know he's strategically trying to manipulate me. Through a trembling whimper, I ask, "What do you want me to say?"

He then stands. I begin panicking from fear. I now start to cry. He sits directly in front of me. He asks, "Why are you crying? Are you lying to me? Tell me the truth, saint. How do you feel about me?"

Through breathless pants, I softly cry, "Wilhelm, I'm too afraid of you!"

"Why are you so afraid?" he whispers.

He just sits staring through me with his other eyes. I literally faint from fright. I wake up, and I realize he has put me in bed. Miraculously, I don't see him again until morning. I take my shower and then go downstairs. It's quiet, but I faintly hear torturous screams coming from the distance. Bitterly weeping, I run to my room and hide in the closet. Someone has been brought home for his sadistic need. It sounds like a child.

My entire body is trembling. I sit in the closet, petrified for at least an hour. I hear thumping and bumping, glass shattering, and then my name. Does he think I got away? I want to say that I'm here, but the fear has paralyzed me. I can't move or speak. The closer he gets, the quieter he becomes. Suddenly, my closet door slowly opens. He's covered in blood.

He calmly says, "I need you. Follow me."

He walks away. I run into my bathroom and vomit. I look at my face. My eyes are nearly closed from crying. I rinse out my mouth and quickly wash my face. I begin to jog so I can catch up to him. I hear his shower running, so I slowly walk toward his bathroom, calling his name.

He says, "Come here."

Now I must accompany him in his shower. How do you remain sane in this situation? You do not. You become diabolical to your core and just cope. I know he did this to break me. And it did! He must have sensed my resistance had weakened. As a result, he tried relentlessly to appear human and lovable the next few days, hoping to win me over. He took me out to lavish places. He even purchased me a ring. It's a seven-carat, flawless, emerald-cut white diamond set in seven carats of emerald-cut black diamonds.

"When's the wedding?" the jeweler asked.

Wilhelm awaits my response. I just stood there, dumb and mute. He waits a few seconds more for me to speak. Then he turns to the jeweler.

"We're just wealthy. All biblical institutions are for the foolish, the weak, and the poor. We make our own rules. We do not need some mythical god's permission to—"

Before this blasphemy continues, I interrupt Wilhelm by kissing him. "This ring is awesome! Thank you!" I tell him.

I turn to the jeweler, who's now repulsed by us. I say through tears, "Thank you, sir, for your talent and time."

Wilhelm just stares as I try to mend this disaster. He turns to the jeweler, giving him an evil look. He then walks out. I quickly follow.

Wilhelm wanted me to say I was in love with him more than anything. He felt if he obtained love from me, somehow he would win this war he was battling. That is what I felt. I never asked, and I don't believe he can even answer that question.

Once we're home, he returns to this loving Wilhelm. I had submitted to his will the past few days, but that encounter at the jewelry store returned me to reality. Once again, I stopped hoping and praying. I accepted I would live with Wilhelm forever.

That same night in an intimate moment, I was gazing into his eyes. They were telling me he loved me. They were persuading me to tell him I loved him. And I wanted to. The emotion was there, saturating the atmosphere. The power of love was overtaking us. I discerned he felt alive and renewed.

I begin to feel as if falling in love with him would set me free from the constant fear and torment. His eyes were entreating me to accept this love. His eyes said, *Embrace the inevitable!*

And as I was being drawn in by his gentle touches and longing eyes, I hear my inner voice saying, *I will never leave you nor forsake you.* Instantly, I begin to draw strength from within. I begin to cry loud for mercy without sparing, deep within. Suddenly, the deception dissipated, and his true self reemerged. He immediately stopped and left me alone. Then I accepted that my search for freedom existed only within.

Zoe's Bed-and-Breakfast

This bed-and-breakfast has been in our family for more than a hundred years. Initially, my great-great-grandmother owned this beautiful land and built a boarding home for young women on her property. I'm named after her, Zoe Lancaster. Once she died, my great-grandmother, Vernice Lancaster, closed the school and opened a bed-and-breakfast. Our bed-and-breakfast housed many dignitaries. People all over the world frequent our lovely getaway.

The vast array of visitors left Grammy Vernice with so many wonderful stories to tell my mom and grandmother. However, the one she treasured most was about an earl out of Britain, Earl Alistair the fourth.

Earl Alistair was ill and needed a secluded place to die. Thus, he built an estate here in Vermont. His son was to inherit his fortune, but his son was treacherous and greedy. Earl Alistair refused to leave his ungrateful son with full authority over his estate. He wanted his family to believe he was still alive even if he died to make sure the whole of his will was in perfect order. He needed three years with another successor in place. He personally put this clause into his will. This would ensure that any person entrusted to his riches was someone he ordained and trusted, someone who was known throughout his community. He had found a young man he fully trusted and admired. He adopted him as a son and made him a lord.

Once all his affairs were in order, Earl Alistair remained in Britain, where he was now able to die in peace. When he would visit our bed-and-breakfast, he had fascinating stories of love and mystery. His real-life stories were more interesting than any book my grammy had ever read or heard. However, the most compelling story Earl Alistair ever told was about the young lord he blessed named Wilhelm York.

The earl said everyone called this young man Lee, but Earl Alistair preferred Wilhelm. It was a strong, distinguished name that deserved a royal title. Usually, people objected to a commoner receiving noble titles, but Wilhelm was so special the only people who objected were those who couldn't conceal their envy of him.

Wilhelm had surpassed the knowledge of his father in his own eyes. Thus, he became attached to the earl. The earl loved Wilhelm, but before he died, he regretted that he bestowed this favor upon him. He learned secrets about Wilhelm that were too disturbing to expose.

The earl lived several years longer than he expected. He witnessed Wilhelm's humble beginnings, his rise to stardom, his elevation to royalty, and his reign in darkness.

"Son, I know you may choose whenever and whomever you desire, but have you thought of marrying and establishing your lineage?" Earl Alistair asks.

Wilhelm calmly answers, "I am my own lineage."

"Come again?"

Wilhelm repeats, "I am my own lineage!"

The earl knows this is a narcissistic answer, but he continues his thought. "Have you considered the Berkley girl? She's fairer than the others, and she loves you."

"I am so tired of hearing that name! Why would I choose her when there is an entire world of women I have yet to meet? I think I know how to end this madness of her!" Wilhelm responds in frustration.

"End this madness of her? What are you talking about, Son? In fact, I will grant your wishes and never enquire of your love affairs again."

The earl knew Wilhelm meant something menacing, and shortly after that, she was institutionalized. Earl Alistair knew Wilhelm wasn't fond of the Berkley women. Still, he had his own motives and interests to protect. Secretly, he had hoped Wilhelm would've chosen her. Eventually, the earl goes to Wilhelm's estate to confront him and ask about what happened.

"Didn't you swear not to ask me about that woman ever again?" Wilhelm asks.

The earl sat without a rebuttal. Wilhelm laughs and says, "See, I knew you were lying! I knew no matter how much you may have desired not to mention her again, you would! So to guarantee my desire would be fulfilled, I silenced everyone myself."

Trembling from anger, the earl demands, "Wilhelm, what did you do?"

"I gave her what she asked for—to be with me forever."

The earl leaves, vowing never to speak to Wilhelm again. His beloved had turned vile, and his heart couldn't endure it. After that encounter, Wilhelm disappeared. The town was consumed with knowing what had become of Lord Wilhelm York.

The earl was questioned day in and day out about Wilhelm's whereabouts and the dark rumors that once evaded the town. The earl was weary because unfortunately, he didn't know what had taken place himself. Clueless about many of the answers concerning Wilhelm, the earl soon hired professionals to help. A few weeks following, someone told him Constance Berkley was carrying Wilhelm's baby. Once the earl heard this, he planned his visit to the asylum.

Constance was a depressing sight. She was strapped down, yet nothing could destroy her beauty. The orderlies assured him she was unable to comprehend anything … except Lee York. The earl tells them he understands, but he still needs to speak with her. He pulls a chair next to her restrained body lying on a gurney. Her belly is full, and it looks as if her baby is almost due.

"Hello, Mistress, I am Lee York's father," says Earl Alistair.

Constance appears to be in a state of unconsciousness, but once the earl says he's Lee's father, she immediately looks at him and smiles. The earl smiles back and asks, "Mistress, is this Lee's heir?"

Her smile leaves. Then she begins to cry. He removes his handkerchief and gently wipes her tears. "Has Lee caused you to cry?" he asks.

She nods yes. He continues, "Can you tell me why?"

She looks over and up as if she's getting permission from someone. The earl slowly turns to see where she's looking. He sees nothing, so he returns his eyes to Constance.

In a soft whimpering tone, she answers, "I promised Lee I would give George a son because that is what Lee asked of me. And then he would stay with us forever."

"Who is George to Lee?" the earl asks.

"The servant who cleans your mills."

The earl sits mortified and equally disgusted by this answer! George Lerwick was a mentally challenged vagabond the earl had taken compassion on, allowing him to clean and live in his mill. The earl wants to have Wilhelm killed for doing this, but he must know if she knows where Wilhelm has gone.

The earl continues, "Mistress, does Lee stay here?"

Suddenly, Constance just begins to wail and scream as if in pain. The orderlies rush in, and the earl is asked to leave. Straightway, he goes to the mill, snatches George, and basically drags him into his office. George is mentally slow but not foolish. The earl interrogates him.

"Did you impregnate Mistress Berkley?" Earl Alistair yells.

"Yes," George answers.

"How? Did you take her against her will?"

"No, sir! Lord York introduced us!"

The earl begins to sob and then asks George to tell him the story. George tells the earl that Wilhelm approached him one night at work with Constance and he asked George if he thought she was pretty.

"I think she's beautiful!" George answered.

Wilhelm professed, "I am your own personal savior. I am your guardian angel. No, I am your own special god.

I can grant your most wanted desires. Tell me, George. What is it you desire most?"

George was in awe and said, "Lord, I want to marry Mistress Berkley!"

"Tonight she is yours!"

Wilhelm began to kiss Constance and then told her to undress. Once she was naked, he whispered, "Grant George a son, and after his son is born, you grant me a son."

Constance was hesitant. Wilhelm added, "This is the only way! If I do not fulfill his request, I am a useless god!"

Constance slept with George several times before she became pregnant. The day her pregnancy was confirmed, Wilhelm planned a celebration for Constance and George at his estate.

He set up an elegant dinner in his home. After they celebrated, Wilhelm said, "Today you belong to George. After much contemplation, I realize I do not want my son born of a harlot but a virgin. Go with him and never bother me again!"

He then put them out. George sat with Constance outside Wilhelm's estate and watched as her mind crumbled. She never returned to sanity again.

Earl Alistair couldn't dispel every rumor, but he requested a town meeting in the open square to allow George to confirm he was the father. On Earl Alistair's authority, the asylum allowed Constance out so that she would be at George's side when he made his announcement.

Because of this story, the name Wilhelm York was burned in my brain. I was always anxious to know what had become of this mystery man! Then on this seemingly ordinary day, he came to our bed-and-breakfast. He was extremely handsome. He looked as if he were airbrushed. No flaws or pores, just smooth, golden tan, baby-soft skin. The woman accompanying him was very pretty, but he just overshadowed everyone and everything present. His lady friend saw me mesmerized! I'm sure she wanted to shout, "Please stop gawking at my man!" If she only knew a smidgen of what I heard about Wilhelm, she would run and take shelter!

Could this really be the missing Wilhelm York? That's impossible! I think, *How can I approach him?* Then miraculously a couple that knows his lady friend comes down for breakfast. They're so excited to see her that she completely ignores him. However, my eyes are fixed upon him! He looks my way and then immediately comes over to me. He never loses eye contact, and once he gets to the counter, he asks me who I am.

"I'm Zoe Lancaster, one of the owners," I answer as I breathe him in.

"My father knew Vernice Lancaster, whose mother's name is Zoe Lancaster. Related?" he asks.

"Yes, that's my great-great-grandmother. I inherited her name as well," I answer with a sound mind, but I'm lost in his loveliness.

"My father is Earl Alistair. Did your grandmother Vernice ever mention him?"

"He was the most interesting person she ever encountered in life, or so I hear. However, I heard that Earl Alistair said you were."

Staring at me with this seductive gaze, he says, "This woman and I are not working out. May I come visit you? Maybe later this week?"

"Definitely!"

He hands me his card and tells me to call him. "Then we can really catch up." He smirks.

He turns and looks at his lady friend, and instantly, the room fills with noise. When we were talking, it seemed as if everything had gone silent, which made his whisper clear and ascending. He's now keenly watching his date, and I can see he's very upset. I think, *Wilhelm, you would have my undivided attention continually!*

He glances back my way and says, "See you soon." He then returns to his date.

After they leave, I come to my senses. I decide to throw this card away. Clearly, he can't possibly be the Wilhelm I seek. Still, curiosity overpowers me! *How is he young? Is this really him?* Obviously, he is a related imposter! What is the truth? I'm not content with fantasy. I prefer reality, so I will call him. This enquiring mind must know.

Victoria's Plan

It has been more than a week, and Peyton is not responding to my calls. I go to the beach to clear my mind. However, looking out into the ocean, panning each end of the shore makes our modest area look huge and overwhelming just as this task of finding Peyton. Nevertheless, once my eyes see Victoria's store, I instinctively know that is where Peyton left.

I never paid much attention to it until now. It looks as if it is definitely owned by a woman. It resembles a straw hut, but it's made out of brick. It had the illusion of straw because of its oat-colored bricks. The beige roof is trimmed in teal and rose as is the trim around the glass doors to the entrance.

I enter, and to my right there's swimwear and sandals. To my left there's beach apparel, jewelry, suitcases, and toiletries. The counter is front and center in the middle of the store. Slightly behind it is a cooler for beverages, and there are sunglasses to its left. And directly behind the counter, about fifteen feet back, there's the rear exit that leads to the public's parking lot.

The walls are white trimmed in teal and rose as well. As I pan the walls, I feel Victoria's eyes. There is a young couple at the counter laughing and joking with her. However, once she sees me, her face goes pale. Her customers abruptly stop their conversation to look my way. I then head to the counter.

"I am so sorry to interrupt, but may I speak to Victoria privately?" I ask.

The couple is more than happy to adhere to my wishes. They retrieve their goods, tell Victoria to take care, and then leave.

Now Victoria and I are just staring at one another in silence. "May I help you?" she asks, smiling.

"Hello, Victoria. My name is Wilhelm. Peyton and I own this estate."

"Oh my God, yes! Hi, Wilhelm! I see you all the time on the beach. It's so wonderful to finally meet you! Can I help you?"

Skeptical, I stare as she pretends as if she is so honored to meet me. I turn my focus to her counter. I am fidgeting with the trial-sized products there. I then return my eyes to her and peacefully respond, "I think you can."

She stands unmoved with this confounded look upon her face. I mimic her look. Then I continue staring as I wait until she speaks. My fixed gazing makes her extremely uneasy. Now with an overly friendly tone, she says, "Wilhelm, I can't help you if I don't know what you want!"

"Who," I interject.

"Pardon me?" she says.

I do not appease her with frivolous answers. I simply stare. Suddenly, she determines she is not going to allow me to overrule her in her own store.

"Will, I don't know what your problem is, but you need to leave!" she tells me.

"Firstly, never call me Will. It's Wilhelm. You and I are not friends. But more importantly, I think you do know what my problem is."

Discerning my agitation, she politely replies, "Forgive me, Wilhelm. You're right. We are not friends, but you're not going to bully me either. I alerted the police, so it'd be wise for you to leave."

"The police that are thirty seconds away? If you alerted them, they should have been here five minutes ago. Why such drastic measures? You don't even know why I'm here."

Pausing briefly, she says, "Well, you need to tell me!"

"Victoria, I am not here to argue. I will take your word. If you do not know anything, all is well. However, if I find out you do know, then you have done something very bad. That holds very severe consequences. Understood?"

We both stand silently glaring at each other. "Well, looks like your day has already gone very badly, so the consequences seem to be yours alone!" she snidely replies. I simply leave.

I exit out of the front door then head to the back of the building. I walk into the parking lot. I look in several of the cars. Then I just stop. Searching now is pointless. I decide to wait until after the store closes and then confront Victoria.

Victoria is an attractive lady. She's tall and very shapely. She has sexy, slanted hazel eyes and short, thick sandy blonde hair that she keeps slicked back because she swims all the time. Still, it fit her well. She has a small gap in her teeth, but it works for her too. It makes her an odd beauty and enhances her sexiness. She is also the local slut. She has a shallow husband who placed his life's worth in his possessions. He would drive his Lamborghini on the beach twice a week to pick her up. They argue regularly because of her constant infidelity. However, he is going solely on his gut feelings. He is too simple to figure out every man she cheated with frequented this very beach. I assumed one day he would put one plus one together and finally get two. Once he did the math, he would then come here on a massive killing spree, so I stayed clear of her store.

Because of her unholy ways, I was confident Peyton would never befriend Victoria. However, in the last few weeks, Peyton began to go to the store quite often. The week of her disappearance, she went every day. I planned to go that particular week with Peyton and finally make my presence known. Obviously, I was a couple of days too late.

Another reason I avoided Victoria was because she was itching for me to know her. She was that whore who befriended women just to get close to their men. She was openly trifling. Peyton concealed that friendship well. Since she is gone, my only option is to get the truth from Victoria personally.

Victoria is locking up, so I come through the back door. I wait until she is by the counter to show myself. She turns and seeing me startles her. She screams. I put my finger to my lips, motioning for her to keep silent. She now accepts I mean business, so she decides to tell all.

"Wilhelm, Peyton was here last, and she went out the back door! Why? I didn't ask, but obviously, she was running. I don't expect you to tell me your problems, and clearly, there are some major ones! However, I'm not going to be your punching bag because she has left you!"

"Did she tell you we had problems?" I probe.

"She never said, but clearly, there were!" she responds.

"Well, what did you clearly see?"

"It was just visibly clear she was abused!" she answers as if she has said something of intelligence.

"Abused? Did you see bruises or scars on her?"

"Well, no! You didn't abuse her physically but mentally!"

"Did she verbally tell you that?"

"N-No, but I just know!" she says, now stuttering.

Perplexed, I ask, "How did you just know?"

Flustered, she huffs and says, "Well, I don't know-know, but I know!"

"You don't know-know, but know what? I'm confused. Will you please explain what you are saying?"

She waves me off and then says, "Wilhelm, I don't have time for this! This is your problem, not mine. Please leave."

I was constantly bending and gesturing, trying to make logical sense of this idiotic conversation we were just having. After that response I stood erect to show her my approval of her last statement.

"Finally, the wisest thing you have said all day. Yes, this is my problem, so why are you involved?"

She stands dumbfounded. She then snatches her purse and attempts to run out the front door. I snatch her and throw her across the counter. She is crying and screaming.

Kneeling next to her, I ask, "Why has every woman in our lives felt the need to interfere? Our life does not concern you. Did I tell your husband what a nasty, unscrupulous whore you are? Never! I let him come here twice a week and be the beach idiot as his wife humiliates him relentlessly! Never once did I feel the need to meddle in your affairs, and I did know-know, as you like to say. So tell me. Why did you think it your duty to help Peyton leave?"

I know she is in pain. Some of her bone had clearly broken. She attempts to answer through her groans of agony.

"There is no good or acceptable answer," I tell her.

She tries to explain again, but I interrupt, "No, Victoria! There is no acceptable excuse! You were glad Peyton left because now I would be another rich man you could seduce. Right? Please do not lie! I despise liars! You already lied earlier today, so here is your chance to redeem yourself! Tell me the truth."

She nods yes and then moans from pain. I whisper into her ear, "And that, Victoria, is very bad."

I break her back. I stomp on her, crushing her spine until she easily fits into one of her suitcases. I then set it behind her store.

I take her cell phone and scroll through, seeking any information on Peyton. And sure enough, Victoria had a secret. She has a sister in college named Morgan. She texted Morgan earlier, asking her to come to the beach before she heads back to school. Morgan informs Victoria she has four friends with her riding back to campus. Victoria tells Morgan she has a friend who wants to leave her abusive boyfriend. Victoria informs Morgan she is going to give Peyton the grand idea to find a SUV filled with bags in the back. Once inside this SUV, she instructs Peyton to hide and allow that driver to get her far away undetected. Victoria told Peyton there was a blue SUV driven by college students, that she should chance and sneak inside.

After she gave Peyton this grand plan, she informs Morgan not to tell her friends and not to attempt to see this woman. Her ignorance would keep her innocent if someone asked her if she ever saw Peyton. She was protecting her baby sis. How special.

I am sure Peyton saw the hand of God in this miraculous SUV filled with clothes and no one ever detecting her presence! Nevertheless, it was not her God but the mighty hand of Victoria—mighty Victoria who is crammed in a suitcase and on her way to the bottom of the ocean. While she was planning the great escape, she should have been minding her own business.

I could have gone to the nearest city and checked hotels or took Morgan's cell number and found her. She deserved a worthy punishment for her deceitful deed. However, that was a waste of time today. Peyton had been long gone for a week now. I actually granted Morgan the miracle of life. Maybe one day I will desire my praise, but today all my attention and energy was fixed upon returning Peyton to me. So for now I just had to wait until she reemerged and then plan accordingly.

When the Lie Becomes the Truth

"Regina, it's after 2:00 a.m. Is Peyton okay?" Casey asks.

I'm crying uncontrollably. I can barely speak. Then I force out the words. "Peyton left! She wouldn't tell me where, but I heard her talking to Ms. Berkley!

"Do you have Ms. Berkley's number?" Casey asks.

"No! I slightly remember how to get to her home! Please meet me at the church. We can go there together!"

Tabitha's home is nearly two hours away from the church. While Casey is driving, I'm calling church members, hoping anyone has Tabitha's address or phone number.

Minister Antonio answers, "Regina, that information is in the church secretary's office!"

I ask Antonio to please call her and then call me back. Twenty minutes later the secretary finally calls with Tabitha's information. Once we get there, we need clearance to get onto her estate. We call, and she's hesitant. Then finally, she says we may come inside. She opens the door, and she looks as if she's been weeping. She seems feeble and frazzled.

Unmoved by her frailty, Casey immediately asks, "Did Peyton come here, Ms. Berkley?"

Tabitha sits motionless for a few seconds. She then says, "Please don't be so formal. Call me Tabitha."

Casey glances over at me and then replies, "Thank you, Tabitha. Have you seen Peyton?"

Tabitha's acting her age today. She's moving slowly and speaking as if she barely comprehends what we're saying. She then asks me to make tea from the already prepared tea setting on a rolling tray behind the sofa. I make us a cup to our liking in the sterling silver tea cups that are trimmed in gold.

Tabitha takes a few sips and then says in a frail voice, "Please be patient with me. I'm an old woman. I cannot endure this constant traumatic commotion."

Casey is getting very impatient. I lean toward Tabitha and explain, "Ma'am, we are so sorry to burden you this late at night, but Peyton may have been abducted by this evil force again. I heard her on the phone with you, and we wanted to know if you know where she may have gone."

Tabitha sets her cup down and then takes a deep breath. "Peyton has always seemed like a lovely girl. However, this evening she brought this horrid demon to my home. I cannot understand why she needed to expose him to where I live before she ran off with him."

I was totally confused by what Tabitha said. As I sit dumbfounded, Casey interjects, "Tabitha, why did they come here?"

"I don't know! He threatened my life, so I begged Peyton to explain the purpose of their visit. I was on my knees, begging for mercy, but they just stared at me like I was beneath them, like I deserved to be begging them for my life. Then they up and left together!"

Casey looks at me, shaking her head. Still, I don't believe this story. It has too many holes! Now I shake my head back at Casey, and then I say, "I heard Peyton ask why you were calling. Why did you call her, Ms. Berkley?"

She looks convicted as she repeats my question. In my book repeating questions buys time to think of a lie!

She responds, "Oh dear, you're right! Forgive my old mind. Yes, I did call her! I had a dream that someone wanted to kill me. I woke up frightened. I live in this massive home all alone. The fear just began to overwhelm me. Peyton has been a pastor, friend, and daughter. I feel closest to her, so I called to see if she would be so kind as to spend a few nights with an old, lonely woman, and she agreed. However, when she showed up, he was with her."

Now my face is twisted up, but Casey's intrigued!

"Did they say why they were here together?" Casey asks.

Tabitha begins to tremble. She pushes a button on her tray, and a nurse enters the room. The nurse asks us to please go into the study so that she can tend to Tabitha privately. We get to the study. Casey instantly calls Maurice, confirming Peyton has crossed over to the dark side. She tells him Peyton ran off with Wilhelm and that he's not kidnapping her! It's one speculation after the other. I stand disgusted, listening to this story of unconfirmed rumors. She notices my painful grimacing, so she gets off the phone and merely shrugs at my disapproval.

"Casey, that old woman is a liar! I came here with Peyton for weeks, visiting this woman. She was more sane and vibrant than you and me! When Peyton got off the phone with Tabitha, she looked hopeless! I believe Wilhelm was already here! She had Peyton come to save her, and he took her again!" I insisted.

"What happened while Peyton was alone with Wilhelm for almost a year? Has she shared anything with you?" Casey confronts me.

"Of course!" I reply with a sneer.

Casey becomes belligerent. "Regina, like what? Please share! All these deep, spiritual testimonies, what happened? They lived in a mega mansion off the water! He bought her luxury cars and jewels! They cruised the Caribbean in a submarine! They had saved friends! I don't know about you, but all this sounds like praise to me! Where's 'he beat me, tortured, and abused me?' All he wanted was love? Really, Regina? Wise up! Our friend is gone!"

I stand speechless. As much as it hurt hearing these words, Casey was right. Peyton never said anything personally negative about Wilhelm other than she felt as if she were in a beautified hell. It was as if the words left her whenever we asked what happened between them. After Casey's reality sets in, the nurse escorts us back to Tabitha. Immediately, Tabitha says, "We overheard your conversation. Unfortunately, Regina, Casey is correct. Peyton has forsaken the way. She has chosen Wilhelm."

House Calls

As soon as Peyton's special report goes off, I prepare to head back to Vermont immediately. My adrenaline is going, and my hatred is so pure at this moment that I have to keep moving. I am pacing the floor like a madman when I hear my doorbell.

I cut off the bedroom light and head to the front of the house to see who could possibly be at my door. There is no car visible in the driveway. I head to the back of the house to see if they parked in the back, and still nothing. A few minutes have passed. I am hoping they went away. Then the bell rings again, so I decide to head to the door.

I call security and ask who was allowed to enter the gates. Security reveals it is Officer Lynn. What can she possibly want? Is she here to detain me? There is no way the police department sent one woman to arrest me, so I open the door. Lynn is standing there in a salmon-colored, formfitting dress. The color looks nude and accentuates her body. I just stare at her dripping wet from the rain.

"Please ask me in. I'm soaked," she says.

As she enters, I look outside for her car. I do not see a vehicle. I ask, "Did someone drop you off?"

She seductively moves her hair to one side of her neck and then says, "No, I came discreetly."

I give her a smirk for her desperate effort. "You walked here?"

"I'm parked in the beach parking lot. I have a badge, so security let me in that way. Is that okay with you?"

I simply nod yes, and she begins lightly clapping. "Yeah! I'm glad. Do you have a robe or anything I can dry off in?"

Lynn has chosen the absolute worst day to come to my home. I exhale loudly, and then I tell her yes.

I go to my bedroom to grab a robe. Then I think of Peyton's room. I go to her bedroom and find a long black satin robe. I can smell her scent as I lift it from the hanger. I then place it up to my nose. I stand there, indulging in the sweet scent on her robe. I then throw it down and bolt out of her room. I take Lynn one of my robes. I begin to tell her where a bathroom is, but she undresses right in front of me. She is not wearing any underwear. She just watches me as she puts on my robe. I watch back, emotionless.

I turn and offer her a drink as I pour a glass of wine. I set it on the table. Then I sit down next to her. I have so many emotions going on inside me. Lynn is clueless about what I am going through. While she was preparing to come and seduce me, she should have been watching the news with her precinct. I am sitting, unable to start a sensible conversation as I watch her moving closer.

"Lynn, why are you here?" I ask as I stand to avoid her advances.

"Because you never called me. It has been at least two months. I thought you understood why I offered my card too. Plus it's not like it used to be, sexy. Women don't have to wait for you men to make the first move anymore." She grins.

I frown and say, "I take pride in the dominant role. I prefer to make the first move. I am terribly turned off by women who want to take my role as the man away."

"Gosh, I'm so embarrassed. Forgive me. My friends convinced me this was the way to go. How humiliating."

She keeps her head down, but today I have no room in my psyche for her. I grab her dress off the floor and take it to the dryer. I return to Lynn, and I see her texting on her phone. I am instantly angered. I snatch her phone.

"Who are you texting? I thought you were discreet about coming here!"

"It's only my girlfriend Blanche," she explains, slightly startled.

I regain my composure and calmly ask, "Who else knows you are here?"

"I swear no one else knows."

"Does Blanche know who I am, how I look, and where I live?"

"No."

"Is she a cop?"

Lynn suspiciously responds, "Yes, why?"

I sense she is feeling threatened, so I change my whole demeanor. I grab her hand and lead her to the great room's balcony. Looking tenderly into her eyes, I explain, "You came at a really sad time. I have lost someone extremely dear to me. She has been gone for two weeks. The pain is unbearable. I am asking because I do not need you and your friends invading my privacy right now."

Rubbing her forehead, she says, "Please give me my dress. I just want to go. I have bothered you long enough."

I go to the laundry room to get her dress, but now I am fighting the urge to destroy Lynn. Having to mention Peyton has enraged me. I try to resist my hunger, but I cannot. I leave her dress in the dryer and come back to Lynn empty handed. I walk over to her and begin kissing her. Naturally, she starts to kiss me back. I remove the robe and examine her bare body. She grabs my hand to lead me upstairs. The room she chooses is Peyton's. I stop at the door. She then climbs on Peyton's bed and motions for me to join her. I stand in the doorway, sickened. I thoroughly examine the room beholding all of Peyton's belongings. Soon I begin to feel as if this woman has defiled the only thing I have left of her.

"Lynn, not this room. This is her room."

"I figured that. I'm trying to help you forget. Come here. I want us to make new memories for you," she seductively says.

"Please not here. Follow me. We shared a bedroom together."

Lynn smiles and then follows me. I take her to a guest room. She climbs on the bed. I follow and start kissing her.

"Did you know her?" I softly ask.

"Who?" she asks between kisses.

She climbs on top of me. I stop her from touching my face by grabbing her arms. "Peyton?" I whisper.

She sighs. "Wilhelm, you're killing the mood. No, I didn't know Peyton, but I knew she was with you."

"How did you know us?"

"Duh, I'm only part of your own private police station."

"I am asking what exactly you knew." I huff, now sitting up.

"I knew through Victoria that you and Peyton were breaking up."

"Victoria?" I ask, baffled. I just killed Victoria a few days ago. I cannot figure out how Lynn could have known to approach me two months ago.

"When is the last time you talked to Victoria? I ask.

"Uh, like … three months ago," Lynn answers.

Peyton did not regularly visit that store three months ago. Now I am feigning to know everything she knows. I ask, "What did Victoria say?"

Loudly huffing, Lynn replies, "Her friend Amina asked Victoria to ask Peyton to attend a marriage conference with Victoria and her husband. Peyton informed Amina that you weren't her husband but a spiritual brother or something weird. Amina sought to find out what was going on with you two. Unfortunately, after that tragic fire that killed Amina, Victoria intervened. Victoria attempted to get Peyton to explain the complexity of your relationship, but Peyton wouldn't go into detail. However, she asked Victoria to mail a letter to a lover in Vermont. After the lover never responded, she asked Victoria to help her get away without you knowing. After this outlandish story, I decided to check your record, but you were clean, an upstanding citizen! I simply wrote both Victoria and

Peyton off as looney and decided I would show them how to make a man like you happy."

Of course, after this information, it was impossible to let Lynn live. Her death was now justifiable. She was a bearer of bad news.

I remove my clothing down to my underwear and act as if we are going to make love. I begin to kiss her inner thigh and ripped through her femoral artery, leaving her there to bleed to death. I am angrier now than I was before Lynn showed up. I must find who this *lover* is Peyton has sent a letter.

I call a cab to take me to my jet. As I am approaching the cab, a police car drives up. I pay the cab to leave. It is Officer MacAleese.

"Hello, Mr. Yoorker. Are you leaving?"

I remove my keys from my pocket to unlock my front door. "Hello, Officer. No, I am actually just getting home. May I help you?"

"Call me Mac please. Do you mind if I come in?"

My mind is spinning out of control, trying to figure out the nature of his visit. Still, I answer, "Sure."

Mac comes in and begins to admire and compliment my home. I close my eyes and just sigh as my blood begins to boil.

"Officer Mac, how may I help you?"

Discerning my irritability, he says, "Oh, forgive me for interrupting your evening, but have you seen Officer Lynn today?"

I do not know if he saw her car in the parking lot or not, but I answer no. He is watching me intently as to read my body language. I remain calm and relaxed.

Displaying a condemning smirk, he says, "Mr. Yoorker, really, I'm not prying into your personal affairs. Officer Lynn was supposed to report to work a couple of hours ago. She never showed up, and she's not answering her phone. Since I'm the law, we checked her cell phone location, and it led us here."

He pauses and then awaits my response. Nevertheless, I am far from worried. I smugly say, "Officer Mac, you are free to look around, but I have not seen her today."

"Okay, thanks," he replies then gets on his two-way and calls for backup.

Seconds after his call, the doorbell rings. It is Officer Blanche Todd. She introduces herself and then asks, "May I call you Wilhelm?"

I simply nod yes.

She is a large manly-looking woman. Her demeanor is meant to intimidate.

"I'm a friend of Lynn, and I know for a fact she was here today. I actually texted her a few times while she was with you. So I know she was here. Understand?"

I do not respond. I just listen with an irked look on my face.

Annoyed, she says, "So, Wilhelm, let's start this again. Where is Officer Lynn?"

"I have no idea. I have not seen her today."

Blanche then takes out her cell phone. She begins scrolling through her and Lynn's texts. She then gives me a damning look. Without losing eye contact, I firmly say, "I understand you are the law and you are used to intimidating people with your premature scare tactics, but your friend wished I would ever invite her over here.

She truly embarrassed herself by handing me her contact information as if I would ever choose to call her. I did not call her then, and surely, I would never call her now. Whatever fantasy she was living through your cell phone is just that, her fantasy. If her cell phone location is in this area, it is not rocket science to decipher this code. Her precinct is on my property. I do not appreciate your threats, and I definitely do not welcome you coming into my home and calling me a liar. So, Officer Blanche, you and Officer Mac can get out. You will be hearing from my lawyer shortly. This unofficial searching of my home and interrogation are the first things I will have addressed."

I then open the front door and say, "Get out of my home now!" They leave silently.

If killing three officers would not attract so much attention, I would have had them join their friend. I call my lawyer as promised. Then I simply drive myself to my jet.

All this wasted time on foolishness has squandered all my patience. I am not concerned about anything except getting to Peyton. So too, I must find who this lover is, the one she supposedly sent a letter. This lover Lynn has put into my mind is driving me crazier than I had been after Peyton's leaving. Everything I dreaded is coming upon me at once. My strategy of planning and then acting is gone. I am reacting purely on emotions. Anyone in my way from this day forth will be terminated.

PRAYER FOR MRS. SCOTT

The church has lost Peyton. We were there around the clock, crying out for her safety, and she just walks out of our shield of protection. Soon after, Tabitha, Casey, and Regina inform me about what they recently learned. This news breaks my heart. Days have passed. Although we're hurting, we're at peace. We assume she has chosen to be with him. Here's another tragedy to add to my life.

After Zoe committed suicide, I never returned to her bed-and-breakfast. In the past my husband and I would spend weeks at a time there, so I have a local post office box near Zoe's. I work for a major magazine, so I chose not to be in a remote area, unable to receive written works.

I had avoided this area many months, but today I took a drive through the mountains just to clear my mind and to see if I received any mail. I view this once gorgeous bed-and-breakfast. It was a beautiful landmark for decades. It's now boarded up. I just shake my head and continue past it.

I get to the local post office, and I find I have received letters. One is in a standard envelope, but it's fairly thick. The return address is from Washington state. These letters were sent approximately ten months ago. Immediately, I return to my car and begin reading.

May 21

I'm compelled to journal.

I fear for my life every second of the day. I have been trapped with this demon for at least two months. I have been cooperative and submissive to it because I need him to trust me.

I pray I escape and do not die here. I've seen and heard the most hideous, frightening things. Just as the word describes his outward appearance is the consummation of all perfection, but it's only a mask.

I don't know what he's saying, but almost every night he speaks in a horrifying growl in some demonic language. He says he's never seen himself, yet he stands in front of a mirror speaking this evil language, staring into his own eyes. I block my ears so I won't fully hear him. I'm protecting myself from any chant that may cause me to submit to it. However, constantly being with him has left me feeling possessed.

I endure a life without music, television, or relationships. The only sounds outside his voice are my hopeless thoughts.

He has provided a very luxurious life for us. I'm in awe how no one sees him for what he is! I'm allowed brief encounters, and some people I meet even go to church! Can the people of God see? My God! How long can I endure?

July 27

I pray this letter finds you prosperous and in good health.

I'm writing because I didn't want to leave this earth and never reveal my story. I'm in the state of Washington off the Pacific coast. My home is approximately forty thousand square feet, dark red brick, and it's gated. I am about a half mile off the main road in Eden Estate. All I truly know is the police station and our home seemingly make up the entire population. I'm sure many are looking for loved ones because we have a dungeon underneath this house filled with the body parts of men, women, and children.

He calls himself Wilhelm Yoorker. I often called him a demon, but he's human. He lacks human emotions. It's as if he's attempting to retrain himself to comprehend human emotions again. Surely, it's a failed attempt.

I thought he may be a vampire, but he scoffed at my Hollywood cartoon monster. In fact, he doesn't need blood at all. He kills, but he doesn't eat human flesh. His idea of feeding is simply killing. He will drink blood, but it's just a desire or maybe a ritual of some sort. But blood isn't needed for him to survive.

I'm writing not to scare you but to warn you. He destroys anyone who has wronged him. When you and your husband saw me that day, he processed that you and your husband purposed to humiliate him. Daily, he plots the perfect annihilation of you both. However, he won't act until he believes he has hatched the perfect plan of attack.

Zoe is dead. He found her repulsive. She was a loose woman. In fact, 75 percent of the people we meet are dead.

We have a semiprivate beach. If we choose, we can make it exclusively ours. The previous owners allowed others to enjoy the beach, so we continued their tradition. We even have a store on the beach. However, the once moderately abundant visitors are now extremely scarce.

One couple would briefly talk with us every time they saw us on the beach. Once they came to our home and visited for at least thirty minutes. I really enjoyed the conversation, so they invited us to their home for a barbecue. We went and met more couples. I thought all was well. Nevertheless, I found them in the gazebo ripped apart, and then they were gone. I don't know how his murders go unnoticed. The police have never questioned us, but there has to be hundreds of bodies under this estate.

Saying no is the most dangerous word used in his presence. I've been milliseconds from being destroyed many times. By a small miracle, he can't imagine living without me. Every time he has purposed to end me, he stops and says, "I need you here." He'd then spare my life. He never hits me or is physically abusive. He simply reveals his true self, which is more fearful than death. As a result, I submit to whatever he requests.

The constant mind games have me going in and out of sanity daily. Answering a question wrong is worthy of a brutal death. I know because I have watched him rip out tongues and hearts and snatch off heads for disagreeing.

I also have been fed blood, and we bathe in blood at least once a month. The covering of the blood protects me from his wrath. He wants to be equal to God, yet he blames God for his demise. My prayer life is nearly nonexistent. He's forbidden me from speaking God's name.

I needed someone to know this. I hope for freedom, but I accept I may never be free, so this must be shared with the believers. The world thinks I'm a great reality show series, but the believers must know this is real. It's the believers he hunts relentlessly. It's the believers he desires most to exterminate. I'm his first attempt to make a true believer serve him.

He's not the devil. He's not merely human. He's not a demon. He is simply a wicked being who has rejected light and found his way to exist in pure darkness.

Please expose this letter. Share it with the world! If I'm not dead by the time you reveal this, know shortly after, I should be, and I am content.

Love eternally,

Peyton Meryl

I feel as if I've read two letters from two totally different people. Nevertheless, I speed to the office and purpose to publicize this letter in my magazine, every church, and the news station immediately!

The Kings Suffer Violence

Harrison and Amina King are interesting. They are just drawn to Peyton and me. Peyton seems so comfortable around them. I know she needs to feel normal in order to accept this life with me, so I allow this new friendship. Harrison talks about traveling and culture, which I know much about. Amina knows how to make Peyton smile. This is something I seemingly cannot accomplish, so she is definitely needed during this time. They come to our home briefly one day.

"Thanks for inviting us to your astonishing home. We're having a small get-together and barbecue Sunday. Will you please attend?" Amina asks.

Submissive, Peyton looks at me, awaiting my answer. The silence is making the Kings uncomfortable.

"You want to go?" I ask Peyton.

"Absolutely!" she answers with a bright smile.

"Well, it's a date," Amina says, clapping.

The Kings head home. I go to Peyton. Kissing her forehead, I whisper, "I hope you know what you're doing for their sakes."

I am gazing down at her, but she refuses to lift her eyes. She gently pushes away, releasing my grasp, and then she heads to our room.

It's Sunday, and we're headed to the Kings' home. They live four miles from our estate. They own a very nice homey house. There are two other couples present and a single man. I cannot accurately recall their names because our visit was fairly short. The only person's name I remember is Minister Rod. He is the unmarried one.

The Kings are Christians. I am sitting motionless while this church meeting is going on, and I am sorely vexed. I put my arm around Peyton and then pull her close.

"Did you know they were Christians?" I ask.

She nods yes. I let out a hearty sigh and then go to the patio. Harrison follows me.

"C'mon, men, let's go out to the patio! The women can have their time inside. We need some brotherly bonding time," he prompts.

If it were possible, I think I would have a migraine. Why would Peyton bring me here? Did she desire to see her saints eliminated? I stand by the patio banister, breathing deeply. Then Minister Rod puts his hand on my shoulder as he walks by.

"Come on, brother. Sit down," he says.

I glance at his hand, and then I go sit down. Harrison and his three stooges are now staring at me. I guess tonight Harrison purposed to lead me to the Lord.

"So, brother, tell us how long you two have been married," Minister Rod says.

I sit silently, watching. He looks at the others, shrugs, and then laughs.

"The suspense is killing us, brother. Spit it out!"

I remain silent for a few seconds more and then reply, "I am not your brother. My name is Wilhelm."

Minister Rod becomes just Rod, I guess. Suddenly, all this brotherly love goes out the window. He now has an irked look on his face.

"Well, Wilhelm, I'm just trying to get to know you. No harm. If you choose not to answer, I'll be fine. I'm simply trying to break the ice."

Harrison is appalled by my behavior. He is frowning at me as if asking, "What is your problem?" Unmoved, I begin looking through the storm doors for Peyton. However, the kitchen light is off, and the women are off who knows where. I instantly think of Peyton using this as an opportunity to flee. I immediately jump up and go into the house. When I enter, Harrison is right behind me. He then closes the patio door.

Genuinely concerned, he asks, "What's going on? Are you okay?"

"No, I am not. I am not saved. Nor do I have a desire to be saved. I do not appreciate this besiege!"

"Besiege?" Harrison says, thoroughly confused.

"Get Peyton and tell her it is time to go."

Harrison refuses to let me out of his sight. He watches me intently as he begins calling for his wife. She hurries around the corner, concerned. With his eyes fixed upon me, Harrison says, "Tell Peyton Wilhelm is ready to go."

Amina glances my way, but she never questions her husband and immediately goes to retrieve Peyton. My personal commotion has caught everyone's attention. Rod and his men as well as Amina and the women all come into the kitchen. I am now infuriated. I tell Peyton to head to the car. These people have encircled me and are unified in their effort to remove me. It left me no choice but to abandon my instant attack.

I speed home and escort Peyton into the house. I tell her to go to her own room. I lock the house. Then I immediately head back to the Kings' home. I drive up with my headlights off. I circle the house on foot and find them in the living room, praying hand in hand. I wait until they finish their prayer.

"Where'd you find that devil?" Minister Rod asks.

Harrison shakes his head and comes up speechless. Amina then explains our relationship.

"It was the wife we loved. They live an extravagant lifestyle. He doesn't appear to mistreat her, but she is unusually meek and severely soft-spoken. He rarely talked as well, so we just assumed they were quiet people. Nothing ever alarmed us. They're a beautiful couple. We've never experienced any hostility from him until today."

"Well, I knew! I discerned he was off. That's why I wanted the men to separate. I knew together we'd figure him out!" Harrison says.

His comment sealed his fate. I am so tired of these people *discerning* after the fact is revealed. Harrison, if you discerned so much, why would you invite me to your home?

Now I am ready to have some fun. I ring the doorbell. Harrison looks out, so I wave. He opens the door.

"I am so embarrassed by my behavior. I had to return and apologize. Peyton is so upset with me. I had to come to you and your friends to make things right," I say, smiling.

Harrison invites me back inside. The women are smiling. Rod is smiling with his eyes. I am 100 percent sure he believes I returned because of his powerful prayer. Amina brings me coffee. I sit it down in front of me and then give her a bright smile. I stir my cream in my cup. All eyes are on me.

"So, Harrison, what are you discerning?" I ask.

Harrison sits, looking perplexed, so I turn my attention to Minister Rod. "Please speak, brother! Tell me what I need!"

"You truly need Jesus!" one man boldly states.

Instantly, I lunge his way and strangle him with one hand. The women are now screaming like banshees. While he is lifeless in my hand, I glare at Harrison.

"Shut them up before I do," I tell him.

Harrison easily submits to my request. The other guy has a gun, so he pulls it on me. I stand still, taunting. "Go ahead. Shoot." He simply stands there trembling.

"If you have never killed, it is much harder than people think, huh?"

I snatch his gun and shoot him in the face. Harrison and Amina are on the floor behind their couch, hugging, crying, and surely praying. I let them alone because they are my guests of honor. The wife of the man I shot in the face charges me, so I rip her head off as she hurtles my way. Her blood drenches the strangled man's wife and Rod. The strangled man's wife faints as Rod dashes out the back of the house. It is dark out, but it only takes me a minute to find him. Once I do, I drag him back inside.

The Kings were frying a turkey. It has been unattended, so it is spewing grease. I throw water on the woman who has fainted. I then instruct her to place the turkey fryer on the stove. I make her turn it up to the hottest level. I then tell her to put a pot of water on the stove behind this boiling hot fryer until it boils. The grease is now overflowing. A massive fire breaks out.

I knocked Rod unconscious, so I place him nicely at the table. I push the woman into the fire. Once she is lit, I push her onto Rod and watch them go up in flames. The bloodcurdling screaming is hurting my ears. I have to leave here. I lead the Kings to my trunk along with this woman's head and body. I then drive to my home.

I move the man I shot into the kitchen and knock the fryer on his head. I did this to conceal the bullet wound. A fire truck and police car go speeding by me. I wanted to take my time, torturing the Kings for their foul hospitality, but I suspected the police would soon come my way. Thus, I ripped out their throats and left them and Mrs. nameless in the gazebo.

I hear the sirens approaching my home, and now my doorbell is ringing. I go inside and hop in the shower, and then I open the door, wet. It is a woman and a man cop. They tell me there has been a tragic fire at a neighboring home. They are quite sure the victims have visited my beach and just wanted to inform me that because of the magnitude of the deaths, there will be news coverage and numerous onlookers. The police suggest I close my beach to protect my privacy. They are merely making sure I am not disturbed because of my neighbor's negligence.

The woman officer is the one informing me. Her name is Officer Lynn.

"People recklessly use those turkey fryers. I wished they would simply take them off the market," she says through wanton eyes. I give her my undivided attention and then smile.

The male, Officer MacAleese, then hands me his card.

"If you have any problems, just call me, and I'll make sure you're not discomforted during this time," he says as I reach for it.

"Take mine as well," Officer Lynn says as she, too, hands me her card. I thank them both and then close the door.

I go check on Peyton. She in under the covers. I assume she's asleep. I do not disturb her. She doesn't know the police were here or anything else, and I desire to keep it that way.

Where Do I Start?

Our ride from Tabitha's is insufferable. I take Peyton to my home. Surprisingly, she does not cry, fight, or speak. I instantly feed off her. No need to make her feel comfortable. I just do whatever I desire to do with her whichever way I desire to do it. No food, no baths, nothing! No niceties at all! Then I stop and just stand over her frail, bloody body, reminiscing.

I remember I had just returned to America. I started a world trip alone. I am a loner. Being around people for hours at a time became wearisome. I lived in California. Once I returned home from traveling the world, I wanted a new beginning. I chose Vermont because it just seemed random and so secluded. I lived among people, but I did not live with the people.

I often made my abode underground where I could not be found. Having televisions and furniture and living like humans was no longer important. I periodically lived in hotels or leased fully furnished condos. I even purchased a penthouse, but my real dwelling place was hidden. I would go into hiding for months at a time.

My need for companionship left me almost immediately after I became immortal. Any intimacy I experienced now was strictly for killing. I desired to be as I am, but I did not want to become oblivious to my human instincts and needs. Losing that would make me a monster. I decided to find a home and live above ground as long as I could possibly tolerate.

The first day I went house-shopping, I saw Peyton. I was meeting my Realtor in Burlington and then heading to the mountains to a bed-and-breakfast once frequented by a family member. Peyton was coming out of a coffee shop. She was sipping her coffee and laughing while on her cell phone. As soon as my eyes saw her, I felt alive. I could not stop watching her. The longer I watched, the more I desired her. I was under her spell. I was inside of the real estate office, yet I could clearly hear her voice. I could smell her scent, and I could feel her warmth. She was genuinely beautiful. She was not your average form of sexy or provocative. She looked arousing and classy, yet she exuded untainted innocence.

Her outfit was not formfitting. Still, I could easily see she had a beautiful body. She is average height. I'd assume five foot five. She has beautiful almond-colored skin. Her ethnicity is hard to determine. She has beautiful soft pouty lips and chestnut bedroom eyes hidden beneath long eyelashes. She has nicely toned running legs and full breasts. I have never been a breast man. I prefer women with small breasts, but hers seemed to fit her well.

It was a little windy out, so as she walked, the wind blew enticingly through her luscious, bouncy hair that she wore completely straightened, making her look very seductive. Her hair is raven black. It resembles Clara's. As I watched, within a matter of seconds, I wanted to make love to her. I had not made love in so long. How did I even remember how making love felt? But I was very aroused. She had awakened some life in me that I wanted back at that moment.

My Realtor had not arrived yet, but I did not wait for her. Once Peyton got into her car, I rushed to my car and followed. She was headed to some meeting. She was dressed professionally, but the others attending were dressed to their liking. I sat in my car for two hours, patiently waiting for Peyton's meeting to end.

Finally, she was driving to a new destination. I followed her to Montpelier for this meeting, but she lived closer to Burlington. She had a grand home. It seemed large for one person, so I assumed she was married, but she was not. I simply watched her go inside. I had no desire to disturb her. I had no urge to hurt her, which was new for me. I sat outside her home, expecting my need to kill to eventually overtake me, but it did not. I sat in the shadows a few hours, and once her lights went out, I restfully waited until morning.

She is out for a morning jog. She looks wonderful in her running gear. I follow discreetly and learn her jogging path. She returns home. Then an hour later she is dressed and headed back to Montpelier. I assume she will be there a couple of hours again, so I go to a nearby hotel and clean up. I purchase a casual outfit and then return to my post. I had purposed to go into her office, but then I chose not to. It's affiliated with a church. I did not want to meet the others. I only wanted Peyton.

I had already decided to purchase the home I saw near Dorset. This freed me to focus on my newfound obsession. I could not comprehend what is happening to me. However, after a month of following her, my obsession was mingled with infatuation. I knew her every move every second of the day, but I would not approach her. If I did not want her dead, what was my purpose in making myself known? There was none, so I continued to watch.

I suffered, watching Peyton yet another month. She had no mate. She had no children. She seemed a loner like me. The day I knew I had evolved is the day I saw her out with friends. They constantly laughed, and everyone seemed so joyful around Peyton. I followed them for a full day. They went to dinner and the theater, and then their night ended. I'm parked across the street. I rolled down my window to hear them interact. A man and woman dropped her off. Now they three are laughing, but I hear her sweet laugh above them all.

Laughing, Peyton says, "Casey, you're being bad! You're not displaying love when it comes to Regina!"

"I guess this is my test from the Lord 'cause she is unlovable!"

"C'mon, sweet, docile Regina? Unlovable? Maurice, help me out!"

Maurice chuckles, shaking his head. He calmly says, "I can't help, Peyton. Casey has purposed to hate her. Only God can help her now."

Casey loudly interrupts, "Whatever! And later for Regina, I'm still on you, Ms. Peyton Meryl! You need a man! When are you going to accept that?"

Peyton's laughter subsides. I focus in on her pure face as she sighs through a faint smile. Seemingly gazing at me through the trees and through the darkness and into my eyes, she solemnly says, "When he finds me, I'll know, and I will love him forever."

She stops gazing my way, but I continue staring at her. Casey replies with sarcasm, "Wow, that was powerful. I felt that."

Peyton bursts into laughter and says, "You just want me pathetically in love, don't you? Sorry, bestie, but I'm afraid that's never going to happen."

Casey pretends to fight her, but as they're playing, Peyton keeps looking in my direction. I'm sure she sees there is a car hidden in the darkness by now.

They are done for the evening. Peyton hugs Casey and then kisses Maurice good-bye. How I wanted that hug. I longed for her kiss. In that moment I decided to have her as my companion. Once they drove off, she stood staring my way momentarily before shutting the door. She then proceeded to cut off every light in her home. I suspected she was planning to spy on me, so once she went to the back, I drove off.

That desire to have a woman had returned with a vengeance. However, it was not a desire for women, but *that* woman! I began to want her so desperately that I ceased from following her after that particular night. I went home and planned my strategy. I even went underground a few days, hoping to rid myself of this rekindled need.

I needed to know if my desire could be fulfilled with any woman, not just Peyton, so I planned a date. I meet a very attractive woman. I take her out, and by the end of the night, I wanted to be rid of her. I really resolved to return her home safely, but she pleaded to stay with me. She begged to go to the water, so I take her to a private lake. Attempting to be romantic and look sexy, she runs to the lake. As the breeze from the lake whisks through her hair, she gives it a photoshoot flip and then runs her fingers seductively through it. Her eyes are closed as I frown her way. She reopens her eyes to me standing a few feet back.

"Come here, Wilhelm. I don't bite," she says and giggles.

I head her way. She grabs my hand and then kneels to the ground, trying to pull me down with her. Initially, I do not budge. She begs, "Please sit with me."

I stare out into the darkened lake momentarily. Then I sit next to her. She is the clerk at the store I purchased clothes from the day after I followed Peyton. She is a really sweet girl. She resembled Peyton a lot that day. I guess I had Peyton in my soul. Tonight she looks nothing like Peyton.

"You're so quiet and mysterious, Wilhelm. You just about know everything there is to know about me. Tell me about you."

"What do you want to know?"

"Anything."

"You have to be more specific for me to open up."

"I'll keep it simple for now, okay?" I nod. "So how tall are you?"

"Six foot three."

"What's your ethnicity?"

"Pardo."

"What's that?"

"Mixed up."

"Ha-ha! Interesting. So what are your races?

"White, Brazilian, and Native American is what I'm told."

"Okay, you look as if you were born in … Brazil, right?"

"No, Britain."

"Ha! No way! Isn't Britain like 99 percent white?" I do not reply. I simply stare.

"Well, I asked because your race is very hard to figure out. You have white features like your dainty mouth and small nose, but your skin color seems too dark for a white person. And your hair is thick, not coarse, but just awesome!" She chuckles. "Wilhelm, you don't look white or mixed. You just look different. But for my sake I'll claim you as my own. I'm deeming you white. So which of your parents is mixed? Hmm, let me guess. Your mom, right?"

"No, my father. His family traveled the world. They had been clergymen and missionaries for centuries."

"Wow. Are you in the clergy?"

"I said had. That generation has long past."

"Well, your dad is still living, no?"

"No."

"I'm sorry. I was supposed to keep it simple. Okay, what's your favorite food?"

"Young."

"Ha-ha! I get it! I'm definitely young! I'm twenty-four. How old are you?"

"Older than twenty-four."

Leaning her head to the side, she huffs. "Wilhelm, I'm trying to get to know you. You seem agitated tonight. Am I boring you? Do you still like me?" She pouts and bats her eyes.

"I do. I think you're very pretty and kind, but I need to get you home."

"Why?"

"It's late."

"I don't have a curfew, do you?" she says and giggles.

I feel my hunger stirring. I stand with my hand outstretched.

"Please let me get you home."

She takes my hand. I lift her. She trips on my feet, falling into me. She's about Peyton's height, so her head lands on my chest. She sensually gazes up at me with a cutesy smile. I'm glaring down at her. She assumes I'm aroused. I am, but not how she hopes.

She gently rubs my face, saying, "God, you're so beautiful."

She lifts my hand and gently kisses it. I then lift her and gently lie her on her back, and before I knew it, her intestines were flowing out of her stomach. I stand admiring the blood spewing out of her. It's then I accepted I had to approach Peyton.

The night of the New Year's party, I did not know what to expect. I was accustomed to Peyton hanging with her friends Maurice and Casey or her friend Regina. I never witnessed her out with a man. I overheard Casey telling her she needed a date, but I did not know they had produced one.

The invited guests are arriving. I am seated with a view of the entrance, so I will see Peyton enter. I recognize Casey. Then comes Maurice. Peyton and some guy, who has her arm, then enter. Consciously, I could not comprehend she was there with a boyfriend. Once I asked and she confirmed she indeed had a date, I had to constrain myself. Had Peyton said she and Juan were in a committed relationship, I would have taken her that night. Nevertheless, seeing Peyton equally attracted to me gave me the false hope everything would go perfectly.

Unfortunately, nothing went as I planned. I quickly conjured up a new scheme. However, this time I did not have the patience to wait months. I barely made it through the weeks I endured. The day I went to her office, I was on the brink of losing my self-control. Peyton's response to me was very belittling. I soon realized I could never reveal I knew all about her. I calmly accepted I had to learn what was needed to gain her trust.

Peculiarly, not my looks or charm won her trust, but her weakness was my wit. It seemed she was more attracted to my intellect, and had it not been for Casey, our rendezvous in Fiji would have sealed our fate. However, the day the Scotts distracted her from me was the final straw. Killing her seemed inevitable, but on our way home, once I had her to myself again, I wanted her to remain. I returned my focus to building a relationship with her.

Peyton shunning me after we visited Zoe's left me without a choice—other than taking her. I sit in total darkness in my sacred haven for a couple of days, but my every thought is consumed by Peyton. I snap out of my meditation and head straight to her home. Peyton is leaving with a group of people, so I follow. This caravan leads to Tabitha's estate. They are grossly engaged in this prayer party. I sit and just watch. I purpose to approach her at work or at her home, but Tabitha's estate is now her new domain. Moreover, even when she goes home, she is never alone. After two weeks I am at my wit's end. I follow her to Tabitha's. After a few minutes of watching them plan my annihilation, my need for her overrules my reasoning. I take who's rightfully mine. I had paid my dues to obtain Peyton, and at that very second, I wanted my reward.

I come out of my thoughts and behold Peyton's helpless, battered body. I want to feel what I felt staring at my date's dead, mutilated body, but I do not. The dilemma I constantly face is as soon as the feeling leaves, it returns with a vengeance. I have attained Peyton to destroy her. My hate for her is real, but this feeling is more real.

I stand motionless, waiting to see if Peyton is still alive. My heart begins beating faster and faster the longer she appears lifeless. My chest tightens as I kneel down next to her. I feel the pain of loss as I slowly reach out to touch her. Breathless, I go to say her name. Suddenly, she flinches, and then my hate returns. I instantly attack her.

Love Conquers All

Finally, it is night. I sit looking through the storm windows, watching the ocean's billowing waves. The house is very quiet. Peyton has been gone for four days. I feel the emptiness. I purchased this estate to share, not live in solitude. I am forced to wait in silence. It's just me, my thoughts, and this maudlin feeling of loneliness. How did I allow myself to get here?

I delve deep into my memory to feel the peace that used to exist in my world. I was a mortal man who once upon a time was content. I had aspirations that superseded most rationale, but that was me in my fullness.

I think of Clara. She was a good lady. I remember how she was the only person who knew how to make me laugh. Although we were intimate, she was only a friend. I knew she wanted to be so much more, but she respected my wishes. She found contentment in our almost platonic relationship.

Clara was rather plain. I would not classify her as an ugly woman, but she definitely was not who others envisioned me choosing. She did not wear makeup or jewelry. She dressed very modestly. Her skin looked as if she lacked sun, yet her hair and eyes were dark, making her look even paler. She was taller than most women, rather thin, and unshapely. However, she was fit and tried to live a healthy lifestyle because she was constantly learning new things in her profession. Many despised me with her, but I did not care what others thought. She made me happy. Because of my status, her connection to me was surreal, and my choosing her made her equally happy. Clara was the balance in my world. I often thought if I ever desired a wife, I hoped she would be as supportive and comforting to my needs and desires as Clara. Whatever I thought or believed, Clara thought and believed with me.

I met Clara at a ball her father had given to celebrate her younger sister's wedding. I was there as a movie star that night. I was paid to take photos and entertain the lady guests. Her father wanted to appear wealthier than he was. He would do outlandish things like hire the most popular celebrity. He would waste masses of money on trivial things to impress people. Clara hated it, but she loved her father. Her sister was the pretty daughter while Clara was considered the ugly one who was never expected to marry. Well, not by way of love and romance but most likely by arrangement or convenience.

This ball was filled with shallow, silly women, but Clara was intelligent and witty. She was a breath of fresh air in this cesspool of wanton women. She was my lady of choice that night and thereafter. As a result, she became the envy of the town. Our now public relationship caused her to receive the respect and notoriety she rightfully deserved.

Clara was actually a genius. What she lacked in looks, she gained in wisdom and intellect. I introduced her to the celebrity and regal world. In return, she introduced me to those who truly knew and controlled all things. My world only had the power to purchase what those in her world possessed naturally. I guess it is how things stay balanced in the world. Clara taught me gratitude and purpose. Our relationship made me appreciate the natural order of things a little more. She was my special needed friend.

There was no way I could have endured Helena without Clara's help. Because of her wealth, Helena often paid the directors or whomever for roles in my productions. Thank goodness I had the power to choose the leading ladies of my films. If ever I would have kissed her, even acting, she would have gone stark mad. She was not like the weak stalkers you see today. She was relentless and open with her obsession. She wanted me as her own beyond what was decent. And she hated Clara beyond hatred. At my request, Clara accompanied me to every event I had to keep Helena away from me.

Helena practiced the dark arts, so she often left little trinkets, bones, and all types of so-called spells and hexes in my dressing rooms. She was hoping to bewitch me into loving her. I could not understand her need then, but I can now. However, she was someone who needed to be locked up, but because of her prestige, no one could touch her. Helena attempted to have Clara killed at least twice. So to ensure Clara's safety, briefly at the beginning of our friendship, I pretended Clara was a relative, but Helena was not buying that story. Clara and my relative status caused others to shun Helena. It curtailed her schemes a brief moment in time, but she was a force to be reckoned with. Helena is a story I cannot forget, but I am trying to think positive thoughts. She is a bad memory of another desired woman gone wrong. I divert my focus back to Clara.

I was twenty-four years old when I met Clara. She was twenty-nine. We were friends three years before we were ever intimate. I cared deeply for Clara, so I asked her about love.

"Have you ever desired to be intimate with someone before?" I ask.

"Well, yes, of course!" Clara answers.

"I'd love to hear about it."

"Wilhelm, no—"

"Please tell me," I whisper.

Although I asked, I would never hope or expect she'd tell about her desire for me. I would stop her if I even thought she would talk about me. I genuinely wanted to hear a story about Clara.

That was when she told me this pathetic story about a crush she had on a college professor.

I replied, "Clara thinks about sex ... rousing." Blushing, shaking her head, she attempted to move away. I caressed her arm and asked, "Where are you going?"

This was the first time I had ever invited Clara into my bedroom. We had removed our shoes and were lying side by side in my bed, casually talking. I knew this conversation would make her very uncomfortable, but this is what I wanted. I needed to see her heart as I seduced her.

Wide-eyed, she says, "I'm simply shifting positions. Well, I've told my story. Tell me a story of a woman *you* wanted, not about the ones who wanted you!"

"Why about the one I wanted? The others are boring, right?" I frown.

"Boring? I wouldn't go that far!"

"Sex is boring, period."

After my last statement, I intently watch her. She tries to stare back, but my gaze is overwhelming her. Looking away, she then says, "Well, if it's so boring, why do you do it?

"You're right, Clara. No more sex for me."

"Are you attempting to be funny right now?" she says sarcastically and laughs.

"Well, no. And you're too far away. Come here."

I pull her close. I can feel her heart pounding. We're now sitting up on the bed, facing each other. My eyes are closed as I hold her by her waist. I lean in as if I'm going to kiss her. I slightly open my eyes, now watching as she closes her eyes and leans in to kiss me back. I slowly pull away and crawl out of the bed. I stretch and then begin walking slowly around my bed, giving her an enticing gaze.

My bed has four huge Mahoney posts. Grasping a post as I circle the bed and walk toward her, I ask, "Are you a clean woman, Clara?"

"Yes," she nervously answers and then looks away.

She's sitting on her feet at the edge of the bed. Initially, she sits facing me, but now I'm standing behind her. I then whisper into her ear, "You don't have to be."

She shivers from my touch as I caress her waist. She then timidly says, "I thought you were done with sex."

Slowly turning her to face me, I say, "I am. I want to make love. Would you please make love to me, Clara?" Trembling, she nods yes. I then ask, "Do you love me, Clara?"

With a confused gaze, she breathlessly whispers, "Yes. Do you love me, Wilhelm?" Her eyes fill with tears.

"That is a hard thing, Clara. You say you love me, but love is as strong as death and its jealousy as cruel as the grave. How have you even prepared your heart for something so powerful?"

She drops her head, shrugging. Gently caressing her breasts, I whisper into her ear, "Know it is only you who has made me even think to ever consider it."

As I make love to Clara, I can feel her submission. I knew I absolutely owned her now. She told me she loved me over and over. As she totally gave herself to me, I began to feel sorry for her. I did not love her, but I did enjoy the moment with her. It was a different experience from all the other women I had been with. I was actually pleased that I made her feel so loved. It was something I thought I was incapable of doing.

Once I went through my transition, Clara and I grew apart. I now found that peace within myself. I needed no one to support, love, or believe in me. I was now invincible.

I couldn't see what I was doing so wrong, but she could. And often I would make her cry. I eventually asked her to leave me alone because it seemed all I did was make her unhappy. She tried to endure, but after a few months, I had changed so drastically. I could no longer stand the sight of Clara. When she told me that she was going to leave me alone, I thanked her.

I can still see the despair on her face, but tonight I can feel the pain in her heart. I now comprehend the agony of wholeheartedly giving yourself to another. Then the person despises you. I feel the longing and despondency of wanting to have her near me … until it is no longer a feeling of want but of need.

I wished I could reach Clara today and tell her I understand what she experienced now. I would allow her the chance to tell me what she did to prepare for such a cruel task. Nonetheless, Clara is long gone. Thus, I will never be afforded that opportunity.

Then I wondered if Peyton even had the heart to think of me? Leaving so abruptly without warning, did she care for a second how I would feel? I do not want my thoughts going down this road. I attempt to fill my head with random memories, trying to curb this need I have for her. I have become accustomed to her being at my disposal, but she is not here. What do I do?

I have absolutely no desire for any other being. I have gone from having any woman I desired to not needing a woman at all to needing exclusively one person! My so-called gift has betrayed me.

Joy? What is that? Peace? I no longer comprehend the definition of it. I had no need for emotions. They left my psyche decades ago, but tonight I am overtaken by them. It's every emotion I despised and thought I had conquered. Needing, longing, and loneliness were emotions I never experienced. Can you imagine having to endure them simultaneously?

Finally, I comprehend why love is as strong as death. Death conquers every living thing. It cannot be contended or vanquished. Once it has you, there is no escape. You cannot be freed from it. In summation, it has left me powerless. I had forsaken all to obtain power, yet here I am stripped of it by love. I guess the word is true—love conquers all.

Curiosity … Kills

Curiosity has its hold on me. I know what my sister said, but I have to see my fugitive's face.

My friends are already wasted, so I could tell them nothing. They would have foiled everything. I had to convince them to stay on this beach for almost three hours, so drinking had to be involved. After an hour and a half, my sister calls and tells me Peyton and Wilhelm have come out to the beach. My girlfriend, Ashland, notices Wilhelm instantly. She's ranting and raving on how fine he is, and she is going bonkers! Ashland's loud and belligerent so I grab her and tackle her to the ground. Her boyfriend picks her up and then carries her into the water.

We're laughing. Then I look over to where Peyton is, and Wilhelm and I lock eyes. A chill runs down my spine. He is beautiful. Peyton goes over to the ocean. She's beautiful too. She has on a royal blue bikini, and her body is nice. I peek to see what Wilhelm is doing. He's serenely sitting in the sand. His knees are up. His elbows are resting on his knees, and his eyes are fixed upon Peyton. My friends are loud and out of control, but Wilhelm isn't distracted. As I'm watching, my best friend,

Cody, comes over to me and then asks, "Is there a reason you brought us here?"

Victoria instructed me not to let anyone know anything. I can't even make mention of her store on the beach. I answer, "It's just so pretty here. I needed to relax before our journey back to campus."

Cody responds, "Cool. Well, I'm going to get shorty's number over there. She's super hot!"

I laugh. Then I realize he's referring to Peyton. I want to stop him, but once again, I'm curious to see what will happen. Cody sprints to the water and then dives in. He begins swimming toward Peyton. I look over at Wilhelm, but he remains poised. As soon as Cody is near Peyton, she promptly gets out the water and jogs over to Wilhelm. I see Wilhelm has her trained. Cody stands, looks at me, and then shrugs. I laugh as I discreetly return my focus back to my subjects.

Peyton's whispering something into Wilhelm's ear. I think they're talking. A few more people are now on the beach. Ashland whines, "Ugh, I'm ready to go!"

"Okay!" I say, pushing to prevent her from blocking my view of Peyton, who's now lying on her back, bathing in the sun.

I walk away from the crowd and call Vicki. "My friends are getting restless. I'll have to leave shortly," I tell her.

"I'm calling now!" Vicki immediately gets Peyton on speakerphone.

"Hey, see the four college students? One guy has on the red and white WSU tee," says Vicki.

"Yes," Peyton answers.

"They're getting ready to go. Sorry, doll, but you must leave now!"

"Okay."

I get off the phone, and I notice Wilhelm is still in his same sitting position. Peyton stands and gazes toward the ocean with him. She looks at him, but Wilhelm doesn't react. Peyton begins walking toward Vicki's. Clueless of the part my friends and I are playing, she enters the store. I turn toward Wilhelm and watch him. Immediately, I tell my friends, "Let's go." Ashland complains she has to use the restroom first, and I want to strangle her. I continue watching Wilhelm, and he's either meditating or asleep because he hasn't moved. Ashland returns. We get into my SUV and then drive off.

We get to Ocean's View Grill, a local restaurant, and there's a table filled with police. Thank goodness because this assures Ashland will be on her best behavior. However, I want to see Peyton's face, so I purposely leave my wallet in my glove compartment. I sneak out and watch her exit my SUV. Vicki gave her a T-shirt and leggings to wear. She's young, very pretty face, but she looks numb. I feel so sorry for her. I watch her safely get into the building across the street. I call Vicki and let her know the mission was a success.

Peyton left a little more than a week ago, so I have been calling every other day to see if anything exciting has happened. I hadn't called today. Then while in class, Vicki texted me:

Vicki: Wilhelm finally confronted me!!!
Morgan: What??? What'd he say???

Vicki: If he finds out I helped her, it will end very bad for me!
Morgan: What!!! Is he crazy??
Vicki: Crazy! But SUPER gorgeous!!!!! Lol
Morgan: I'm in class, will call u in an hour!
Vicki: Ok

After class I call, but Vicki never answers. After several hours of no response, I call Tony. He doesn't know where she has gone. The next morning my family and I are worried sick. My parents and I go over to Vicki's home, and Tony exposes my sister's adulterous lifestyle. It is now a fiasco. Tony's worried and infuriated at the same time. My mom is worried and mortified. I'm sitting there, wondering if I should tell them what I know. My dad is the only rational person in the room. I take him to Vicki's bedroom and tell him what I did. Now my dad's upset with me. He storms downstairs. Then he and Tony head to the police.

"We made a report to Officer Lynn. I don't trust the men there. Vicki had an affair with one of them," Tony says.

We're relieved the police were informed, but now all we can do is wait.

Months have passed, and Vicki still hasn't returned. I tried to finish my semester, but I'm mentally unable to study statistics and economics during this dreadful time in my family's life. I'm spending my last few nights at my apartment before I head home permanently. Then someone knocks at my door. I look out the window and see a black foreign luxury car in my parking space. Out of sheer curiosity, I open the door. It's Wilhelm.

. . . *Kills*

Things have gone awry. I have found Peyton, but I am filled with rage. I return to Washington one final time to ensure all was still intact at my old estate. Afterward, I begin to feel ill-treated, and I desire revenge.

It is well into the evening. I am standing in the dark, deep in thought, admiring our former residence. This is a gorgeous estate that could have been our perfect home. Feeling cheated, I go down my list in my head, and I remember Morgan. She was someone who definitely deserved to be punished. I immediately head to her apartment. I had researched and found Morgan initially, but during that time I was too focused on finding Peyton. I did not want to bring extra attention to myself by adding Morgan's disappearance.

I get to her apartment, and it is on the second floor. Experience has taught me I should prepare to kill more than one person. I knock twice, and she opens the door without hesitation. I enter, staring. She stands there, stunned. Still, I say nothing.

"You're welcome to sit down," she nervously says.

Now sitting, I continue to stare without responding. "Wilhelm I don't know where Peyton is, but do you know where my sister is?" she boldly asks.

"I found Peyton."

She begins to cry. Then someone knocks at the door. She turns and looks at me. I extend my hand toward the door, letting her know she may answer it. Her friend enters. He sees she is crying, but initially, he acknowledges me.

"What's up?" he says.

I nod. Then he returns his focus to Morgan. I sit and observe them. I let her whisper to him briefly.

"It must be nice being able to visit the one you love without a legion of people getting involved," I comment.

They both stop whispering and begin listening. "What's your name?" I ask.

"Cody."

"Cody, is this your girlfriend?"

"No, Morgan's my best friend."

"Is that by choice, or is it because that is the only way you can be near her?"

Cody swallows from nervousness and then looks at Morgan. Gazing into her eyes, he answers, "It's not by choice."

Morgan shakes her head and then yells, "Why are you here?"

"Cody, it is not my choice to be away from my girl either. But thanks to you and Morgan, she is far away." I stand.

Perplexed, Cody looks to Morgan, seeking answers. She suddenly cries out, "Did you kill Vicki?"

Cody instantly grabs Morgan and pushes her behind him. He shouts, "This is Wilhelm? Morgan, call the police!"

"Morgan, if you love Cody, you will not call anyone."

"He's bluffing. Call the police!" Cody yells.

I grab Cody and slam his head on the floor so hard it bursts open. Morgan starts screaming uncontrollably. I get in her face and put my finger to my mouth, telling her to be quiet. She starts gagging, so I push her away. She throws up all over the couch and table.

Repulsed, I say, "It is disgusting in here. Wash your face and change your clothing. We are going for a ride." She does as she is told. Then we get into my car.

Morgan sits, emotionless. I am certain she is in shock. I drive her to a remote area in the mountains. I have no desire to explain what she has done wrong because she knows. Plus I think her sanity has left. I park on the side of the mountain. I lead her to the cliff and then shove her over. I could have been nice and brought Cody, but why bother? I am mentally drained. I have grown tired of hatching new schemes. I cannot be traced or caught. My fingerprints lead to a dead man who no longer exists. My car will lead to a nonexistent woman in Canada, so I simply drive off.

Casey's Confession

Regina is on the phone with Antonio. He's convincing her that Tabitha and I are wrong. Regina's sobbing like she just lost her mother. I love Peyton, but these two act as if she's 100 percent pure. This conversation is grieving me, so I politely ask Regina to get off the phone. Regina sits quietly—pondering my request, I'm sure.

"I have a question to ask, and please hear my heart. Why aren't you upset? Do you think Peyton going through this is a joke?" Regina asks in anger.

"What are you talking about, Regina? Because I'm not believing the lie and accepting the truth, you have a problem with me?" I shout.

"Casey, you're the liar creating the lie! I have been silent way too long! Since it's just you and me, I have to say it. Do you want Wilhelm?"

I yell, "Oh my God! Stop worshipping Peyton like she's a god! You all know she has to be sleeping with this man, yet you all act as if she isn't! It's obvious she wants to be with him, but you all act like she's being forced! Tabitha just revealed she came and voluntarily left with him!"

Regina begins to laugh through her tears. She's utterly appalled by my beliefs. With a gagging gesture, Regina yells, "You are sick! Is that all you're concerned about, that she may have slept with him? If she's riding him from sunup to sundown, who cares! Our sister has been missing for seven months, and now she's gone again! We want her back safe and in her right mind! That's our concern, not that he's screwing her!"

Regina leaves. I want to call Maurice again, but I can't. I must confess that I initially wasn't too fond of Peyton. Peyton and I have been friends a little more than five years. I met her through church. Her parents were missionaries—Charleston and Malan Meryl. They actually funded the building of our church, making Peyton our *golden child*. She seemed distant and untouchable. Her entire life had been rooted in church, so I assumed we had nothing in common.

I was your typical wild child. I went to college. I had boyfriends and sex, and I partied too. Then one day I was invited to our ministry and found Jesus. I had much zeal and ambition like most to save the world! Therefore, I wanted to work in every auxiliary. Because of my willingness to work, I was introduced to Peyton, whose life consisted only of church work. Once we started doing ministry together, I fell in love with her. She was an excellent example. However, I still wanted relationships and to have fun outside of the sanctuary.

Don't misunderstand me. Peyton was very enjoyable to be around. We traveled together and everything. Our relationship only began to broaden once I started dating Maurice. Maurice is saved, but he wasn't as involved as Peyton and I were. Once he and I established a committed relationship, I wasn't as dedicated as I used to be to my duties. My commitment to church hasn't changed, but moving toward marriage will consume more of your time. It is written that the married woman is concerned about the things of the world and how she can please her husband. Granted, Maurice and I aren't married yet, but soon we will be. So marrying him was now my main focus.

Maurice was very fond of Peyton. He often attempted to find her a man. Whenever we went out as a group, his friends were constantly begging Maurice to introduce them to Peyton. She was a gorgeous girl and an extremely classy lady. Then by some miracle, Peyton was dating!

He was a man of God, and he was very attractive. He was a minister. Thus, he wanted to be married immediately. But Peyton wasn't having it! She wasn't moved by his vehement love for her. She found every flaw he possessed and ultimately ran him away.

Six months later he was married and starting his own ministry. Peyton was relieved, but I was so angry.

"Well, you blew it, Peyton! God will never send anyone that perfect your way again! You're just too picky and ungrateful!"

She thought I was overreacting, so my words didn't move her one iota. After that nightmare, I left her dating life alone. Then it was the issue of no life outside of church! Oh my goodness! Peyton's parents left her wealthy. She never wanted for anything. Nevertheless, I thought she needed a career as an outlet to meet new people. A place to coexist with the secular world, but that, too, was a disaster.

Peyton wasn't that fanatic who couldn't say a sentence without adding Jesus. Nor was she so spiritually spooky you couldn't relate to her. However, she wanted nothing to do with this world. I understood her stance, but personally, I couldn't fully embrace it.

We were slowly drifting apart, but Maurice insisted that wasn't wise. He comprehended she was just used to being alone. She was an only child who had lost her parents and had learned to exist contently on her own. He asked if I would mind if he got a little involved because he thought he knew how to crack her hard shell. And sure enough, he did!

He wanted her to hang with us without us pressuring her to date or lecturing her about getting a life. He learned that if you just allow people to be who they are without imposing your will upon them, they will eventually share their hearts. Then you can be helpful.

"Casey, the reality is you don't know her. You refuse to let her be Peyton. You make her feel as if being Peyton is all wrong yet being you is all right," Maurice explained.

After Maurice chastised me, I left Peyton alone, and she surely opened up. She admitted she could be too hard on her dates and that maybe she would soon start a career. Peyton's newfound lifestyle was in full bloom. We invited her to the New Year's Eve party expecting her to decline, but she said yes! We told her we wanted to get her a date, and she agreed to that too! Now my mind was blown! I already loved Maurice, but now he wasn't only my man but *the man* in my world!

Peyton and I went to Maurice's office right before New Year's. We hang with him a couple of hours, and then we head to the mall. We then go to the coffee shop to relax.

I say, "Now that your watchdog Regina isn't present, please tell me why you won't date, Peyton? Men love you. Maurice has texted me several times already, saying how his coworkers are feigning to date you!"

Blushing, shaking her head, she answers, "I don't know, Cass!"

"You do know! Tell me!"

"Lately, I have been thinking about love. I see how happy you and Maurice are, and I want to have that too."

"So go get it! What's hindering you?"

"Being too picky, I guess. I just don't want to choose a fool. I want him to be sexy and fine, smooth and cool, but he has to be wise and love God as much as I do. That seems so hard to find. I don't need some counterfeit to deceive me. If I feel anything wrong about a man, I immediately end the relationship! That's just me." She shrugs.

"I fully understand your concern, but there's no perfect man. Sorry you can't marry Jesus. He's our brother! Plus that's disgusting!"

She thought that joke was pretty funny. It made her laugh, but I could tell she received a revelation in it as well. I then say, "You'll never find him if you don't at least date and see, right?"

She nods. I then show her a new text from Maurice. Juan wants her to be his date for the New Year's Eve party. I pull the phone back and then say, "Here's your moment of truth. Yes or no?"

She nods yes and then covers her face, shaking her head. I tell her Juan said great. She shoves me as we laugh like high schoolers that received a note from our secret crush. Peyton and I spent the next couple of days finding the perfect dresses.

The night of the party, I called that morning and had Maurice tell her that we were celebrating life. We were going to have a champagne toast after midnight, so she had to participate.

"Well, of course! What's the purpose of going if I don't intend on joining in the festivities?" Peyton laughed.

We didn't want Peyton to drink regularly or date weekly. That wasn't our goal. We simply wanted Peyton to enjoy life just a little. She was almost thirty, and she had never had a sip of wine or an intimate kiss. She was such an amazing woman. We didn't want her youth and magnificence wasted because she was unwilling to get out of her own way. Finally, she understood our hearts. I knew this night was going to be awesome!

Our party consists of eight people—Maurice and me, Peyton and Juan, and two other couples. The atmosphere in this place was sheer energy. Truly, we have never had as much fun as we all had that night. Everything was perfect. The icing on the cake was when Wilhelm approached Peyton.

Words can't describe the awesomeness of this man. I must admit that when I saw him, I hated I was there with Maurice. Wilhelm was the perfect height. He had some type of accent, but it wasn't too heavy. It was sexy and perfect! Everything about him from his clothing to his skin was perfection. His aroma was perfect. His tuxedo fit perfectly. He was simply *perfect*! Easily, he had a room of at least five hundred people captivated!

Inwardly, I thought, *This just isn't fair! Peyton gets the absolute best in everything!* Then when he came to the table, every woman in that place wanted to die and come back as Peyton! Even after Wilhelm left and Juan knew his dream of dating Peyton had been eradicated, he still was excited to be there. I think everyone was intoxicated, but not from alcohol only. We were high on life. We were young, wealthy, healthy, and ready to conquer this new year together. However, after a few days, I noticed Peyton was going back into her comfort zone. Then when I learned she hadn't called Wilhelm, I immediately intervened. I begged Maurice to find her something to do in his firm. He did, and I was thankful.

My trust in Peyton's stability started to wane the day she told me she blacked out and awakened to Wilhelm standing over her. That was insane! But she goes out with him again? I trust my friend, so I do not meddle. Then she casually invites him to Fiji? A woman who's not sexually active doesn't invite a strange man to go on a vacation with her, especially if he blatantly told her he wanted to have sex with her … on their first date! Who does that?

I didn't hesitate to go to Fiji because I was truly concerned about my friend's state of mind. Her desire to see him still had me fully convinced she had slept with him that first date and was now infatuated with him. However, the conversation that convinced me she had been intimate with him was about the day she ran into the Scotts. She stopped calling me and Wilhelm. The day I called to see why she was avoiding me, she began ranting about some mystery woman named Zoe and how all she did was work for Jesus! Blah, blah, blah. It was just a weird feeling.

I have never known Peyton to be a liar, so I couldn't accept she was fabricating these stories. I accepted Wilhelm obviously had some type of superpower. I didn't write that off as a bold lie, but what I wrote off were her unspoken truths. I wanted her to admit she was into him. All this fame and new celebrity, but all she exposed was how he killed and how he had supposedly sold his soul. She talked of how she prayed and resisted and escaped. She preached salvation, which was all good, but why did this homicidal maniac need her there? Was she killing too? What was her purpose?

Peyton was a true saint to our church. Everyone believed she was kidnapped. Even after Pastor White announced she was in the hospital because of stress or some garbage, Regina and Antonio were still telling everyone she had been taken. I knew talking to Regina would be useless, so I reached out to Antonio.

One evening he and I went out to eat alone. After his deep story about visiting Tabitha's estate, I say, "Did Peyton tell you that man may have raped her, but she still dated him and invited him to Fiji with her?"

Antonio's jaw is dropped. "What! Casey, that doesn't even sound like Peyton! You're tripping."

"I'm her best friend. She tells me everything! Remember how I flew out to Fiji and then Hawaii with her so she wouldn't be alone with him? I know it's hard to believe. Hell, I'm closest to her, and I'm in disbelief. But trust me. She's been with him. She hasn't been our

Peyton since she met him! Antonio, she got on TV and asked him if he raped her! So why are my beliefs so far-fetched to you people?"

After that meeting Antonio and Regina started building an army against me. Even my Maurice started siding with them. I was so frustrated I wanted to leave that church until I talked to Pastor White's wife, Sister Cecilia.

"Hey, Casey, I'd like for you and me to talk this evening. Are you free?" Sister Cecilia asks.

"Yes, Sister Cecilia."

"Great! Meet me in an hour."

I meet Sister Cecilia at a restaurant. I expected Pastor White to be there too, but it's only us.

"Thanks for coming, and this conversation is strictly between you and me, okay?" I nod, so she continues, "Regina's mother told me she overheard Antonio telling her husband a detective seeking information on Peyton visited him. Has anyone contacted you?"

Sighing, I answer, "Yes."

Antonio's such a pussy. Vaughn told us not to reveal this to anyone. I never expected this secret to get out. So too, I didn't want anyone to know what I told him.

Vaughn approached me one evening at work. He was an attractive older man. He seemed very intelligent and extremely wealthy.

"Casey, Wilhelm's family is very dear to me. They're very prominent and respected people who love the Lord. Did you know Wilhelm is a church leader in his country?" Vaughn asks.

"Wow! No!"

"Yes, he's very well respected. He was only to be here for a short time, but somehow your friend has convinced him to stay. Has she contacted you explaining why they've left like this?"

"No, she hasn't, and several of our church members seem to think he abducted her and that he's demonic."

"Demonic? What in heaven does that mean?"

"Absolutely nothing! Just a bunch of spiritual foolishness to make Peyton seem purer than she is!" I say, rolling my eyes.

Vaughn goes on and on about Wilhelm's innocence in this madness. I tell him I think Peyton's choosing to be with him, and he confirms she is. He tells me that he's seen them interact several times and that she's willingly with Wilhelm.

"Casey, I can't reveal their whereabouts. His family pays me very well for his privacy. But I've heard those viscous accusations from several people. It's really traumatizing to hear these people speak so negatively about such a great individual. Please reveal this truth to your church family and to anyone you hear spreading these malicious rumors."

Sister Cecilia didn't really comment on what I revealed. She thanked me and switched the conversation to church business, and then we left.

After telling her all that, I tried to tell Maurice, Antonio, and Regina, but they refused to listen. Then God vindicated me. A week later Peyton returned home. She had no idea what Vaughn had revealed to me, so I'd question her, hoping for the truth, but to no avail. Peyton spoke with such conviction I didn't know who to believe.

But once her interviews started, I was leaning evermore toward Vaughn's story.

Then to add injury to insult, after Sister Cecilia and I spoke, she became distant as ever. Antonio ended up telling me she saw I was too envious to rightly judge what was going on with Peyton. My believing Vaughn over our church members proved I wanted Wilhelm myself. I was offended and humiliated, but finally, things were calming down. One producer blatantly called Peyton a fraud, yet my church overlooked it.

Peyton supposedly halted her interviews, although I read networks stopped using her because she was a phony! But who could I tell? In these pathetic people's mind, I was just too jealous, so nothing I said held merit anymore.

Those of us not blinded by her untainted image of purity could see clearly that Peyton was no longer pure. She wanted to be with Wilhelm. The day I asked what Wilhelm wanted from her and she answered by saying *love*, I learned her true purpose. Why wouldn't she reveal that? Why was that information so sacred? I was grieved, and my complaints against Peyton had Regina ready to brawl.

Regina and I were never friends. We were simply connected through Peyton. She was Peyton's groupie in my book. I can't expect Peyton's most loyal fan to turn on her. I happily decided to avoid Regina altogether.

The night Regina and I went to Tabitha's brought the answer to my deepest prayers. Tabitha witnessed this twisted relationship with her own eyes. Hearing her tell naive Regina that Wilhelm and Peyton came and left together caused me to let out a sigh of relief. I had known—not just now but for years—that Peyton was not perfect. I hated that the truth had to be exposed so drastically, but people needed to know.

I was slightly envious the night Wilhelm approached her. He was gorgeous and wealthier than any of us could have imagined! But God knows best. God knew she needed to be humbled. She appeared genuine. We deceived ourselves into believing she didn't think she was better than us, but she did! This public exposure was the move of the Almighty.

The world still didn't know, but the church had to know. Peyton was a fraud. She fell for Wilhelm like any other woman would have! Her pride and arrogance made her hide and then act as if he had her against her will. This disappearing act was just that, an act. We thought she was dead a year ago, but she returned. And she'll return again. The word is true. Just confess your sins to one another. Confession frees you and me.

Regina's Discretion

Casey sits there, looking extremely stupid, but she has seemingly calmed down. "Why don't you believe Tabitha?" Casey sincerely asks.

Trying earnestly to help Casey comprehend Peyton's horrific tragedy, I respond, "I forget you weren't there when Wilhelm took Peyton. We had been talking to Tabitha for weeks, and nothing was wrong with this woman! Tabitha and I witnessed him turn the entire area black and then magically disappear while a dozen or more of us were watching! Antonio was there. Ask him! Peyton sacrificed her life for Tabitha, and to see this old witch change on Peyton is sickening! Those of us who were there know she's being held against her own will, and we know he's demonic!"

Of course, Casey has no rebuttal. Casey has always envied Peyton. It was Casey finding Maurice that allowed her not to envy her as much, and that enable the two women to build a relationship. Peyton knew Casey envied her, but her character allowed a friendship to develop despite Casey's motives. This is not the time for jealousy and envy to take precedence in her heart. Someone had to confront Casey and stop this assassination of Peyton's character during the most traumatic time of her life.

We're now back at church. After my last tirade, we remained silent. I exit her car quietly and then head to my car without looking back. I am officially finished with Casey. Our friendship only existed through our connection with Peyton. Now that Peyton's gone, Casey and I have nothing in common. I'm thrilled to be rid of her! I just wished it could've ended through the death of Casey, not the loss of Peyton.

My family took Peyton in once her parents died. She was an adult who could live on her own, but my parents clung to her. They felt as if they owed everything to the Meryls. Being there for the Meryls' only child was the least my parents could do to show them their love and respect.

When Casey first joined our ministry, her disdain for Peyton was easily detected. I often warned Peyton to watch her back around Casey, but Peyton simply wasn't that person. Peyton gave everyone a fair chance and shunned no one. Peyton was wise, so she wasn't ignorant to Casey's jealousy. However, once Casey started dating Maurice, he helped her see Peyton's goodness. Then she seemed to genuinely be a friend to Peyton.

When Peyton said she wasn't attending church service New Year's Eve, I wasn't pleased. I asked why, and she gave me an earful of nothing but excuses that sounded like Casey. I just listened.

"I hear you, Casey, but how does Peyton feel?" I ask sarcastically.

"Regina this is me. I really want to go. I desire to experience something new." She laughs.

"Because I trust you, I won't worry too much, but please be careful. And no drinking."

She hugged me and then left. Surprisingly, after her party, I hadn't spoken to Peyton in a couple of days.

Weekly at the church, we need volunteers to pass out flyers in the community. Casey happened to be there with me. I overheard her talking about the party, and she begins to tell of Peyton and Wilhelm. Now why is she telling this member, who only knows Peyton as a leader here, about this party? It seems innocent, but there was nothing innocent about Casey when it came to Peyton. Her motives were never pure in my sight. I could easily see she secretly wanted Peyton dethroned. She thought Peyton was placed too high on a pedestal. Thus, Casey felt it was her job to knock Peyton off it!

Because of her inexorable quest to bring Peyton down to her level I worked relentlessly to keep Peyton in her place of honor. Peyton was an honorable woman who deserved her respect despite what this silly woman thought. Maurice is a sweetheart. He loves Casey, but even he confided in me about his fiancée envying Peyton. He was careful in his dealings with Peyton, whenever she were around. If Casey ever knew he exposed that information to me, she would despise him. Maurice's secret was safe with me. Since he knew the truth about her, he obviously could handle his relationship.

I tried to accept Casey, but once she convinced several members that Peyton wasn't telling the truth concerning Wilhelm and that she was demonic herself, I was done with this woman. I noticed her envy escalated once Wilhelm approached Peyton. Peyton was missing, but all I ever heard Casey talking about was Wilhelm. Members were coming to me, revealing what she was exposing. Minister Antonio called me one night extremely upset.

"Regina, you know I'm above gossiping, but had Peyton told you she may have been raped by this man but continued to date him?" he asks.

"Who told this blatant lie, Casey?" I ask, livid.

"Well, she started it, and now it's circulating through several members."

I assure Antonio it's a lie, but the rumors continued because of Casey.

Antonio confided in me, telling me he blamed Maurice and Casey for what Peyton was going through. He was convinced Peyton would've never chosen to go to some party over church to celebrate a new year. He'd only hang with them now solely to protect Peyton.

"If they ask her to do anything stupid from now on, I'll be there to rebuke them sharply," Antonio said.

After Peyton's return, one Sunday after church, the usuals decide to go to a movie, and then afterward, we grab coffee.

"I'm glad you want to return to the office. Although Maureen has your old position, you have favor with the boss." Maurice winks as he tells this to Peyton.

Surprised, Casey asks, "Oh, you're going back to work?"

Nodding, Peyton answers, "Yeah. I need some normalcy in my life."

"Mmm. You're done being a movie star?" Casey smirks.

Casey's remark makes everyone uncomfortable. Yes, Peyton was pretty much a celebrity now, but we knew not to mention it amongst ourselves. We knew never to speak of this tragedy in casual conversation.

"Really, Casey?" Maurice says, agitated.

"What's your problem?" Casey snaps.

"You! You're all of our problem right now!" Maurice shouts.

Maurice has never gotten upset with Casey publicly. The humiliation she feels is displayed upon her face, and she can't shake it. Everyone stares at Casey as she stares at Maurice, so ashamed.

"Please, it's okay. Please don't fight," Peyton says.

Maurice asks to be excused and then walks away. Everyone has a straight face, but I'm hollering inside from laughter. Casey is so loud and simple acting most times. She's such a foolish woman. I will never comprehend why Maurice is with her.

Antonio attempts to change the subject by talking about Pastor White's sermon and the movie we just saw. Peyton and I engage in his conversation, but Casey just sips her coffee in silence. Although we were out like old times, things were certainly new. Our crew was divided, but no one wanted to admit it.

Finally, Maurice returns, but he doesn't apologize or try to get back in Casey's good graces. I can see Peyton feels responsible for their fight, so she says, "Maurice, I appreciate you, but I don't mind talking about my journey." She looks at Casey and then says, "I'm okay. Let's talk about it."

Maurice, Antonio, and I look at one another, but Casey's staring at Peyton with a devious look on her face. She then asks, "So please tell us—what were you and Wilhelm doing all that time?"

Maurice is biting his bottom lip because he's so upset. Casey simply rolls her eyes at him and then returns her focus to Peyton. Peyton responds, "I don't understand your question."

"What don't you understand?"

Antonio interjects, "Be more specific, Casey!"

"Why's everyone so upset? Am I wrong for being curious? Isn't this why you've been on television for months? So why are you guys so upset? Peyton clearly didn't tell the media every intimate detail, which is wise. So I'm asking as her friend! Am I wrong, Peyton?"

"No. That's just a broad question. Antonio's right. I want you to be more specific."

"So Wilhelm murders people, right? And he's evil, right? So did you aid him? What'd he have you do?"

"He didn't include me in that part of his world. He exposed that side of himself the first week I was with him, but after that, he concealed it."

With an inquisitive glare, Casey asks, "So how did you live?"

"Pretty normal, but he just wasn't normal."

"Huh? Can you be more specific?"

"Casey, he's possessed, so his beliefs are contrary to ours. We love God, but he hates Him. We love people, but he hates them."

"So what did he want from you?"

Now through squinted eyes and a small smirk, Peyton answers, "I guess nothing."

Antonio huffs as he shakes his head at Casey. Maurice and I are just staring at each other, hoping this awkward moment will pass.

Now with a smug smirk, Casey replies, "Well, that's good to know. I hoped you weren't in a relationship because I met his girlfriend. She's a lawyer, real pretty, but she's surely unsaved. I guess she fits perfectly into his wicked world."

Unconsciously, we all look at Peyton. She tried to keep an expressionless face, but I could see that information devastated her. I yell, "You're such a b-witch, Casey! Shut your stupid mouth! You talk too much!"

"What's your problem, groupie!" she says, laughing.

Maurice knocks everyone's coffee off the table and then says, "Someone get her home. I'm out!"

Coffee's all over Casey and Antonio. Casey calmly grabs napkins and wipes herself off. Antonio wipes himself and then says, "Let's go, Peyton. You too, Regina. Casey's a big girl. She'll get home."

Peyton yells, "Stop it! Why's everyone so upset? I can answer Casey!"

"Thank you!" Casey responds, scowling at Antonio and me as we all move to another table.

Peyton sits up straight and then asks, "How long have you been wanting to say that, Casey? Obviously, it's been festering inside you for a while. But I thought we were best friends? You should feel free telling me anything. But I see you don't. Next time you want to shock me, don't!

Whatever you think you know about Wilhelm, keep it to yourself because I don't care. I'm free and very thankful for it. I guess now she can tell you what you're really itching to hear. Hopefully, hearing about him through this *wicked* woman will satisfy you."

"Peyton!" Casey calls out as she hurries away.

Antonio runs after her, but I sit, glaring at Casey momentarily. Through tears, she says, "Go away, Regina! If you all had a backbone, she'd get free! But you all sit around and act as if nothing's different about Peyton when we all know full well she's not the same!"

"We know, but we aren't God. Her telling us her deepest, darkest secrets can't free her. It'll tantalize our ears, but then what? Casey, the reality is you need to get Jesus for real. Somewhere you're surely lacking His wisdom and love."

She simply flips me off and starts crying. I place a hundred-dollar bill on the table and then leave.

I had never personally met Wilhelm, but I knew he was a sight to behold. His beauty had not only deceived our Peyton but taken a hold of Casey too.

Peyton's return was almost as glorious as the second coming. Our church and community praised God continuously for her. Her interviews were so convicting, but the media didn't want anymore. Every person in Peyton's presence sensed her strength and wisdom.

Peyton returned to us very somber, and who could blame her? No one but Casey. Casey was trying to convince everyone Peyton was demonically oppressed, but so was she. Peyton shared much more with me than she did the others. She revealed to me, Casey's wanting him, was Wilhelm's greatest power.

She confided in me, saying, "Regina, thank God you never met him, or you'd behave just like Casey. Every woman who saw him wanted him. My resistance is what keeps him intrigued, I guess. That was and still is my daily struggle—that I do not fall."

She shared some stories, but all were horrible. I couldn't stop crying, but she barely cried. She explained she cried so much the past six months that she was often tearless.

Casey was entrapped by Wilhelm and didn't know it, but how do I reveal this? Casey will not accept this, and others will reject it. It was my burden to bear this discretion until my own truth could fully be exposed.

Constantly on My Mind

Helena doesn't deserve to be called mother. The only positive thing she has ever done is introduce me to Lord York. She didn't introduce us physically, but through his film and media. How I want to be close to him. Some suitor comes to this castle at least daily, requesting my hand in marriage, and Helena defiantly attempts to find devious ways to grant their requests. Helena only allows me outside the castle to go to confession. She has no respect for the church. This is her form of punishment. I pretend to hate it, but it's my only outlet.

I actually met Lord York entering into the church. My driver greets him and introduces me.

"Good morning. Mistress Constance Berkley does not need an introduction," Lord York responds. He walks over and kisses my hand. "I would love to come to your home and ask your mother Lady Berkley if I may court you."

I'm in disbelief. I'm so happy I just know I'm in a dream and will soon awaken.

"Forgive me. Please go to confession. Although I cannot imagine what you possibly have done wrong," he says, smiling.

Lord York then turns to my driver and says, "Please relay my request to Lady Berkley and let her know I will be coming this evening. Hopefully, my visit will be welcomed."

I enter the church, but I do not go to confession. I sit in the pews, musing over the wonderful thing that has just happened!

We get home, and I go straight to my bedroom. The driver goes to Helena to deliver Lord York's message. I look out my window and watch until the driver leaves. I begin to look through my gowns, envisioning which dress Lord York will like the best. I carry my favorite teal dress to the mirror, and my joy overtakes me. I begin to laugh and cry from bliss! As I'm laughing through my tears, I hear my room door open. I turn to see who it is. I'm greeted by a forceful slap from Helena. I fall to the floor with a nosebleed. Blood is all over my teal gown. I stay on the floor, staring at my blood-stained dress.

"Get up, you vile, deceitful girl!" Helena yells.

I rise slowly only for her to kick me in my stomach. I fall backward, but Helena snatches me up. "How did Lord York see you? What did you do?" she screams.

I go to explain, but the sound of my voice enrages her. Whatever I say causes her to beat me. I huddle in a ball on the floor, concealing my face as she kicks and hits me until she's satisfied. Then Helena bolts out of the room, shouting blasphemies. Despite her attempt to stop me, I'm ready and poised by five in the evening, awaiting Lord York's arrival.

Helena's a saint in his presence. She goes to greet him with an embrace, but he moves away. "We have met several times, Helena. No need for embraces."

Helena begins to sob. Lord York then stretches out his hand to me. I take his hand, and Helena gives me a deadly scowl. Lord York kisses my hand.

"I will have her home before dawn," he says, gazing into my eyes. We leave.

Lord York has dinner prepared at his estate. We eat in silence. After dinner he escorts me to his porcelain room for tea. He remains silent, but I discern he's waiting for me to speak.

"Lord York, thank you for having me."

"You may call me Lee. You and I do not have to be so formal when we are spending intimate moments."

I smile and nod in agreement. I felt special calling him Lee. Helena once said he harshly corrected her, demanding she call him Wilhelm. Only those in his family were still allowed to call him Lee.

"How old are you, mistress?"

"I'm a sixteen-year-old woman." I answer. He chuckles at me.

In a docile tone, I ask, "May I ask how old you are?"

"I am whatever age you desire I am."

"Hmm. I would say you're twenty-two?" I grin, dropping my head.

"Why two? Let us just say twenty. It's neater." He smirks.

"So you're twenty?"

"Yes, and I always will be," he whispers seductively into my ear.

He kisses my cheek and then returns to an upright position. This is truly the best day of my life. He returns me home just before dawn. Helena is sitting in the darkness, but she doesn't speak or approach me. I acknowledge her presence. Then I go to my room.

Religiously, Lee comes to get me three times a week. The first few times, Helena beat me. She left a noticeable bruise on my back. Lee confronted her, demanding she never touch me again. Helena would never disobey Lee. However, she was hell-bent on knowing how Lee had seen my back. Naturally, I must have removed my clothing for him to see this bruise. Thankfully, she feared displeasing Lee because she would have definitely killed me with her own hands. After it was known Lee and I were intimate lovers, Helena was tormented. Her screams echoed throughout the castle. Lee showed no emotion regarding her torment. Although I should have basked in her agony, I couldn't. Secretly, I was tormented myself.

The truth of our intimate relationship was that it was nonexistent. Lee refused to sleep with me because I was a child. I'd try to seduce him, but he was never tempted.

"Once you become a woman, then we can be intimate. Will you wait for me?" Lee asked.

"I will wait for you forever, but I'm a woman now, Lee! These age requirements are merely man-made rules that are calling me a child! I thought you weren't ruled by man's or God's laws but only your own!"

"Constance these are my rules. I never mentioned an age. I will not touch you until you are a woman in my eyes."

I was unequivocally in love with Lee. I would express my love and need for him relentlessly, but his only response was, "Constance, I do not love you."

After a year and a half of being with Lee, he began to invite another woman over. He would have his driver take me home once she arrived. I could never reveal this was going on to Helena. My pain would be her pleasure. My only peace in this madness was that Helena was suffering.

After a few weeks of this other woman, I refused to leave. Lee's only other option is that I stay and endure his time with her. I hated leaving him, so I would stay while he was occupied with this woman named Amelia.

Amelia is older, so I'm sure he's sleeping with her. She's totally clueless to my relationship with Lee. I've seen her at the church, confessing for hours. Seemingly, she's a good-hearted woman. Unfortunately, good-hearted people do not fit into our world.

I'm finally eighteen. I'm now a woman by all laws regardless of what Lee thinks. This evening waiting like a silly girl as he spends time with his so-called woman, I find it's no longer tolerable. I quietly sneak into his bedroom where they are. I discreetly peek inside and see Amelia's bare back sitting on top of him. She leans down and kisses him. I enter the room, undress, and crawl into bed with them. Amelia screams and then jumps from the bed. I turn to look at Lee, but he's not there! I see a black shadowy figure. Suddenly, I wake up. I'm fully clothed and seated on the couch in the living room.

Once I realize where I am, the butler greets me. "Mistress Berkley, Lord York's car is prepared to take you home."

"No, where's Lee?" I ask as I jump up. I quickly head to his bedroom.

However, his bedroom is back neatly groomed without him or Amelia. I then look at the clock and realize it's his dinnertime. I know Lee's routine. He eats dinner. Afterward, it's time for tea. I wait for Lee and Amelia to arrive. I promise him after tea I will go home. Lee doesn't respond. He simply watches me. I offer to fix their tea. Amelia's so giddy and naive that it nauseates me. Does she even care I interrupted them? Seemingly, she has no recollection of me entering Lee's room! Perhaps my status has her afraid to confront me. Whatever her reasoning, it's still ridiculous. I fix us all tea. We drink in silence. As soon as I take my last sip, the butler escorts me out. I get home and cry myself to sleep.

Lee changes his routine. He picks me up the very next evening. I get into his car, and he's not pleased. He immediately says, "Well, now you owe me a huge favor."

I agree because I poisoned Amelia. I knew once she fell asleep, she would never wake up again. I have waited and endured too much to obtain Lee. I refused to be forced to witness him replace me and not retaliate. Lee would choose one woman and date her exclusively. The only reason he overlapped our relationship with his and Amelie's was due to our shared contempt for Helena. He knew Helena was evil, but he never witnessed it in me. I thought I was nothing like Helena. Poisoning Amelia revealed a part of me I didn't know. Murdering her awakened a strength in me that I didn't want stilled. I was relieved to know I had the strength to kill for my love if that was needed. Lee has no fear of my aggression, but he has begun to despise me. He felt trapped and needed a way to be rid of me.

Helena could no longer endure the torment of this relationship as well. She had begun to openly confess her love for Wilhelm even more aggressively than she ever had in the past. She was publicly humiliating my father. She became foul and vulgar with her disrespect of us.

The community sees the Berkleys as a family worthy of honor and to be revered. Helena's antics are quickly blamed on Lee's evil bewitching. They even secretly blamed him for Amelie's death. These accusations caused him to hate Helena and me equally. Thus, I was willing to do anything to make him accept me again.

The following evening after Amelie's death, Lee takes me to Alistair's mill. He leads me to a back door and knocks. A scummy-looking middle-aged man opens the door. His name is George, and he looks as if he hasn't bathed in several days. George actually resides at the mill in a small room hidden in the back. George pulls out a chair for me. I sit down, but my eyes are fixed upon Lee. George pulls out a chair for Lee and then offers us something to drink. I'm disgusted, and I say no in such a detestable way, assuring he knows exactly how disgusted I am.

"George, you know better than that. Sit down," Lee commands George.

Lee stands, lifts me up, and then leads me over to George. Immediately, George stands to respect me. Lee asks him if he likes me. George goes on and on about how beautiful I am and how he loves me and wishes I was his wife. His praise almost makes me vomit. George is speaking, but my eyes are locked with Lee's. While George begs Lee to grant his request, Lee moves George out of the way. He begins to kiss and caress me. My first truly intimate moment with Lee was in this filthy hole with this repulsive man watching us. Lee allows me to kiss and touch him unreservedly. He then tells me the favor I owe is to give George a son. I instantly stop kissing him as I slowly release his face. I stand wide-eyed and speechless. Lee simply stares back, awaiting my response.

I look over at George, who's lustfully gazing my way. Frowning, I yell, "Lee, I will never do such a repulsive thing! I will only make love to you! I want to have your son!"

Lee merely listens, expressionless. I continue to explain why I'd never grant this request, but he just stares. Unfeeling, he simply responds, "You owe me." Still, I unrelentingly refused.

"Fine! This is the last time you will see me. Enjoy your life," Lee responds.

He goes to leave. I grab him as I fall to me knees, bitterly sobbing. "Do it, or let me go!" he says.

I just begin to undress. "Receive your answered prayer from me," Lee tells George.

"Thank you, Lord York!" George says, ecstatic.

This allowed me to see the dark side of Lee. There were rumors of his darkness, but I refused to see it. Life would become meaningless and void without him. However, my darkness was revealed to him as well. I guess it left him feeling justified in what he had decided.

Lee leaves. He doesn't even stay to take me home. I sit in front of the mill crying until morning. I ask the master of the mill to contact Earl Alistair because I needed a ride home. The master assures me he has Earl Alistair's authority to get me there discreetly. I get home to Helena's wailing. I go to my bedroom and soak in the bathtub for hours.

I then decide I will not have this peasant's child, but each time we meet, Lee threatens to leave me. My heart and mind cannot endure that, so I continue to submit.

Lee faithfully picks me up. However, my intimate visits to his home were now for George and me. After a month of sleeping with this horrid man, I beg Lee to have a doctor check for my pregnancy. The stars have finally aligned in my favor. I'm pregnant! Lee kisses my forehead and then whispers, "We must celebrate. George will be pleased to know I am able to grant the impossible."

He sends me home, telling me to put on my best clothing and prepare for tonight's grand festivities. The dinner Lee prepared is fit for a king. George has been cleaned and groomed, and he actually looks like a gentleman. However, neither he nor I can outshine Lee's matchless beauty. We eat and dance and really celebrate, but I know all this is too good to be true. It's now past midnight. Lee congratulates George and me on our new baby. He then tells me that my impurity doesn't agree with his morals. He gives us his blessing. Then George and I are aggressively escorted out. I could feel my sanity fleeting.

I want to cry, but I can't. I want to fight, but I can't. I have even forgotten how to walk. I collapse outside Lee's estate's iron gates as they lock. I gaze up into the night sky, but then George's face covers my view. He smiles, so I close my eyes to avoid seeing his dreadful face. Everything starts becoming unrecognizable. I squeeze my eyes tighter, trying to remember, but I'm unable to decipher where I am. Suddenly, I hear whispers of Lee's voice. My mind keeps replaying Lee's face and name in my head. I go to speak his name, but I have lost the ability to utter a word. I slowly open my eyes. I see my sanity dissolve into the night sky. Life as I knew it was now nonexistent.

Will Someone Please Listen to Officer MacAleese?

The death of the Kings was a gruesome tragedy. The fire basically incinerated everyone in that house. How the gas line was exposed so quickly no one can logically figure out. It has only been three bodies identified so far. The Kings' remains and another victim's wife's body are still missing. I saw the black Maybach owned by Mr. Yoorker speeding past Officer Lynn and me the day of the fire. It really stood out to me. Why? I don't know, but I was more concerned about him speeding past me than the fire at that moment. There were so many people catering to this scene that I wouldn't be missed. I wanted to go without Lynn and investigate Yoorker. Once I told her I needed to go inform him, Lynn perked up and tagged along with me.

We get to his door, and he opens it, still wet from a shower. Lynn's in heaven, and I'm convinced he's not innocent. I don't want to alarm him of my suspicions, so I simply pretend I'm there to prepare him for the heavy traffic of onlookers and media. Lynn and I both give Yoorker our cards, and then we leave.

My shift is over. I get home, brew a pot of coffee, and then start my search on Mr. Wilhelm Yoorker. This Yoorker is worth more than eighty-eight billion dollars in America alone. He's some kind of dignitary from Britain. He's basically a sole heir, and that estate is not required to reveal their net worth or the full extent of their lineage. Oh, the joys of the unscrupulously wealthy. You can murder if the price is right!

Yoorker never as much as had a parking ticket. The only information I can find on him is that he purchased a home in Vermont. He wasn't born here, so that information was hidden in Britain. I couldn't find his parents, nothing, but that doesn't deter me.

I have two weeks' vacation available, so I decide to use my time and visit Vermont. However, this is a dead end. I go to the Realtor who sold him the home. She tells me the day they were to meet, he left before she arrived. She never met him. Then Yoorker had his lawyers and his *people* do everything.

His home is secluded. He has few or no neighbors. No one in that neighborhood knows him, and his address is untraceable. I asked his Realtor for his lawyer's information, which I know will probably get me nowhere. Obviously, he has a lawyer to shield him. Still, I try.

His lawyer's name is Vaughn Pharris. He's an older man, very professional and dapper. He's overly friendly and seemingly too eager to help. He has been Yoorker's lawyer for more than a decade. He tells me Yoorker came to the States because he was young and ambitious. He wanted to be productive not live off his family. It's the same sweet talk every rich kid deceptively gives. For sport, I ask what he's accomplished. Though his accomplishments are massive, they were easily attainable because of his wealth. Yoorker's into real estate and technology and has stock in every prosperous Fortune 500 venue, so I'm not impressed. In my book Yoorker has done absolutely nothing. Pharris has been doing this speech so long I think he believes I'm buying it. I then take my chances and ask if I may talk to his car salesman. Pharris's disposition immediately changes.

"Of course not. Now it's my turn to question you. What's your interest in my client?"

"I'm just an admirer." I shrug.

"Well, my best advice is that you admire him from afar like everyone else. He prefers privacy. My job is to ensure his preferences are kept."

"Wow. Well, thanks for your time." I let out a hearty laugh.

I leave, but Mr. Pharris has to know I'll be researching him next.

Unfortunately, Vaughn Pharris is another dead end. All his t's are crossed, and i's dotted. His life is an opened book. He's well-known and loved in this community. Yoorker is simply one of his many rich clients. Yoorker desiring privacy is the norm in that world.

After wasting two days of my life, I decide to head home. I'm sitting in the airport, eating breakfast, and reading the local paper. I come across a story about a missing woman named Peyton Meryl. She was abducted about five months ago, and the reward for any information on her whereabouts is one hundred thousand dollars. This reward has been raised by a local church.

Peyton? That name stood out to me for a reason, but at the time I didn't remember why.

I board my plane and head home. I get home and my friend Jason May comes over. He's also a policeman. We call him May. I told no one what I was doing, so May asked where I went.

"This is between me and you, but I don't trust this guy Yoorker. I found nothing, but something irks me about this guy," I confess to May.

"Yeah, I feel you. I think it's called envy or jealousy!" He laughs.

"I'm serious, May!"

"Speaking of Yoorker, he offered to pay for the remodeling or demolition of the Kings' home after the authorities are done with their investigation. You know how that community hates raggedy property and negative press in their neighborhood. As a result, county has petitioned for the police to accept it was an accident, demolish the home, and sell that luxury property as soon as possible!"

"Wow, how convenient! May, this guy has something to do with this fire! I feel it in my gut!" I grunt out through gritted teeth. "Is he married?"

"I don't know, but Victoria and Tony should."

"Yes, their store on the beach!"

He has to go to work, so I head to Victoria's store. Victoria and I had an affair a few years back, so I try to avoid her, but she was my only link to this Yoorker character.

Victoria sees me enter the store. Frowning, she jokingly says, "I plead the fifth!"

"How are you doing, Vicki?" I smirk.

She gestures her hand expressing she's so-so.

"What's going on, Mac?"

"Do you know Wilhelm Yoorker?"

She shakes her head no but answers, "I've seen him. His girlfriend comes to the store periodically, but lately, she's been coming more frequently.

"Do you know her name?"

"Peyton."

My heart rate has doubled! "Is she from Washington?" I ask.

"I don't know. I know they aren't married and that Peyton seems timid and afraid. The only people they actually socialized with were the Kings." Now I'm back at square one.

After I find out Yoorker's lady friend's name is Peyton, I decide to follow them. This particular day they seem happy and in love. He's taking her on a shopping spree, I guess. I don't want to get too close, but I need to see her face. My cell phone camera is useless. I follow them back to their estate. Then I go purchase a real camera. I even ask Vicki to try to sneak a snapshot for me.

Vicki calls me a few days later. She informs me that Yoorker and Peyton are on the beach. I need to hurry if I want to see her. I walk into Vicki's store. She franticly rushes over to me, closes the door, and then turns me to face out of the window.

She whispers, "Mac, Peyton just walked out! That's her in the white bikini!"

She's a petite lady. Her back is toward me. She approaches Yoorker as he stands. He kisses her. Then they head to their home, hand in hand. They're now out of our view.

"Well, you may not have a photo yet, but she gave me an earful today! Your police instincts are good because I asked her if Wilhelm was her husband and she said no. So I said, 'Oh, you're just living together?' And it threw her for a loop! She then explained her relationship with Wilhelm is more spiritual than romantic!"

Vicki abruptly stops and then stares at me. I ask, "Okay? What does that mean?"

Vicki bursts into laughter. "Who the hell knows! It sounds twisted! Maybe he's her cousin or brother, and she doesn't want people to find out they're sick and twisted!"

Vicki's dramatic, but that was a very odd answer. I tell her to keep spying for me and keep trying to get a picture of her.

Once I'm home, I decide to search the Internet for a photo of the missing Peyton in Vermont. The photo I find is of a very attractive woman, and she's something of a heroine in her community. This missing Peyton is a church lady from a lineage of religious people. Her and Yoorker's lifestyles were total opposites. The day I followed them, they visited a jewelry store. I asked the jeweler if he knew them. He tells me that they're atheists. After this information I decide to stop my research.

A few weeks later, I see Peyton in Washington catching a cab. My partners and I are having lunch at Ocean's View Grill when she walks right past me. I tell everyone to go get seats and that I will catch up. I discreetly watch her from across the street. She's underdressed for her status. She's on her phone, so I hope Yoorker is meeting her. He doesn't show, and then she gets into a cab. I find that odd, knowing her boyfriend is a billionaire. I go eat, so my partners don't become suspicious. I make up a reason to leave early. I get in my car and call Vicki. She tells me Peyton has left Yoorker, and that's all she knows.

A week later Vicki's missing. The following week Peyton appears on television. She's telling a paranormal story about Yoorker, but she never mentions his name. I almost break my neck falling from my chair. I immediately call Lynn! She doesn't respond. I need a witness! Peyton's story is so far-fetched I can't particularly say why to just anyone. Lynn's the only person that'll go without a needed explanation. I instinctively know I need to confront him as soon as possible!

Lynn is nowhere to be found, so I page her friend Officer Blanche. Blanche tells me Lynn's at Yoorker's! Blanche had just seen the story as well, so we both rush to his estate. He's very disrespectful, and then he puts us out of his home. Blanche and I agonizingly wait to get the proper paperwork to arrest him, but he was gone that same night. The next morning that house was totally empty! People have been painting and renovating around the clock.

I track the bank account paying these people, and it leads me to Vaughn Pharris! In fact, Vaughn Pharris owns this estate! Wilhelm Yoorker was no one. We have a search warrant for Wilhelm Yoorker's property, but that doesn't exist. By the time we get through all the red tape and legalistic deception, it was a new home. Wilhelm Yoorker was a phantom literally being sought out across the nation. I was slightly reprimanded and put on a stress leave with pay. Peyton's ghost story discredited my and everyone involved story. We weren't considered witnesses to a murderer but a ghost. Pictures of the missing 1900s actor begin to surface. All Wilhelm's elderly fans are emerging, giving frivolous accounts of his mysterious gift of eternal youth. Yoorker and Peyton became a clown show to most, but I know I'm not crazy. I haven't seen a ghost or demon. I saw a maniac who's still out there somewhere.

Business as Usual

Officer MacAleese visiting my office instantly alarmed me. I love Wilhelm. I consider him my son, but his secrets are deeper than even I can possibly continue to handle.

I'm done for the day. I lock myself in my office, and then I prepare to hear what Wilhelm needs from me. I call, and he answers. There's melancholy in his voice.

"Hey, Will, are you up?" I ask.

"Yes."

"An Officer MacAleese came to visit me not too long ago. Do you know him?"

"Mmhmm," Wilhelm grunts.

"Help me, Will. Tell me what's going on. Where are you?" I beg, now frustrated.

"I am in Washington."

"Are people missing?" I ask, dreading his answer.

"Mmhmm."

"All right, I'm flying to your estate today so I can get everything in order immediately."

On paper I have been Will's lawyer for about a decade. The truth is I have known Will for almost thirty years. My daughter saw him at a function, and she fell in love.

I introduced myself as a favor to her and then offered my services as well. Surprisingly, he needed a new lawyer. His previous lawyer had recently passed. Once I started working for Will and learning his affairs, things seemed extremely weird. He told me he was thirty years old. I was shocked. I would've made him twenty-five or less, but his wisdom and maturity convinced me he was indeed older. He lived in California when I met him. California was his permanent residence, although he traveled constantly. However, once I found out his net worth, I was in total awe.

Wilhelm says, "I will pay you whatever you ask and more if you remain loyal. Handle my affairs and ensure I am anonymous. Then I promise you and I will never part."

I told him I could handle that. I gave him my price, and he tripled what I asked for. Hence, he was my new best friend.

I was with him all day, getting all his belongings out of his deceased lawyer's name and into an alias. However, I noticed his lawyer's name was on documents thirty and forty years old. I assumed his father had the same lawyer, but I recall Will telling me his father passed before he was born. I didn't want to start off asking him all these cryptic questions. Obviously, they had legitimate answers, so I overlooked everything bewildering and just did my job.

Will was an easy client. His affairs were in immaculate order. He merely bought expensive toys and traveled the world. He'd be gone years at a time. He'd need me for nothing, but he paid me without fail. Our dilemma started when I could no longer ignore the fact that he wasn't aging. He supposedly was thirty-one when my daughter was twenty-six. Ten years had passed. My daughter looked thirty-six, but Will looked the same. I accredited it to his wealth and stress-free life. Then I put the thought out my mind. Then about fifteen years into our relationship, he needed me to work a miracle for him in Australia. I went there, and as soon as I saw him, I was in disbelief. He looked like a brand-new person and very young. He's the same man I encountered fifteen years ago.

A man attacked Will over a woman. Supposedly, he killed them in self-defense. That was his story. I made that go away. Then immediately, we boarded his jet and headed to California. We're talking, but he notices my eyes are transfixed. I'm trying desperately to pretend as if I don't notice his youthfulness.

"I wanted us to ride together because I trust you. You may ask me anything, and I will answer you honestly," he says.

I'm honored yet afraid at the same time. Contemplating if I should ask, I take a deep breath and then ask, "Will, by now you should be nearing fifty years old. Why are you still young?"

"I think I involuntarily sold my soul," he answers nonchalantly.

"Wow. I don't know how to respond to that! Please tell me your story."

He willfully exposes all his secrets to me. "I need you to protect me," he states candidly.

"Was your story about that couple true?"

He admits it wasn't. He confesses periodically he must kill and that he desires blood. His secret was safe with me.

I kept him away from my family because they met him young and would naturally have questions.

Only once did Will and I almost part ways. My niece met him at a business event, and she was hooked. Coincidently, I was in the same hotel at another event and saw her sitting with him in the hotel's restaurant. I hurried to the table, letting my niece know that I knew Will. I then asked him to walk with me.

"Pharris, you are making a scene," he says, perturbed.

"Will, that's my niece, so avoid her!"

"I have, but she keeps finding me. She is stalking me. I do not fare well with stalkers, so I remove them," he explains.

He heads back toward the table, but I grab him. "Will, don't kill my niece! Where's your loyalty to me?" I plead.

He snatches his arm. His heartlessness frightens me.

"Pharris, you do not know this part of me. I will feed. If you remove your niece, find me someone else speedily."

My heart is racing. I turn toward my niece, but she's gone! I'm in a state of panic. Cell phones aren't popular yet, so I'm forced to endure the agony of not knowing if he has killed her or not. Days have passed, and Will and my niece are missing. Will leaves a message with my secretary after a week. She informs me he's in Russia. However, my niece is never seen again.

My so-called coincidence was anything but that. This event taught me nothing occurs by happenstance. Had I not been in that hotel, I would've never known Will could betray me so callously. I vowed to expose him, but after watching my sister cry and hope for the return of my niece, I refused to be the one to break her spirit. I wanted to tell my wife, but I just couldn't. How could I tell my family that I've been supporting a monster knowingly for years?

I'm planning my exit from Will. Still, I decide to keep his secrets. He calls me that following Monday morning at my office. He's back in the States. He tells me he's across the street and then asks if he may come to see me. I allow him to come. He enters with his head hanging down. He then remorsefully says he's sorry. He reveals to me that he has no physical needs. Women are his easiest prey because they're always willingly accessible to him. My niece was in his suite when he got there, and the rest is history. Once his desire is stimulated, he fulfills it.

He explains, "Pharris, this is not a moral-friendly gift. This is a bloodlust that needs to be fulfilled immediately. I will use whomever to fulfill this thirst. It can be a man, woman, or child. Do you understand?"

I'm not proud to admit this, but I did understand. My perverted comprehension of him somehow tightened our bond. Him traveling and fulfilling this desire abroad made my life simple. Will never having relationships was perfect. However, once his desire returned for this mystery woman, all hell literally broke loose. I was putting out so many fires that my head was spinning. I wanted her gone. I needed him to destroy her immediately. His obsession for this woman wasn't only a hazard to himself, but it also began to affect me and my empire.

Officer MacAleese's visit let me know the walls were starting to close in on us. And fixing that madness in Washington was beyond repair. I needed to make a few phone calls and work some magic. It was now time to intervene. I needed this woman's name.

Nothing Is as It Seems

I've been at the church forty-eight hours. I'm totally burnt out. I'm ecstatic about getting home into my own bed and shutting myself in for a week! I stop, grab takeout, and then head home. I'm walking up my driveway when a sharply dressed older man calls my name. He walks up, extends his hand, and introduces himself as Detective Vaughn. He shows me his badge and then asks if he can come inside. I invite him in and make us coffee. After we're settled, he asks, "Minister, may I call you Antonio?"

I say yes, and then he continues, "Antonio, I'm investigating the case of Wilhelm Yoorker and your friend Peyton Meryl. There's so much to this story that we don't comprehend."

I chuckle and then reply, "You and me both."

Detective Vaughn then asks me to please tell all that I know about this situation.

The night Wilhelm came in the midst of Tabitha's community Peyton seemed too comfortable when he appeared. The other men and I were locked and loaded. Then Peyton just walks in front of our guns. It seems as if she knew him. I never shared this with anyone because I didn't want to assassinate her character without allowing

Peyton to explain her actions. The public's opinion was so divided it really began to sway me. Those of us present didn't see Wilhelm do anything heinous to her. What we witnessed was Peyton stopping our attack by approaching him with no fear. Next, all the lights went out, and then they were gone.

A few days later, Peyton appeared on television with a sketched drawing. The facial composite artist confirmed Peyton and Tabitha Berkley gave the authorities an old photo of a 1910 actor, and Peyton's rationale simply was to tell the artist, "This man looks exactly like him."

The composite artist was a little leery, but what else interesting was going on in this secluded area of Vermont? This quiet town was in the midst of a massacre, and the only witness was Peyton! Thus, the media permitted him to use it.

After Peyton met Wilhelm in jail, no one saw them leave or heard from them again. Wilhelm was no longer a suspect. It was impossible for one man to single-handedly kill all those people. It was done too quickly without a weapon. This mystery man—oddly, no one at the jail could remember him—became a fantasy. Peyton's accounts seemed fictitious. The only real story belonged to the people killed, not Peyton's.

Our pastor went to the news station and police precinct to see what had become of the story and of our missing sister. He was told that Wilhelm and Peyton's lawyer came and informed them that Peyton was mentally ill. She was now in Wilhelm's care, receiving the best treatment offered. During service that announcement was made at church, and the congregation returned to their lives. However, those of us who were involved in the process had no rest. We knew Peyton's story about Wilhelm being supernatural wasn't completely false. A small nucleus of us never stopped praying for her safe return. However, once she returned, those supportive of her became divided.

The press never gave Wilhelm's name, and the name Ms. Berkley kept quoting belonged to a man who had been deceased for nearly a century. We were now torn because Peyton never said his name. Was she delusional? Most were caught up in knowing his name, but the story that caught my attention was Casey's accusation that Peyton had been raped.

I go to the hospital with Regina's parents by using our clergy credentials. We inquire about the night Peyton claimed she was there, which was the night when the massacre took place. Her story was confirmed. She had received a rape test that same night. They found no semen, but she definitely was not a virgin. Now I'm not gullible. I know many women and men have lied and said they were virgins when they weren't, but Peyton was a virgin. Learning she was no longer a virgin surely confirmed he raped or had consenting sex with her. However, Regina's parents and I kept that information to ourselves. If she returned, we decided we would confront her, but if she never returned, that was her business to keep.

After that story I had nothing more I cared to share. I hoped I answered some of Detective Vaughn's questions. We talked for approximately an hour. He thanked me, and then he left. I was glad he was gone. Talking about Peyton with Wilhelm was grievous.

I was fairly new to Peyton's ministry. I thought she was beautiful, so I began to pursue her. I initially joined her church to remain close to her. When possible, I made sure I was involved in every event Peyton supported. Cunningly, I befriended Regina. She and Peyton were like sisters. Regina would keep me informed about Peyton without Peyton being aware of my motives.

Regina had a strong dislike for Casey. I had no problem with Casey, but after she convinced Peyton to attend that party, where she met Wilhelm, I did! Regina and I became thick as thieves as a result. Anytime I'd hear Casey make mention of Peyton negatively because of Wilhelm, I wanted to punch her in her face.

Initially, like Casey, I was convinced Peyton was exaggerating her fear of Wilhelm. I mean, why wouldn't she give the media his name? Even after she returned, though her interviews were very interesting and entertaining, they just seemed scripted. She was so well versed that many people saw it as another introduction to some paranormal or Christian show for cable.

I eventually hated Casey. Had she not tricked Peyton into going to that party, none of this would've happened! She and Maurice were the culprits, yet they were crying and leading search parties like they were so innocent and distraught. After Peyton was missing for so long, not to mention the ambiguousness of her recorded accounts of Wilhelm, this Wilhelm became almost imaginary. Still, he was very intimidating to me.

Maybe she was pretending, but I was taunted. I wanted one chance to prove I was the better man in her presence. Frustratingly, the most agonizing part of this story is I had seen him and missed my opportunities!

One day the office was in disarray because of Peyton's boyfriend. I was catching the elevator up to my office, and I rode up with a very distinguished gentleman. He was tall and attractive, and he smelled great.

"Hey, what's the name of your cologne? I usually wouldn't do this, but I have a woman I'm desperate to possess." I laugh.

"I honestly do not know. So that I stay current, I have others style and dress me," he says as he merely glances my way.

I was a little turned off by his response, but I knew he wasn't lying. He couldn't help his lavish lifestyle obviously, so I got over myself.

"It's great to be you," I respond.

He gave me a look of scorn, slightly smirked, and then exited the elevator on Peyton's floor.

I get to my desk, and then fifteen minutes later, I hear women cackling like hens. I go disrupt their circle.

"What's so exciting?" I ask.

"Peyton just got in a Bentley with an angel! Well, his looks are angelic, but if it were me, nothing saintly would be going on tonight!" a coworker says.

The women listening agree in laughter. I give a fake grin and then walk away. Hearing the women's response to Wilhelm stayed in my head. I assumed Peyton felt the same way. I then realized she wanted him. She'd been on several dates with him in the past. If he was so wicked, how was that achieved?

The ministry noticed I wasn't as active once Peyton left. They had bestowed all these titles upon me, so I felt obligated to stay, but she was my real motivation for being so involved. I would even hang with Maurice at the office to get information from him, but he was useless.

However, my most devastating moment in all this was the day Peyton disappeared from the church. I realized I actually saw Wilhelm in the sanctuary. The church was packed, but I was more interested in keeping up with Peyton. I wasn't consumed in prayer. I was sitting on the altar, observing Peyton until she exited the sanctuary. I then noticed this young man gliding through the crowd. I saw him go into the back offices. I assumed he was related to our pastor or simply had to use the restroom. I thought nothing more of him once he was out of my sight. Then Regina called, and I instinctively knew it was him I had seen only a few hours earlier.

I wanted to share that story, but for what? Supposedly, Peyton voluntarily left the church with him. I only sided with Regina because I wouldn't accept Peyton wanted him. I promoted Wilhelm took her against her will. Then miraculously, it was confirmed the day that magazine article was released. All the lies had been dispelled. The truth was she hated him, and that was my peace. The magazine article was encouraging. Still, things didn't end so simple.

After the police did a full investigation, they reported Wilhelm Yoorker was an alias. His real name is Vaughn Pharris. He's a well-known local lawyer. Detective Vaughn was actually Wilhelm in disguise? He was himself, disguised as himself, inquiring about himself?

This wasn't true. Nor did it make practical sense. And to top all, Vaughn was now missing. He hasn't been seen in months.

I knew Wilhelm was real. I saw and talked with him! Casey, Maurice, Juan, Tabitha, and countless others—if you factor in the ones at my office and that New Year's Eve party—knew how he looked! He was young, not old.

Once the news spread that Wilhelm didn't exist, I left the ministry altogether. Seemingly, Casey left too. I noticed her absence just before I stopped attending. However, I didn't seek answers to her nonattendance. I desperately needed a hiatus from everything connected to Wilhelm and Peyton.

Prove Me Right

After a couple of days of the congregation mourning the loss of Peyton, I'm desperate to prove she's still alive somewhere, basking in willful bliss with Wilhelm.

Luckily, no it's not luck, but predestination. It was ordained by God that Peyton would call me first, and then have a cell phone number under my name. This let me know where to start my search for the truth. Although she didn't call Wilhelm from this number, I'm able to trace the store location where she purchased it. The area is in Washington like she said, so I take a week off from work and head to the West Coast. The area is very beautiful as I expected.

I go to the local store where Peyton asked me to wire her money. This has to be the most elegant convenient store I've ever seen. I take my receipt to the counter and ask about the day of that transaction. There's an attractive young woman at the counter. I'll assume she's a high school senior or college freshman. The young lady tells me she's a college freshman home for the weekend. Her mom owns this store and is in the back. I ask if she'll please get her. She obliges and then leaves me waiting at the counter.

The mother enters the store. She's not as attractive as her daughter, but she looks wealthy and seems extremely snobbish. I begin to ask questions, and instantly, she says, "Yes, surprisingly, I do remember her. She looked quite distressed. She didn't look familiar. By her apparel I assumed she wasn't from this neighborhood."

I'm proven right yet again. This woman is haughty. She's probably embarrassed I'm in her store right now.

I respond, "Great! Can you recall if she came here alone or had she been accompanied by someone?"

She seems to perk up once I ask this question.

"Well, she came alone, but I needed her address and identification to receive such a large amount of cash. And surprisingly, she lived in Eden Estate."

"Ma'am, I'm from Vermont, so I'm not familiar with that location."

"My heavens, why are you way over here?"

"I'm searching for my friend. I wired her that money, and I haven't seen her since." I lied, but I needed to make the story more interesting.

Now carefully examining me, she says, "I'm sorry to hear that, but Eden Estate is right outside of Ocean Shores. It's a very exclusive estate only owned by the ultra wealthy."

This is my chance to pretend I'm wealthier than this highbrowed woman. Lowering my eyes, I nonchalantly reply, "Oh, okay. Well, will you please assist me in finding this location? Am I near her estate?"

Now with a pretentious scowl, she answers, "Because I don't know you or your missing friend, it's probably best you go to the authorities. Until then, I'm not comfortable giving out any more information."

"I wholeheartedly understand! Thank you, and have a blessed day."

What a shrew! She was so arrogant. She was highly offended I treated her bragging of her neighborhood with contempt. Nevertheless, she had already given me the information I needed. I GPS Eden Estates, but it keeps leading me to Ocean Shores just as she said. It's only seven miles from this location, so I get into my rental car and head to Ocean Shores.

The area is breathtaking. I see a restaurant, so I go inside and ask if someone can direct me to Eden Estates. I enter, and miraculously, there's an officer at the bar. I walk over to him and read his badge. It says, "Officer May."

"Hello, Officer May, my name is Casey Dalton. I'm looking for Eden Estates. Am I near that location?"

He stands and puts his finger up, telling me to wait. He then begins paging an Officer Mac. After he briefly converses with him, he informs me how to get there.

"Ms. Dalton, you're less than five miles from Eden Estate. It's not plural. Officer Mac will meet you outside the gates. He has his car lights flashing, so you'll know it's him."

"Thank you, Officer May. Have a blessed day."

Police escorts to get on an estate? Fancy, but I just follow his orders. I see the police car's flashing lights, so I park behind him. I get out of the car, and his facial expression instantly turns to disappointment. He has hurt my feelings, but I'm cute to myself. I mentally remove his unwelcoming glance. He appears very serious as he puts on his shades. I know my looks aren't on his mind. I remove my silly thoughts and focus.

I say, "Officer Mac?"

"Yes."

I extend my hand, but he doesn't shake it. He faintly smiles and then says, "How may I help you, Ms. Dalton?"

"I'm looking for my best friend, Peyton Meryl. I believe this is her estate."

Officer Mac is cleaning his shades, but he instantly stops. He quickly glances my way. I guess mentioning Peyton made me worthy of eye contact. His stern demeanor softens as he answers, "Peyton no longer lives here. She and Yoorker moved out about eight months ago."

"Yoorker? Oh, Wilhelm! By any chance do you know where they moved?"

"Trust me. I wished I did, but I don't. Who are you again, and why do you need to know?"

I now have his undivided attention. I explain, "She needed money to get back to Vermont. I wired her the money and got her home, but now she's gone with Wilhelm again. No one can find her."

I tell him my full story. Instantly, Officer Mac begins telling me some of his suspicions. He describes how they'd hold hands and kiss in public. He tells how they would even walk from the beach to their home, holding hands. We then both come to the conclusion Wilhelm is no demon. He's merely a bad guy protected by his money, and Peyton is in love with him. After conversing outside of this massive gate, Officer Mac explains how the beach is now private. Visitors could no longer enter without the owner's permission. I thank him for taking the time to speak with me. It's now late, so I ask for a good hotel to use. He suggests the Royal Hotel.

Officer Mac is right. This is a stunning hotel. I go to the concierge and pay for my room, then as I'm getting my key card, I see Wilhelm entering an elevator. Can I really be this good? Of course not. My steps are being ordered!

I jog toward him, yelling, "Please hold the elevator!"

I enter and say hello. Wilhelm doesn't look my way, but he nods, acknowledging my presence. He pushes floor seven. I'm on the fifth floor, but I pretend seven is my floor too. He's dressed in black from head to toe in his tailored suit. He smells divine. His cologne gives the perfect scent. It's not overpowering or too faint. It fills the elevator perfectly. I try not to stare, but I just can't help myself. I discreetly examine him from top to bottom. He is flawless. We get to his floor, and he's an absolute gentleman. He allows me to exit first. I want to follow him, so I stop and act as if I have received a call. I get on my phone and begin speaking to my imaginary caller.

As I hang out by the elevator, he looks my way. He looks deep into my eyes as if he's gathering my thoughts, but with an ominous stare. I had seen Wilhelm briefly at the New Year's Eve party, but seeing his entire face so closely was majestic. He was an angel just as Peyton proclaimed the first night she met him.

He approaches his hotel suite. He doesn't have a key, so he knocks. Unfortunately, I can't see who opens the door. I record the room number and then return to the lobby and request a suite on floor seven. I'm fortunate enough to get the room adjacent Wilhelm's. I try to eavesdrop, but the walls are solid. I even use a glass, but that's a failed attempt.

Lying in bed, I decide to text Maurice. I let him know I'm fine. I lie and say I'm visiting my sick aunt. I tell him she's recovering well. Maurice trusts me, so he simply texts, "Praise God!" He's content, and so am I.

I'm dozing off when I hear distant moans. I jump up and then run to his wall. I faintly hear high-pitched screaming. I immediately think maybe Peyton is being naughty over there. As I listen, I determine these aren't faint screams of passion. I tiptoe to my room door and crack it open, hoping to hear clearer from the hall. I hear nothing. I close the door and return to the wall with my ear next to a glass, intently listening, but it's quiet. I listen a few more minutes, and then I stop.

I put my glass on the table and start undressing. Then there's a knock at my door. I look out of my peephole. It's Wilhelm! My heart is racing! Those screams have me feeling very uncomfortable. I was confident I was right about Wilhelm and Peyton's relationship. And Officer Mac increased my confidence even more! I wholeheartedly felt finding Wilhelm would prove me right to everyone back home, but now I feel I'm very wrong.

I step away from the door, contemplating what to do. He then knocks again, but this time he says my name.

"Casey, is that you?" he calmly asks.

I'm terrified, but I can't pretend anymore because he knows who I am. I take a deep breath and open the door, and I see he's covered in blood. I move back with my hands covering my mouth. I know if I scream, he may kill me. His glare is evil and piercing through my soul! I go to fall to my knees, but he quickly grabs me and says, "You do not want to do that, Casey."

He lifts me back to my feet and then tells me to bring him all my towels. I go to the bathroom immediately. He hands me a face towel. I wet it. He cleans the few sprinkles of blood off his face. He then takes the bath towels and soaks the blood off his clothing. The blood isn't visible on this black suit, but his hands are drenched. He wraps his hand in a towel and then leads me to the dining area.

He motions for me to sit down. He then washes his hands in the kitchen sink. He puts a towel in a dining chair and sits across from me. By some miracle or perhaps from shock, I don't cry. I'm petrified, but I'm more interested in whose blood is on his hands and what he has to say. However, he doesn't speak. He just glares at me until I feel the urge to start the conversation.

I ask, "Wilhelm, who's hurt? Peyton?"

"No. You do not know him—or you might, but that's not important. Why are you here?"

"I'm looking for Peyton."

"She's gone away."

"Where? Are you running off together? I'm not here to stop you. I just need to know the truth."

Perplexed, he says, "Peyton never told you the truth?"

I tell him all the terrible things Peyton has said about him. I tell him about Detective Vaughn, Officer Mac, and what Tabitha confirmed. He listens intensely as I reveal everything I know.

"You don't think any of that is the truth?" he asks.

"I know you're different and unique." I pause and then say, "I know Peyton willingly chooses to be with you."

"Why do you believe she chose me willingly? Did she ever tell you that?"

Shaking my head no, I answer, "I just believe in my heart she wants you. She never said she was intimate with you either."

Wilhelm begins to laugh. His mouth is wonderful. His teeth are luminous and glistening. His smile is bright and white. I know it isn't that terrible bleaching some celebrities get. Their teeth are so white they look ludicrous. Wilhelm's teeth are naturally white, and his laugh is inviting and sexy.

"Casey, it's called being an adult and classy. Who kisses and tells at our age? Nevertheless, you have thought incorrectly. Everything Peyton told you was true. She does not love me. Nor did she choose me. I am not who you hoped and, I sense, fantasized I would be. I am who she said I am. Your desire to go to Peyton and her peers and say, 'Aha! Just as I suspected," will never come to be. Your insatiable need to prove Peyton wrong has destroyed you. You covetous and treacherous friend, you have been defeated by Peyton yet again! Luckily, today is your last time feeling those cruel pains of jealousy. Casey, you should have known that always wanting to be right is just wrong."

A Clean Heart

Morgan and Cody did not satisfy me. I am headed to my jet, thinking of how to curb this need when Pharris calls. He asks, "Hey, where are you?"

"In Washington."

"Whew! Perfect! I'm in Ocean Shores right now at the Royal Hotel in suite 772. Meet me there."

I get to his suite, and Pharris is talkative and hyper. He runs down all he has concealed. Naturally, everything is tightly shut, untouchable, and untraceable.

"Thanks, Pharris. You have never failed me."

I just watch as he keeps this painted-on smile. He fidgets as he returns the paperwork to his briefcase. I sit quietly, observing him a little longer.

"What's going on? Is there something you need to tell me?" I ask.

Pharris stops and looks into my eyes. He's now looking through me with his lips tightly pressed.

Pharris is my confidant and friend. He considers himself a father figure, yet he is still very afraid of me. Anytime he sensed I was displeased, he became disturbed. However, this night he should be because I am severely pained. Pharris refocuses and then begins shaking his head no.

"Is there something more you need to tell me?" he asks.

"Yes, but I can handle it."

He drops his head, nods, and then says, "Well, that's it. You're officially nonexistent. You're free to hang out with me or go. The choice is entirely yours."

Still carefully observing his body language, I move to the couch. I then respond, "Pharris, I am extremely upset tonight."

He silently glances my way as he takes out a handkerchief to wipe the sweat forming on his forehead.

"Ask me why," I say.

"Why, sir?" he reluctantly asks.

"I hear you have been talking to Peyton's people."

He instantly stops what he's doing and sits on the couch. Then he gives me his undivided attention.

Nodding my head, I continue, "Yes. And my orders were to keep her name private, never seek her out because she was strictly my problem."

He opens his mouth to speak, but I stop him and say, "You get one chance to explain yourself."

"Will, you have heard incorrectly!" he answers.

But I had not heard incorrectly. Pharris inquired about her name while pretending he was the new owner of our home after the Kings incident. One of the workers of the landscaping company I hired jokingly mentioned how he would miss seeing the woman of this house.

"Oh, you knew the woman of the house?" Pharris asked.

"Yeah. She was pretty friendly and very nice looking! Ha-ha!" The worker laughs.

"Yes, she is a very charming woman." Laughing, Pharris asks, "What was her name again?"

"Peyton. I liked that name, so I remembered it."

"Yes! That's right. Peyton!" Pharris deceitfully responds.

Once Peyton and I left the precinct that evening in Vermont, Pharris had no idea if she were dead or alive. Naturally, he assumed dead until the landscaper revealed my secret. This is Pharris's expertise, so he learned everything there is to know about Peyton. I had no need to follow Pharris or keep records of his whereabouts because supposedly he worked for me. I was engrossed with Peyton, not her people, so they were fair play. Pharris easily gathered them one by one.

He had undercover detectives pretending to be church members and coworkers. They knew every step she made. However, they needed to find a moment I was not lurking so they could remove her. Peyton became Pharris's enemy because of my need for her. He saw her as a complete threat, and the only way to cure me was to end her existence. But that was not his call, only mine.

I reveal this information to Pharris. He patiently listens. Once I finish speaking, he doesn't deny any of my accusations. He simply sighs and then says, "So what now, Will?"

Amazed by his response, I lean back in my seat. I sit deep in thought. I think on my life. Meeting Peyton has disrupted every course of it. For more than a century, I did things my way. I existed without longing or wanting for absolutely nothing. Peyton had annihilated all peace and contentment in my world. Even when she was with me, I had no peace. I spent every waking moment ensuring she would not escape me. Any moment she was out of my sight, anxiety would overtake me. The fear of looking up and her being gone ruled me. Still, she was worth every sacrifice to me. Pharris was out of order. With a blank stare, I repeat his words.

"What now? Interesting reply."

Pharris is a true friend. He has sacrificed his own morals to accommodate mine. Many will say it is the money he is loyal to, but I will strongly disagree. Pharris willfully shielded me from everyone and everything. There was nothing or no one he ever exposed my secret to. For years his family had no idea I still existed. He sought out Peyton anonymously. He never revealed to anyone I was the root of his motive why he wanted her dead. He was willing to let the authorities trace her murder solely back to him if needed. I am his son. He wholeheartedly loves me.

His logic in ridding her from my life was simply, "I thought you deserved much better, Will. She's not worthy of you. You can't see it, but I can. And I wanted to see you happy. You are above men. You are regal. You are my king, and I desired to protect your throne."

Pharris's words do move me. They are sincerely from his heart. I shed a tear because he is dear to me. He is loyal to me, but my loyalties are only to myself. Peyton was off limits. His good intentions disobeyed my rules.

He is kneeling at my feet. I stand him up and kiss him. Then I destroy him completely.

Tying All Loose Ends

My identity has been tightly concealed. Peyton's attempt to make me real to the masses is a failed mission. Her closest friends know I exist, but they will wholeheartedly keep Peyton's secrets confidential. However, there is one uncertain acquaintance who knows I am real. I met her on my first date with Peyton. This person is her assistant, Maureen.

The people connected to Peyton were hardened liars and deceivers. Maureen is no exception. She is a professional liar. The first thing she ever said to me was a lie.

Peyton has been long gone, and Maureen has nicely settled into Peyton's old position. Maureen even has her own assistant. How wonderful. I get to the office around five to learn Maureen's schedule. After three stakeouts, I learn Maureen leaves around seven fifteen in the evening. I park by her car in the garage and wait until she comes out.

"Hello, Ms. Reagan."

She screams as she turns to face me. I give a large smile and say, "I'm sorry. I was not trying to scare you."

She laughs while holding her heart, and then she says, "Will, right?"

I act impressed. "Yes! You remembered my name. How flattering."

My smile fades the longer I stare. Hence, her laughing has now ceased. Giving an uncomfortable giggle, she asks, "Well, what's going on? Can I help you with something?"

Her politeness instantly irritates me as I stand motionless, thinking. She bucks her eyes and then says, "Will, I have to go."

She turns to get into her car. I respond, "I'm sorry. I was pondering if I wanted to expose our intimate business, but yes, you can help me."

I allow her to get inside of her car so not to frighten her. I am standing by her window, but she does not let it down. She opens a small crack and then asks, "What do you want, Will?"

"I gave Peyton something very personal that I need back. She said she left it in her office. May I please look in the location she told me and retrieve my personal belongings?" I act saddened.

"You'll have to come back tomorrow morning and get it. I'm not returning to the office tonight! Please understand!"

"No problem. Thanks so much, Maureen," I say as I slowly back away. She gives a pinched smile, rolls up her window, and then skids off.

I see her peering through her rearview mirror. Once she leaves the garage, I get into my car and follow her. I park a few houses down and then circle her home on foot. She is in her kitchen. She pours herself a glass of wine. I learn she has a pet toy dog. It is a Cape Cod home, allowing me to see all of the rooms. It seems she lives alone. She undresses and then lies in the bed. I immediately check all of the doors. Her storm door is unlocked. I quietly walk to her bedroom. As soon as I go to enter, she is right there. She begins to scream uncontrollably. I grab her and carry her to her bed. I lay her down and then climb on top of her, restraining her.

"Please stop screaming. I am not here to hurt you. I just need some help. Will you please help me?"

Although she's still crying, she nods yes. I then explain, "I am going to let you up. Please just listen."

I stand, pulling out my pockets and then removing my blazer.

"See, I have no weapons. I come in peace. I simply need someone to help me, okay?"

She agrees, but she cannot stop crying. Fortunately for her, I decide to overlook it.

"Have you seen Peyton? Now before you answer that, I remember you are a liar. Our first encounter is very different from this encounter. Lying tonight will not be tolerated. So please—I am begging you—please answer me as honestly as you possibly can."

Maureen's taking in quick breaths as if there is a shortage of air. She then forces out, "No! She left our office about eight months ago!"

"Well, what do you know?"

Again, she begins crying loudly. I grab her by her neck, slightly choking her, and say, "Stop crying and answer my questions! Your quick responses increase your chances of survival. Live today and then cry tomorrow. Sound like a plan?"

She attempts to nod yes. I release her, pushing her against her headboard. I impatiently wait a second before she franticly responds, "I swear I don't know! Maurice is her only friend on our floor, and he keeps everything about her private!"

My voice now escalating, I ask, "Peyton never cleared her office? She left her parents' photo there? She removed nothing?"

"She hired someone to remove her things! Who, I don't know! Maurice promoted me. When I returned to work Monday, her office was already empty!" she stammers out.

"So you know absolutely nothing about why she has left? Nothing, right?"

She sits lethargic, recollecting her thoughts. She then answers, "All I know are rumors. Another man from her church named Antonio works a couple of floors up. He told someone Peyton was kidnapped by her stalker. Other than that, I heard nothing!"

I sensed Maureen brought up the word stalker to taunt me. In her attempt to belittle me, she foolishly exposed she knew much more than she claimed.

"A stalker? That's interesting. Knowing that information, you never called to check on Peyton? You didn't care about her well-being?"

Maureen's demeanor instantly turns cold. Annoyed, she answers, "I simply worked with her. We weren't friends."

Feeling deceived, I begin to pace the floor. I ask for her cell phone, but it reveals nothing. I hurl it against the wall, smashing it. My anger causes Maureen to cry, so I warn her again. I see her heightening fear, so I calm myself. I need her alive. I sit silently thinking for at least a half hour. Then I have an epiphany!

"Did you meet Vaughn Pharris?" I ask.

She now sits deep in thought as if she is wholeheartedly trying to think. Through squinted eyes, she answers, "Yes. Detective Vaughn came to my office."

Baffled by this title, I respond, "Detective? When and what did he want?"

Now the floodgates have opened! Maureen carefully explains, "Vaughn questioned me a few months after Peyton disappeared. He said he needed my help and that it required my secrecy. I was his secret agent per se, so I kept him knowledgeable of how much the office knew. Vaughn had recently interviewed Antonio. We both provided him all Peyton's personal information. He strictly needed my help to inform him of her return to Vermont. However, Peyton never returned to the office. Therefore, my services weren't needed."

"Did he say why he needed Peyton found?"

She starts shaking her head with her eyes tightly shut. She now covers her mouth as tears run down her face.

"Your life depends on this answer, Maureen!"

Abruptly, she shouts, "He needed her gone! She was a menace to our society!"

"What? How so?"

Loudly, she wails out, "She was destroying his upward mobility as well as mine by simply existing!"

Polite, professional, highly educated, seemingly sane Maureen was willing to aid in Peyton's assassination for a six-figure salary. Maureen, the hired help for Peyton, had given Vaughn every lead he had in order to have Peyton killed or permanently removed. Peyton was a thorn in her flesh. Peyton often praised Maureen on her expertise, unaware she despised serving her.

I begin to laugh uncontrollably. I laugh until I cry. Maureen just sits watching me trembling in fear. I laugh until I am content. I sit down on the edge of the bed next to her. As I regain my composure, I exhale. Then my laughter abruptly ends.

"You are a wicked one. You people are hateful and certainly twisted. Yet I am the one you all have called the devil? Peyton's life was worthless to you. You sat pretending, in her face, Maurice's face, and every coworker in that office's face. You concealed a secret for almost a year in the hopes of aiding a stranger in murdering Peyton for money?"

Maureen begins to repent for her wrongdoings openly, leaving me somewhat confused. I then ask, "Oh! You go to church, Maureen?"

"Sometimes," she whimpers under her breath.

"Have you ever read the Bible, Maureen?

"Sometimes."

"Apparently, you have not! Since we're exposing secrets, I'll share my secret too. I was raised in the church! I even taught the Bible! And it clearly states you cannot serve two masters! You will love one and despise the other. Maureen, church should have taught you. You cannot serve God and money!"

I snatch her up by her legs and rip her in two. I stand admiring her death for a few minutes. I then wrap and tie her body in her comforter. I take her with me and dispose of her in a secluded area.

Old Endings and New Beginnings

When I awaken from my daydream, I whisper into Peyton's ear, "You want to see who I am? You have been trying to figure me out since we met. Well, here I am!"

I show her the beast that lives inside of me. She wails out a bloodcurdling scream. Then she goes into a state of shock. I have never seen myself. I refuse to acknowledge my inner entity. I need to feel my power is all mine. I kneel over her, and as soon as she awakens, I begin to feed ravenously upon her. I know I have only a day or so before she dies.

The next morning I notice she is not moving. I lift her and then franticly shake her. She starts to breathe, but only faintly. I softly ask, "Are you dying?"

She weakly exhales. I feel her heart beating extremely slow. I kiss her. I then pant out in a whisper, "I love you. You are the only person I've ever loved."

Three, two, one beat. Then she is gone. I weep bitterly. I lie there with her dead body for hours.

I rise up and look into the mirror. I am more attractive than I have ever been, but behind me stands the real me—a vile spirit that has taken my soul. His appearance is his seal of approval. My spirit stands behind me slightly shifted to my left. It had my height and body type—an identical black shadow of myself. However, it is a black darker than any shade of black described by man. It has magnifying, deep royal blue eyes. My dark eyes masked its eyes. Others only saw a blue hue through my natural eyes. It has facial features. It looks as if they are penciled in like a sketched drawing. It has a shiny, wet glow all over its body. It's the wetness I felt in that mirage of a hallway. I felt its body inside of mine. Lastly, it has a very pleasing yet distinct smell. Its smell is comparable to all the fragrant anointing oils described in the Bible.

The darkness I experienced in that hallway was it consuming my body and replacing my soul. My heart, sight, and mind were all replaced in that moment.

My eyes are transfixed upon it as it gazes back at me, mesmerized. Although I remember absolutely nothing during my coma, I am sure it was remaking every part of my existence during that dead period. It was preparing a desired home where it could comfortably reside for as long as I could possibly house it.

Today it has granted me more youth. My renewed youth is always my reward.

I stare at myself for a moment more. I then turn and remorselessly toss Peyton's body into the fireplace and watch it burn to ash. Instantly, I have a feeling of relief. I burn that fire for days, never leaving that spot in front of the fireplace until I know every part of her is consumed.

I prepare to leave that area and search for a new place of solace. However, I returned to Washington one final time. I told myself I was making sure all things were still in order. Truthfully, I went to say my final good-bye to a time in life I learned to love.

The same day I knew Peyton was not returning, I put our estate on the market. I sold it in less than thirty days for much less than what I had purchased it for. While I waited for a buyer, I took the house through major renovations. There was no sign that Peyton or I ever lived there. I even purchased Victoria's worthless store for a very handsome amount. Her husband was extremely pleased. He had only kind words to give. I simply endured more blatant lies from another imbecile oblivious to my identity.

I had the store demolished, and the beach was now a private beach. The new owners were older, and the amenity they sought most was privacy. They desired a secluded community for their children and grandchildren. I put more gates around the perimeter of their property and added "no trespassing" signs. The signs were beautifully written in the opening of each gate. My special room underneath this estate was now concealed under tons of steel and concrete. It was neatly covered by an indoor pool.

Returning to Vermont was the start of my new beginning. Before I left our estate, I destroyed most of Peyton's belongings. However, I could not destroy everything. She had a chest at the end of her bed that I decided to take with me. Because of the abruptness of Peyton's departure, I did not get the luxury of taking time to pick and choose what I would have wanted to keep. And I never felt relaxed enough to sit and go through her chest. After our first encounter on the yacht, I knew I would have her back in my possession soon. As a result, I could endure seeing her things again.

I open the chest to her black diamond ring. It's in its original box on top of a Bible and a few other books. Most of these are how-to books for creating scrapbooks and crafts. She has a digital camera filled with ocean shots, families, and children. It even has a few photos of the front of our home. It is really much of nothing inside here, so I return to her books. I notice she has made several journals. I thumb through each one page by page and find nothing.

I pack her things back into the chest. I find a journal made of seashells she created from a pocket notepad. A few pages are ripped out, but all the other pages are empty. I then go through every single thing in that chest all over again, searching for those missing pages, but to no avail.

I must find these missing pages. I am certain they will reveal Peyton's heart to me. I have been pursuing Peyton for nearly two years, and I know nothing. I had never told Peyton what she meant to me before I killed her, but she meant my life. And she never revealed anything to me. I know her heart is hidden in those pages, and I am desperate to find them. I do not know how, when, or where, but I am determined to know before I depart.

Her missing words are the key to my existence or nonexistence. I keep the notepad and then destroy everything else. It is a keepsake that keeps me … I guess the correct word is *hopeful*.

I Blame You

Hope is a new emotion for a brand-new Wilhelm. I was strong enough to destroy the only thing I ever loved. Hopefully, my power and strength is being renewed.

Before I seek a new dwelling place, I take a detour to the person who deserves to see me most. As I am riding up the driveway, the gates open as if my arrival has been expected. The front door is open. I walk in, but no one is in sight. I go over to the window overlooking the woods and wait patiently for Tabitha to appear. I feel her presence, so I slowly turn to acknowledge her.

"Please come and sit with me," she says.

She sits on the couch. I sit in the chair across from her. My eyes are attentively fixed upon her, but she refuses to look up. She motions to the table, offering me tea.

"You want anything?" she asks. I simply stare.

Exhaling, she finally looks my way and says, "Will you please make me like you? I have waited and hoped for so long that this day would come! I feel as if I'm in a dream! You can't comprehend my joy! You are awesome! Make me like you!"

I sit, staring at her, expressionless. She reaches out her hand to touch me. She pauses to make sure I will not object. She begins lightly rubbing my face. She gives a sigh of relief as she touches me. Now sitting at the opposite end of the couch, she grabs my hand. She gently places it on her wrinkled cheek, still seeking my approval or disapproval. She then kisses the inside of my hand. I remain unmoved. She looks up as a tear runs down my face. She immediately drops my hand and moves away.

"Why are you crying?" she asks.

My eyes are still fixed upon her, but I say nothing. She returns to her seat and then asks, "Where's Peyton?"

The mention of her name is like a sword through my chest. I know the pain is displayed upon my face. Tabitha is not afraid of me, so she comes to embrace me. I stand, putting my hand out, stopping her.

"Why do you care?" I ask.

"I know you love her and desire her as your own. I'm only asking because she's not here with you."

Angry, I reply, "Peyton is dead."

As soon as I say this, Tabitha covers her ears as her mouth drops open. My anger immediately turns to confusion. Why is she shocked?

"Aren't you happy she's dead?"

"Of course not! How did this happen!" Tabitha responds.

"I killed her!"

Gasping, she cries out, "But why?"

With a perplexing scowl, I beg, "Please make me understand your feelings."

Tabitha can barely get her words out as she drags her trembling body across the room farther away from me.

"Wilhelm, I thought you loved her! Why did you do this?"

"Because you and a host of others never left us alone!"

"What? What do you mean?" she cries.

I am extremely lost. Tabitha's reaction has me discombobulated.

"What do I mean? It was you that requested her! It was you that distracted her from me! It was you that wanted her dead most!"

"Wilhelm, that is so untrue! I loved Peyton! We all loved Peyton! I'd never want to see her hurt!" she groans out, dejected.

Her words are taunting me. What did she mean she loved Peyton? I reply, "You did not love Peyton. You love me!"

"Yes! I love both of you!"

I walk to the staircase. I am so upset I begin pacing. I cannot listen to this confusion. Suddenly, rage overtakes me. I rush over to her, yelling, "*If you loved us, why didn't you leave us alone?*"

Her thin, frail body falls to the ground from fright. She cowers in a ball as I approach her.

"Why? Why would you put her on television and surround her with those people if you loved us? You Tabitha! You never gave us peace! You made her feel as if she had to save you from me! Everyone I destroyed and blamed, but you are the blame! You are the curse! Your wicked grandmother and twisted mother set me up! Your birth has utterly destroyed me!"

Tabitha crawls back to the couch, demoralized. Her saggy, frowning skin turns pale and lifeless. She sits on the floor with her back against the couch.

She admits through a blank stare, "I am cursed. I dedicated my entire life to finding you, and now I have nothing. No husband, children, or family. My entire life has been spent searching for you. I never imagined you wouldn't love me. I only saw you would love me and renew my youth. Then we would live happily in love forever. Your love was worth every sacrifice I had ever made. The one person equipped to obtain you for me took you from me! She was simply supposed to lure you to me, but you loved her. The man devoid of love fell in love in front of my eyes! I couldn't understand how she could resist you. I thought it was merely Constance that Helena had cursed. However, it seems she cursed not only those who love you but even the woman you would love."

I reply, "You're wrong. Peyton got away. She is not cursed. Helena, Constance, you, and I have received the same fate, but Peyton is in peace. You do not know, but I know. I walk in a different dimension. I see through different eyes, and Peyton is gone. I cannot find her. You just may see me again, but I will never see her again. Your selfishness took her from me. I blame you and you alone."

Tabitha begins bitterly weeping as I approach her. Glaring down at her, I continue, "As much as I would like to kill you, I think life in this decaying, old, feeble body is worse than death. Living and knowing you will never see me again is a harsher punishment. Your dream of kissing me and me loving you will never come to be. Every fantasy you had of us, I actually lived out with Peyton. You waited seventy years, but you do not have seventy years more. All your dreams and hopes have been dashed! The thing you dreaded most has been granted! My only desire for you is that you rot in this dark, lonely, dismal mansion miserably and then die and go to hell!"

She falls back, hyperventilating. I ring for her nurse, who rushes in. I calmly instruct her, "Make sure she does not die!" Then I quietly leave.

Let It Come to Pass

Soon Tabitha will have to leave this castle, or people will start to ask more questions.

My husband is dead.

My daughter is dead.

Lee's parents are dead.

That despicable Earl Alistair is finally dead.

How dare he reveal Constance's secret! How connected the Berkleys would have been to Lee's affairs had the people believed Tabitha was his daughter! Helena Berkley and Lord Lee Wilhelm York's name would have always been spoken together in the same sentence! Lee and I would have been family forever!

Society is changing so drastically. Privacy is no longer valuable to the majority anymore. Our population is diverse and expanding. Youth and novelty is so important now! Lee's desires were years before his time. He was wiser than the rest of us and planned well for this foreseen future. How did he know this day would soon come?

I see that horrid Clara was too daft to even know Lee's heart! What a fool! I pray she's dead! I had one moment of joy in this wretched life. And that was learning Lee had abandoned his treasured Clara! Unfortunately, it was only a fleeting second of joy.

Although Lee surely lives, his absence leaves him dead to me just as all the others. Simply knowing he's alive is worthless, so how do I find him? Tabitha is my last hope. I have sacrificed much to obtain Lee, but now she is all I have left to give.

I'm no longer that vibrant young girl who hoped and believed my dream would come true. All the commitments to darkness have failed me! Everything ever prophesied to me only came to pass to torment me. Tabitha's prophesy needs to be true! I need Tabitha to find Lee right now—today! However, wisdom has assured me that will never come to be.

Wisdom is an annoying woman whom I avoid because she thinks she knows it all! Therefore, I reject her today as I always have! Her ways are too restricting! That's why I have unrelentingly rejected her!

I am a dreamer! I hope against all hope! I don't need hope or wisdom, only my dreams! Daily, I dream of Lee with me. He and I were, are, and always will be the same! We are one!

Sadly, I have aged. I don't want him to see me this way! If he resisted me then in my beauty and youth, he will certainly reject me today! How much more rejection must I endure at the hands of Lee? All I wanted was to love him, and all he has ever given me in return is hate! Where's my reward? Where's my justice?

If I'm brutally honest with myself, I have always clearly seen what my gift has to offer. Seeking love for the joy of love or peace for the serenity of peace will never be granted! I should have learned by now if I ask for beauty I will receive it, but at what detrimental cost? What is the price? What must I sacrifice in order to ensure Tabitha finds Lee? Asking she finds him and he accepts I'm his soul mate and then we raise her in peace will never happen! That desire is too good. Why hadn't I figured out before now that my future is in the hands of malignant fate?

Evil never produces good! Evil produces after its own kind! A tree is known by its fruit! I can't expect a thorn bush to produce berries. Thus, I can't expect evil to produce good!

As I look into the mirror, I see a fool! I found the secret to my success too late! I did not grow old gracefully. Constantly crying and hating has left a permanent scowl upon my face. I have no soft laugh lines only hard frown lines. And seeing Tabitha makes me frown even more. Tabitha's beauty is by far much less impressive if compared to Constance's beauty. Constance's father was handsome and regal. Tabitha's father was a simpleton and unflattering to look upon. Tabitha has nothing to offer except her mother's name. What can she possibly add to this family?

The truth is that her conception is a blemish to our family's name! It's degrading to need Tabitha. She's the seed of a beggar. How can she possibly obtain Lee?

It bleeds my heart, and my heart is failing. Soon I will be dead! The past forty-five years of constant heartache has damaged it. I can sit here as I'm deteriorating and continue to hope for a happy ending, but that's just foolish. If only I had been as brave as Lee to step into the darkness.

It was September 13, 1913. I saw Lee entering his favorite restaurant. However, now everyone called him Wilhelm. Lee was dead. He was a constant traveler, so seeing him in town was rare. I knew he had returned home, so I waited for him to come out the entire day. In the evening he finally left his estate and headed to the restaurant.

It was rumored he and Clara were over. I was anxious to ask him if it was true. I discreetly entered behind him. I demanded I be allowed to join him in his private room. I just assumed it'd be some woman accompanying him, but he was alone. He kept the room extremely dark. The only light was a single candle burning in the center of his table.

My mother had raised me in the occult, so there wasn't much I feared. Nonetheless, entering this room with Lee was dreadful. It was at least seventy degrees outside, but it was freezing inside this room. I stood by the door entrance as I heard the maître d' lock us inside.

"Helena, why are you here?"

Lee sounds as if a soft echo is speaking with him. Still by the door, I squint, hoping to see his face. I call out, "Lee?"

"Respect who I am, Helena. Call me Wilhelm. Things have drastically changed since I was that nineteen-year-old boy. You've been obsessing over for more than a decade."

"Forgive me, Wilhelm, but I'm here to see you. I've missed you."

"Well, come see me."

The closer I get to Wilhelm, the colder it becomes. Finally standing in front of his table, he tells me to sit down. I sit, and he pours me a glass of wine. I look intently into the dark corner he's hiding in trying to see his face. He's leaning back in his seat and breathing deeply. The coldness in the air is visibly seen each time he exhales.

"Wilhelm, it's so cold. May I request they turn off the fans?"

"No, this is my preferred temperature. I am extremely hot. If you're uncomfortable, I suggest you leave."

I pick up my wine and sip without responding. After a few minutes more in silence, I then beg, "Wilhelm, let me see your face. I've missed you."

He slowly leans forward, and his face is as beautiful as it ever was. However, his pupils are nearly neon blue.

"W-What have you done to your eyes?" I stammer.

"Helena you're not afraid, are you?"

Through my quivering voice, I answer no. I wanted to say I'm terrified.

Suddenly, he stands and then squats next to me. Black eyes, blue eyes, neon eyes, I still want Lee with all my soul. As I reach out to touch his face, he tightly grabs and then snatches my arm, saying, "Helena, Lee is dead. I am someone else. Say what you want, and then leave."

He then throws my arm and moves back into the darkness. Massaging my throbbing wrist, I say, "I want to be someone else with you! Is Clara new too?"

"Do you want to find out about Clara or me?"

"You!"

"You and your mother seem to enjoy anything unholy. Why haven't you already been converted?"

"I don't understand your question."

"Why are you still a wretched human?"

"My mother taught me to keep my options open. Never sell out completely to one side."

"Well, your perverted witch mother is a fool. Being lukewarm gets you rejected by God as well. He wishes you were either hot or cold. Because you're too cowardly to make a choice, He vomits you out of His mouth! Your straddling the fence is detestable to Him also."

"Lee? I-I'm so sorry. Forgive me! Wilhelm, have you chosen a side?"

"Yes. Will you join me?"

"Will you love me?"

He leans in, allowing me to see his face, and then whispers, "You won't need love."

Pleading, I say, "I will join you if you promise to love me first."

"Helena I am devoid of love, so that will be impossible. My time is valuable, and I need to feed. Make your decision now. If you choose me, feel free to stay. If not, heed my advice and leave immediately, or we will make your decision for you."

I no longer only hear Lee's voice. There are voices. Even more than two, it seems. I hesitate for a split second, and then fear grips my heart. Before I know it, I run to the door, screaming. I violently kick it while begging the maître d' to open it! Once the door opens, the maître d' snatches me out. He quickly locks the door behind me. He's sweating profusely, and breathlessly, he asks if I'm all right. I nod my head continuously as I try to comprehend what just happened.

He escorts me to the door, hugs me, and then whispers, "I heard Lord York now serves Satan. We're praying he goes to America and never returns. Go in peace, Lady Berkley, and may God be with you."

I nod and then head home.

Shortly after that encounter, Lee did seem to live in America. He traveled constantly. Seeing him was nearly impossible. I hadn't seen Lee in years. Then he showed up at my door to court my daughter. I tried to tell him I had decided to serve with him since our last meeting. Tragically, he would have nothing to do with me. My opportunity to be with Lee was gone all because I was too fearful to reign in darkness with him. As a result, I never forgave myself or anyone for that matter.

I hated life and everyone in life except Lee. I was certain Constance would choose to serve with him, but obviously, he never offered her the opportunity. I felt chosen, knowing he never asked her. After he destroyed her, I desperately needed to find him! I needed one last chance to convince him I was no longer afraid to submit to his will. I prayed for years he'd return, but that prayer was never answered. Now I have a new prayer.

Today in my last days of life, I pray Tabitha finds Lee and suffers my same fate! I pray her daughter captures Lee's heart, and she must endure seeing his desire for another daily! I pray her pain is just as excruciating as mine is every second of every minute of each day!

I pray she's older and more displeasing to behold than I am today. In fact, make her double my age when he finds her! Her likeness will represent everything Lee has despised most—aging! Let her be deceived as I have been deceived into believing all her sacrifices will pay off! Let her spend her life alone, hoping and dreaming of Lee's love but never attaining it!

However, my last prayer request is for my beloved Lee.

May he find the thing that will destroy him. May he suffer the same fate he has caused all who loved him to suffer. Let him realize what I learned, only when it's too late! As I sit here dying and finally learning the truth of my so-called gift—namely that it's a curse—grant Lee the same fate! I pray with all my strength and being that he's alone. I pray there's no one around that loves him or he loves. He then learns he is deceived.

Although I will not live to see that day come to pass, I pray, let it come to pass.

A House Divided

Casey thinks I'm her fool. Her aunt is well? Which aunt is this, and when has she ever mentioned an ill aunt out of state? I text back a simple religious response to appease her. I then think upon Peyton.

I've done everything in my power to keep Peyton near me. I surely thought giving her a position at my office and us working so closely would eventually strengthen our bond. I had completely convinced Casey I was only getting involved in their relationship to save their friendship! I couldn't care less about that friendship. I only care about being near Peyton. In fact, I can't imagine having to spend all that time with Casey without Peyton.

I was surprised Regina never noticed I was in love with Peyton. I believe Regina purposely overlooked my love for Peyton. I think she's in love with me herself. Regina would reveal little information on Casey, hoping I would leave her. Truth is that my heart left Casey the moment I met Peyton.

My constant matchmaking for Peyton surely convinced Casey and Regina my motives were pure. My introducing her to my firm's COO, Juan, certainly deceived them into believing I wanted no one but the best for her. However, Juan was the least of my friends. I knew he would never win Peyton over, so I purposely chose him to be her date that night. Internally, I was laughing at him and his excitement. He was my personal inside joke, but once Wilhelm appeared, the joke was surely on me.

Wilhelm decimated all competition. His presence made you feel impoverished and unattractive. I was devastated seeing Peyton so enthralled. Her eyes were filled with awe and desire. I put on my best performance that evening. After he walked away, all joy had seeped out of my soul. I was already upset. Then on our ride home, Casey talked about Wilhelm nonstop. Her voice started to irk me. By the time we got to her home, I dreaded kissing her good night. I mustered up the stomach to kiss her, and then I drove home feeling defeated.

The day I saw Wilhelm in the office was even more upsetting. Seeing him at my firm made me feel as if he had invaded my personal space. Peyton was in my territory. He was trespassing on my property! I immediately headed over to Peyton's office to confront him. Once I approached him I found he was only an inch or so taller than me, but he made me feel as if I were coming against a giant! He just looked like an abundance of new money. I'm all man, but I must admit he was distractingly attractive. He was so attractive I couldn't stop staring at him.

I went over to show my authority, although he was very intimidating. However, I refused to show any inferiority in his presence. I stood my ground well, but Peyton was very irritating because she was obviously into him. I knew she hadn't seen him since the New Year's Eve party, yet she seemed overprotective of him. She acted as if she didn't want me questioning him at all! She literally interrupted answering my question to him as Wilhelm stood grimacing at me as if I were a peasant who didn't deserve to breathe his air. My ego was crushed! Still, I invited them over without having anything planned.

Despite losing this battle, I couldn't rest knowing Peyton would be with him that night. Of course, they didn't come over, and Casey ran over to her home to hear about Wilhelm like a female dog in heat!

After Wilhelm and Peyton's date, Casey wouldn't stop talking about him, but I didn't care. I needed to know his every move with Peyton, and if it was through Casey's mouth, then so be it!

Casey visited her imaginary sick aunt, and I never heard from her again. The congregation and our acquaintances expected me to leave the church, but that was the furthest thing from my mind. Once Casey was gone, I became more active in church! This was the perfect time to stay! I was praying harder than anyone present, hoping that Peyton would return. Her return this time meant I could pursue her in peace.

My new commitment to church had Regina stuck to me like glue and vice versa. If she was my link to Peyton, I was willing to get engaged to her too! In fact, I already befriended all of Peyton's friends! However, Casey's departure allowed me to interact with them freely. As a result, Jonathan Scott and I have become close. In fact, I am one of the first to know that his wife's magazine article comes out today.

As soon as the magazines hit the stands, I call Jonathan to congratulate the missus. He and I are meeting for breakfast to celebrate, but mostly, he will fill me in on Peyton's unpublished letters. I had exposed my heart to Jonathan, letting him know that I loved her.

As I'm pulling up to his home, I drive past Wilhelm, and our eyes lock. I immediately call Jonathan to let him know I'm following Wilhelm. He doesn't answer his phone, so I leave a message and continue following. Wilhelm leads me to a local landfill. Who has unrestricted access to a landfill? This guy seems to be able to do whatever he wants! The availability of everything and everyone to him was too high for my mind to comprehend. Figuring out his unlimited privileges was too complex to decipher in a few minutes. I mentally push his advantages compared to my disadvantages out of my head. Legally, I can't enter with him, so I simply wait patiently until his car drives back out.

I've been sitting at least twenty minutes when Wilhelm appears at my door. He calmly says, "Looking for me, Maurice Carlson?"

It takes everything in me not to cry out like a little girl. He looks so demonic that my heart briefly stops beating.

"Since you are brave enough to follow me, get out of your car and face me like a man." He taunts.

My fear is at the highest level, one I never imagined it could reach! However, this man has bruised my ego so many times I won't let him demean me anymore. Although I'm terrified, I'm angrier because Peyton has exposed her heart to Mrs. Scott.

I bravely respond, "If you step away from my door and give me some space to get out, then I will!"

He moves back very slowly with a murderous glare.

"What? Are we supposed to fight?" I jokingly ask.

He remains still, breathing deeply, watching me. I soon remember what he is, so I try to calm him down.

"Wilhelm, I don't want to upset you. I've accepted Peyton loves you. We all have! We just want to know that she's well."

"Why do you all feel the need to keep telling me this lie? Did Peyton tell you she loves me?" he asks, annoyed.

"Yes!"

"Oh, she speaks to you from the grave now?"

I'm confused by his question. "What do you mean?"

"Maurice, why have you followed me? Tell me what you want to know quickly. My time is valuable."

"Wilhelm, I was supposed to meet Mr. Scott for coffee, but he never answered his phone. Then I saw you leaving his home, so I assumed you would lead me to him."

"He and his nosey wife are in the trash where they belong."

My heart is pounding against my chest. Frenzied, I ask, "Where's Peyton?"

"I assume in your heaven … or just dead!"

"What do you mean? Is she in this landfill too?" I yell.

Wilhelm now softens his face. He relaxes his shoulders and begins to examine me.

"Have you even been missing Casey? She and Peyton are probably together. I doubt it, but in your happy, all-loving world, I am sure they will meet."

"Casey? Huh, what? Where's Peyton? You'd better not have touched her!"

He rushes to my face. "Or what? What possibly can you do to me?" he says and scoffs.

I trip and fall, attempting to back away from him. He walks my way. Now standing over me with a condescending look, he says, "You poor little man. You settled for Casey because you weren't man enough to get Peyton? You had to plot all sorts of schemes to trick her into wanting you, yet all I had to do was show up. Man, it has to be really emasculating being you. What, Mr. Maurice Carlson? What do you want from me? You want me to tell you how to get her? Are you as pathetic as your dead fiancée and hope I will reveal our intimate secrets with you? *What do you want from me?*"

Extremely humiliated, I begin to cry. I'm crying so hard I'm choking. Of course, his words are degrading, but that's not my reason. I'm crying from pure fear. He's no longer a man. Both his eyes have wholly turned a dim royal blue. A tear runs down his cheek.

"I am in pain too," he groans out.

I overwhelmingly feel his pain through my fear. He then closes his eyes and begins to speak.

"Maurice, why you and Casey chose to follow me to seek the truth bewilders me. What is the purpose of all this brotherly bonding if you do not even trust what the other says? All of you were supposed to be unified, yet everyone in your circle had their own version of what was true and didn't believe anything your so-called brothers or sisters said. I must have spoken to everyone connected to Peyton, and I can honestly say no one was in agreement. That's pretty pathetic, yet you think I'm on the wrong side? My partner and I have never been divided!"

He snatches me up and then throws me in the backseat of my car. He begins pulling my flesh from my bones. I'm screaming in a pitch higher than any octave on the scale! My skin looks like string as he rips it. It feels like a jagged knife slicing through me! I then think how his outward appearance caused me to overlook what he was. I should have known not to provoke my enemy.

My life plays out in front of my eyes. I repent as I begin losing consciousness.

Let No Man Put Asunder

The Scotts think they are celebrities.

After a few days of seeking, the authorities find our old home in Eden Estate. However, it is no house of horrors. That underground pathway they so desperately sought has long been filled. It is a deep, narrow pathway to its location that only required cement and water to rid its existence forever. The Scotts are months behind already. I properly left that area, and the new family is very pleased with their new home.

Oh, Mrs. Scott's magazine is the most coveted literature not yet published! Moreover, she has done everything except openly confess she is the heroine to this story. I try wholeheartedly to move past Peyton and fight daily to renounce self-destruction. Nevertheless, faithful Mrs. Scott has sealed my fate once again.

Peyton's escape deferred my plans to remove these people. It was truly their ignorance that ruined all. The day I took Peyton to Zoe's, I had resolved to persuade Peyton to let me make her as I am. However, they were the ones who led her to Tabitha. Tabitha's nonsense ensured that I had to take Peyton against her will. Had the Scotts never lured her to Tabitha's, I would have won

Peyton over without her knowing every secret I possessed. By the time she learned of me, she would have been mine wholly. I had planned my night to approach Peyton for countless months, and it fared perfectly. Convincing her to trust me enough to go to Zoe's was a magnanimous feat! All my hard work was vanquished by a twenty-minute conversation. Once Peyton met Tabitha, it consumed her. Her desire to have a productive, normal life with love and a career had been robbed from her.

This learned blindness is needed to accomplish uncontested servitude. I needed Peyton deluded in order to conquer her. It would have been easy, but the Scotts' disruption made it tragically hard!

I see Mrs. Scott's magazine at the gas station the very morning they release it. I see Peyton's face, and I remember I never killed the people who put us asunder. I search the magazine for an address and pay for my gas, and straightway, I head to Mrs. Scott's office.

It is a couple of minutes past five in the morning. I cut my car off and sit in a hidden parking spot across the way, waiting until she walks out. Six on the nose, she comes out, and people are hugging her. I am sure they are comforting as well as praising her. I just want to rush over and rip her guts out! However, I remain composed because she did not accomplish this alone. Her weak, useless husband is just as much at fault.

She begins to drive, and her office is less than ten minutes from her home, which is perfect for me. Before she closes the door, I greet her from behind and walk in with her. Mr. Scott is preparing to leave for work. I greet him with a handshake and then politely lead them both to their living room couch.

I request the actual letter, and Mrs. Scott informs me it is in her office desk. She stands, hoping to take me to it, but I tell her to please sit back down. Mr. Scott is sitting with gritted teeth yet crying and praying.

"Mr. Scott, if you want to drown in your own blood, keep praying. Be quiet if not!" I tell him.

I guess he knows his prayers are worthless because he instantly stops.

"So much for faith, huh? You want to live! Won't you be in heaven if you die? I guess it's not all you saints claim! No one is willing to die once they see me. You all submit to my will!" I say, laughing.

He just stares at me with a stupid look on his ugly face. Then Mrs. Scott shows she has the balls by confronting me.

"Why are you here?" she asks.

I answer, "Well, obviously for your life!" She instantly stops speaking.

"I saw your texts to Zoe. Be truthful. Did Peyton ask you to ask Zoe about me?"

Hesitating momentarily, she answers, "No."

"No? So you wanted to know what?"

"What does it matter!" she screams.

I snatch Mr. Scott's face from his skull because I am tired of looking at it. It's grotesque! He is now bellowing in pain. Mrs. Scott starts to wail.

"Tracey, shut up! Be quiet, and then answer my question."

I jump back as she vomits over the arm of the couch.

"I wanted her away from you!" she cries.

"Why?"

Breathless and trying to clear the bile from her throat, she forces out, "I didn't want her tainted! She was a very good girl! I was only attempting to help a friend!"

"Did you know me?"

"No! No!" she shrieks.

"So why would you seek to condemn me before you even knew my character?"

She just begins to sob uncontrollably. I watch her and her pathetic husband as they moan, both weak, beaten, and defenseless. I whisper into her ear, "Mrs. Scott, no more condemning."

I rip out her tongue. The Scotts are now unconscious together. The pain has knocked them out. I behead them both and then put their bodies in trash bags.

I walk around their home, searching for information on their son. I know him. I could be cruel, but his death would be a waste of time. The ones who will grieve him most are already dead. Plus, I may need him in the future. I return his picture to the mantel. I leave and dispose of the Scotts in a landfill. They were filthy trash in my eyes. I get a hotel room for the night and then prepare for my flight to Tahiti.

Riding to my jet, I remember Mrs. Scott mentioning how the original letter is in her desk. I break into her office. Lo and behold, she is not a liar. Peyton's letter is in her top desk drawer. I put it in my pocket and then head to my destination.

I refuse to read the letter until I am alone in a stable location. After I am in the air and my attendant is done accommodating me, I let her know not to disturb me. I take out Peyton's letter. I know all was supposedly put in the magazine, but I need to see for myself what she has written.

I guess Peyton's supposed lover was Mrs. Scott. So many lies and mind games, especially at the hands of Peyton's so-called friends. I needed to read this letter for myself, or I would always feel Mrs. Scott had somehow deceived me.

Those who lie and scheme for the *good* of their friends are held in high esteem to most, but not in my eyes. I knew I was deceiving and scheming, and Peyton and all her friends hated me for it. But they loved one another for it. That often vexed me and ignited my hatred toward them. But I digress. I return my focus to the letters.

Magazines are infamous for using what sells and deleting what they deem unsellable. Therefore, a written magazine article would never satisfy my curiosity.

I take the small pieces of paper out of this manila envelope. I see her beautiful handwriting, and my desire to see her starts to grip me. I reread the printed letters, but lo and behold, there are journals that were not printed. I begin reading.

August 12

Everyone is dying. My last hope is Victoria. I must befriend her and get her to aid me. I need my people to know I'm alive and on the opposite side of the country. They deserve to know. Tracey has this magazine, and her PO box is the only address I slightly remember. Lord, make me accurately remember!

September 1

Please protect Victoria. If he even thinks she's aiding me, she'll die horrifically.

Writing frees my mind. I have to reveal my heart, or I'll explode. Maybe I will send this. I can't keep lying to myself.

After all the fear and the horrors I've seen and experienced, I do not want him dead. I don't even want him hurt. You know all things. I might as well say it. I don't want to leave, but I must.

I don't want him to love anyone but me. I don't want anyone to get to know him. He belongs to me. I want him exclusively for myself.

I want him delivered. The man Wilhelm is in there somewhere. I see him. I hear him. Daily, I touch, feel, and taste him. He bleeds. He feels. He loves.

I tell myself I do not, but I do. I ask myself, "How is this possible?" I ask myself, "Why

would you fail your people? Why would
you fail God?" I have failed all.

I must get out of here! I must escape him,
or I will soon tell him that I love him.

There is a sticky note clipped to the top of this page that says, "Do not publish in case Peyton returns. We do not want her image tainted. Once she is fully recovered, we will allow her to reveal her own story. —T. Scott."

I thought finding out she loved me would strengthen me, but it completely destroyed me. Learning I accomplished my goal and then having to accept I single-handedly destroyed it made me want death. I did not want to remember anything or anyone anymore.

Love Defined

He is the only man I have ever loved.

Wilhelm is sitting on the couch with his eyes shut. His head is tilted back, but his back is straight. His hands are resting on his inner thighs. I just finished bathing and came downstairs to see if he's in my world or his world, the one that I do not have access to.

I have on my satin black robe and its matching gown. I'm moisturizing in this new fragrance I created. I hope he likes it. I put on my body butter in the chair across from Wilhelm, but he's still unresponsive. Once I'm done, I hesitantly creep over to the couch where he's sitting.

I sit down. Now he's glancing at me from the corner of his eyes. He doesn't change positions. Nor does he display any emotion.

"Are you all right? I just came to see if you needed anything," I ask with a comforting smile.

He looks without responding, closes his eyes, and then shakes his head no. I slide over and tuck myself away in the corner of the couch.

"You smell nice," he says softly.

"Thanks. I hoped you'd like it."

I remain next to him for at least an hour, but he's zoned out. Today I wished I knew where he goes in his times of meditation. In the past, seeing him oblivious to this realm would frighten me. He'd be gone, and I'd dread his return to this dimension. But today I long to be wherever he is. He has no interest in me tonight. That disturbs me. Is his desire for me fading?

Wilhelm would be engrossed by my thoughts twenty-four hours a day. He wanted to know what I was thinking every second. In the past few weeks, his distance has been painfully troubling. One thing about Wilhelm is that he'll tell you exactly how he feels. He doesn't know or possess the will to be kind and polite. Because of this attribute, I'm afraid to ask him why he has been so distant lately. I have no fear of him. I only fear him saying he no longer desires me.

Tonight I need desperately for him to swoon over me because tomorrow I will be gone. I finally confided in Victoria. She wasn't my person of choice, but she was all I had left. I purposed to let Amina know and allow her and Harrison to aid in my escape, but Wilhelm destroyed that plan literally. After Amina's death, I didn't have the time to establish a brand-new relationship. Victoria was the next best thing. She devised the perfect plan. We decided tomorrow would be the day.

I knew my feelings for Wilhelm were evolving. I wholeheartedly planned to be gone before my love was in full bloom. Many times before my planned day of departure, I changed my mind and didn't want to leave him, but I had given Victoria the wounded woman act so strong that I would've looked foolish staying. Then if ever I truly wanted to leave, she wouldn't help again if she perceived I was an unstable person given to change.

I sit watching Wilhelm for hours, and now I need him here with me. I can't leave without being intimate with him one last time. He's still sitting comatose in the middle of the couch. I stand over him, examining his lovely face. Unfortunately, he's fully dressed, forbidding me to admire his strong yet supple physique. His skin is glowing, and his lips are heart-shaped like the lips on a perfect drawing. He has strong cheekbones, long luscious eye lashes, and he always smells delectable. His scent is natural. He hates perfumes, but he desired natural oils on me.

Now sitting next to him, I lean over and kiss his hand. It's still neatly placed on his lap. I slowly rise up and scoot away because I see his eyes moving under his lids. He covers his face with his hands and sighs, and then he opens his eyes. He turns his head to face me, so I smile. He sets his hands on the couch next to his sides. I gently lift his hand and set it snugly upon my face. He just watches me. I softly kiss the inside of his hand and then return it to my face. Still, he doesn't react. I then stand to head upstairs. Seemingly, he's disinterested in my out-of-the-norm advances. Then thankfully, he grabs my hand and leads me onto his lap.

I climb on top of him, straddling him. He's not speaking, but I know he's pleased.

"You're very beautiful." I whisper. He continues watching in silence.

I kiss his lips, his neck, and then his ear. I lay my head on his shoulder. He gently pushes me up to face him. I know he's trying to interpret my actions. He kisses my lips and then softly tells me, "Just say it."

I know he's telling me to finally say I love him. Although I have never spoken the words, my actions exposed my love for him this night. It's my last night with Wilhelm. Can I at least tell him the truth before I leave? Does he deserve to know the truth? Will this truth make him happy or make him feel as if he has completed his task? I don't know the answer to these questions. Admitting I love him isn't as easy as it'd be telling a natural man.

As he waits for me to speak the words, I return my thoughts to him and answer, "Tell me what you want me to say, and I'll say it."

Wilhelm has never used the word love except for saying "making love." I surely thought I had foiled his plans, but then he boldly says, "Say you love me."

I sit on his lap, stupefied. I desperately attempt to utter the words, but they're trapped in my throat. He begins to kiss my neck, my chest, my lips, all over, and he keeps whispering, "Say you love me."

After seconds of my silence, he stops asking. He gently pushes me off his lap and then goes away. I'm now alone in this big, dark room, struggling with my emotions. I want to be with Wilhelm desperately tonight, but his heart is far from me because I refuse to admit I love him. All I need to do is follow him and tell him, and then we'll make love and live happily ever after! Sadly, I know that's a dream destined to turn into a nightmare.

A few minutes later, I head upstairs, and our room door is shut. I stare at the door, heartbroken. I want to go inside, but I don't know who will be present. My longing and fear are equal in this moment. I'll assume because he closed the door, he doesn't want to be bothered. I shed a tear. Then I go to my room and restlessly fall asleep.

Wilhelm is used to me not answering him when it comes to exposing my heart. I have a headache because I've been stressed all night trying to figure out how to reveal the truth to him. Throughout the night I had decided I would stay, but his now frequent vacillations from this realm to the next leave me fearing he's preparing to leave me. Therefore, I change my mind yet again and choose to go ahead with my plan.

He's been in his secret world for most of the day. Wilhelm comes out of hiding in the evening and is ready to accompany me to the beach. It's a quiet day. I see a group of young people and a couple of families, not too many people are out. I ask Wilhelm to come swim with me, but he declines. I run into the water. I dive underwater and then peek at Wilhelm with my body submerged and only my eyes above the surface. He's looking in my direction, but he's not focused on me. I begin to cry. How did I allow myself to get here? I fought this untoward relationship for months. Now here I am despondent because Wilhelm is starting to act as if he can live without me.

Standing, I notice a boy swimming in my direction. I immediately exit the water so this stranger won't see I've been crying. I return to Wilhelm, yet he's zoning out again. I simply start small talk. He nods, but again, he has left me.

I hear my phone vibrating in my clutch. It's Victoria. She calls to warn me that it's time to act. I say okay and then return my focus to my Wilhelm.

I lie on my back next to him, hoping he'll respond, but he doesn't. After a few minutes of sunbathing, I stand to see if he'll simply look my way. Wilhelm is gone, deep into his realm of thought, into the unknown. Wherever he is, he surely no longer needs me here or there. I hesitate during my departure, but before I burst into tears, I behold with admiration my beautiful Wilhelm. Then I leave.

Once I'm in the city, I call Casey. Now I'm waiting patiently for my cab. While waiting, I realize I need to develop and memorize an acceptable scripted version of my story to tell. I'm grateful to be free. I know choosing to stay with Wilhelm would've been damnation for my soul. It is a divine intervention that made me accept it was wiser to leave. Nevertheless, I still need a plan. I can't tell anyone I love him. No one will understand.

Amina King was my friend sent by God. I needed to tell someone the truth of our relationship. The day the Kings come into our home, Amina and I get in the water and converse. Harrison and Wilhelm stand in the distance and hold their own conversation. Well, Harrison is speaking as Wilhelm blatantly watches Amina and me.

"Wilhelm's quite intense," Amina says, glancing toward him.

Faintly smiling, gazing his way, I ask, "Why do you say that?"

"He's just watching you as we speak. It's as if he never wants you out of his sight." She chuckles.

Amina is probably in her late forties or early fifties. She's around my mother's age if she were alive. It's then I decide to expose my secret. If my mother were here, I'm sure she'd understand. I'd tell her everything.

I reply, "That's because he doesn't."

"Really? I don't know if that's good or bad. Let's face the ocean and speak."

I glance at Wilhelm once more and then turn my back toward him. Amina then asks, "What's the story behind your relationship? How long have you been together?"

"Since January. Well, really, March."

"Oh? So is he your husband?"

"No."

"You've only dated since March and live together already?"

"It's not like that."

"No?"

I feel myself feeling embarrassed because I'm supposed to live holy and this just sounds ridiculous.

"He kind of tricked me into living with him. This is temporary," I answer.

"Okay … I'm listening." She sees my frustration, so she says, "I won't judge you. I believe God has me here. I only want to be a friend." She smiles.

"It's complicated, Amina. I didn't want to be here. Now I do. I need to leave, but I can't. Well, I won't. I don't know what I want anymore."

"What kind of a man is he?"

I glance toward him and then say, "Sometimes he's everything I asked for. Then other times—"

"What? Say it."

"Other times he's just not."

"Please explain. You know he's going to interrupt us soon. Say it, Peyton."

"He's not who he appears to be," I whisper.

Perplexed, she shakes her head. I continue, "We're more spiritually connected than anything."

"Ooookayyy … what does that mean?"

"I believe I've been connected to him for a greater purpose than—"

"Than what? Hurry, Peyton. He and Harrison are headed our way!"

"Than love."

"So you have fallen in love with him already?" I nod yes with tear-filled eyes. "Is he saved?" she asks. I shake my head no.

"Love is unconditional, believing, and long-suffering. Love is powerful, but that power is detrimental when you love the wrong person."

"Or thing?" I whisper.

She gives a confused scowl. I continue, "I thought only wicked people willingly chose the wrong things and/or people to love. Am I wicked?"

"Now you have me totally confused, Peyton! Is he wicked?" she asks, glancing back at Wilhelm.

"I deceived myself into thinking I could easily reject his love. I wholeheartedly believed that because I knew right from wrong, I could remain with him and never fall, but that isn't sound wisdom, is it?" I say.

"No, the Bible clearly says, 'Do not be deceived. Evil company corrupt good habits.' The longer you're with him, the more you'll accept him!

"You're so right, woman of God! I'm not swaying him toward my ways, yet he has almost fully persuaded me towards his."

"What's his ways?"

I look up, wide-eyed and dumbfounded. She then says, "The love's too strong now, huh?"

"Who's in love?" Harrison interrupts as he grabs Amina's waist.

Wilhelm is intently watching me, awaiting an answer. Amina stares as I stand speechless, staring into his eyes. Wilhelm then asks, "Yes, who?"

Amina's watching Wilhelm, and she then looks at me. I drop my head. She then answers, "Why it's me telling of my love for you, husband!"

"I knew it!" Harrison laughs as he kisses her lips.

Wilhelm and I stand emotionless, watching them interact. Wilhelm obviously wanted to learn the truth of Amina's and my conversation, so he invites them up to our home. However, Amina wisely talks only of our house.

I should have purposed to escape long before now. The murders and the shrilling screams throughout the night didn't bother me much anymore. Now my rationale was simply. *He has to feed!*

My fall was my burden to bear. However, I felt commanded to share my newfound wisdom. Unfortunately, exposing all your shortcomings doesn't make people stronger. It gives them an excuse to be weaker. They ignorantly tell themselves that experience is the best teacher! That's a cliché enslaving the multitudes! Ultimately, all those around me will find a reason to fall because of my words from the heart instead of using those same words and excelling.

I regretted sending that letter to Tracey. I hoped she'd never think to find it. I prayed she wouldn't reveal my secret. Nonetheless, if she does, I'm prepared for the challenge. Daily bearing the agony of leaving my beloved Wilhelm lets me know I wholeheartedly can endure anything.

Visions and Dimensions

Wilhelm and I are riding home from the hospital, and he's asleep. I'm thinking, *Wilhelm, you've already missed the entire first month of 1913! Wake up!*

I'm staying with him for a few days … or for as long as he needs. Once we arrive, I tap him so that he can walk himself inside.

"Wilhelm, we're home. Wakey wakey," I softly say into his ear.

He slowly opens his eyes and gives a chilling gaze. He doesn't speak.

"Are you well? Shall we return to the physician?" I ask.

He gives a look of annoyance as he shakes his head no. He immediately exits the car and quickly enters his home without waiting for me to accompany him. I send the driver away and enter, but Wilhelm is gone. While calling his name, I see one of his servants. Her name is Tilly. I ask her if she's seen him.

She answers, "Yes, Miss Clara, but he specifically asked that he not be disturbed."

"I'm sure he's not pertaining to me. Where has he gone?"

"He has gone to his bedroom, Miss Clara, but I'm certain he has requested absolutely no one is to disturb him!"

I pat Tilly on her shoulder to ease her anxiety. I'm solely here to care for Wilhelm, so it's impossible he doesn't desire my company. I instruct her to make tea and then bring it to his bedroom. She nods and then heads to the kitchen.

It's early in the afternoon, yet the halls seem dark and cold. The comfort and coziness I would usually feel walking through the halls and corridors feel dismal. I feel an uneasiness as I approach Wilhelm's bedroom door. I lightly knock and then walk inside. I see him staring at himself in the mirror. I softly call his name, but he's unresponsive. As I slowly walk toward him, I realize he's whispering very fast. I reach out to touch him, but he immediately stops speaking. He turns to face me.

Agitated, he says, "I told Tilly to make sure I was not disturbed!"

"Tilly told me so, but surely, you desire my company! I'm here to watch over you as the doctor requested."

"I am well. Please leave."

I want to plead my case, but he gives me this piercing glare that makes me afraid. I look away and ask, "Do you need anything before I go … to a guest room, I guess?"

"No. Good day."

I glance up, but he's still glaring at me. And as soon as I walk out, I hear him lock the door. He stays in his bedroom the remainder of the day.

It's now morning, and I'm in the dining room, ready for breakfast. Everyone is working in silence. I see Tilly, so I follow her. She's headed toward Wilhelm's bedroom. She is sprinting. I shout to stop her.

"Tilly! Is Lord Wilhelm coming to dine this morning?"

Tilly quickly turns and motions for me to keep silent. She runs toward me, grabs my arm, and then escorts me down a hall away from Wilhelm's bedroom. Frantic, she whispers, "Miss Clara, Lord Wilhelm is not well! I pray, and I know something evil is with him!"

Baffled by her accusation, I ask, "Why would you say that, Tilly?"

Tilly seems terrified, but as she goes to complete her thought, Wilhelm comes from around the corner. He seems jovial and excited as he kisses Tilly's forehead.

"Good morning, ladies. I am starving. What happened to you last night? I thought you were supposed to watch over me while I slept?" Wilhelm says, hugging me as he escorts me to the dining room.

I glance back toward Tilly. She's standing in the middle of the hallway with a blank stare, gazing into Wilhelm's room. She clutches her rosary beads and uses her hands to do the sign of the cross, and then she enters.

"Wilhelm, you put me out of your room! You weren't yourself at all last evening! I think you need to go back to the doctor."

"Are you mad? I feel great. I did feel strange the first few hours, but after resting in my own bed, I feel fine."

Wilhelm is back to normal, so I didn't mull over his unusual behavior the night before. And I definitely didn't mull over Tilly's religious antics.

Berkshire studios booked an American tour that he has to be on in a few days. I choose to overlook everything bizarre because I don't want to dampen his moment of bliss. I assume I will travel with him, but I'm not invited. My heart is broken because I want to be anywhere Wilhelm will be, especially since he'll be gone for months. Nonetheless, his desire is being fulfilled. I focus on my work and give him his space.

After his departure, the first couple of weeks, Wilhelm called me every night. After a month I only heard from him weekly. However, by the third month, I couldn't find Wilhelm. Approximately four months later, Wilhelm returns home. However, he only comes to see me via my urgent request. He has exciting stories to tell. America is in love with him as we knew they would be, but Wilhelm is different.

I'm awakened in the middle of the night to find Wilhelm sitting in the chair by my vanity. I turn on my lamp and then rise to tell him to come back to bed. Strangely, I'm unable to wake him. I watch him all night, but there's nothing I can do to get him up. It's now eleven in the morning, and I feel as if I need to call a physician. Worried, I begin dialing the doctor. Then suddenly, Wilhelm stands up.

"Oh my God, Wilhelm! You've been in a coma since midnight! You have to return to the hospital!"

He shakes his head no as he grabs my hand and leads me to the bed. We sit down, and he begins to share his heart.

"I am not sick, Clara. Nor am I in a coma. I am having visions of a different dimension. I know I sound insane, but I am not. I have had a life-altering change. Remember when I told you I desired to stay as I am today forever? Well, I accomplished my goal."

His story is beyond reasoning. I'm speechless as he tries to tell me what he has experienced. His story is very vague as he gives outlandish accounts of dismal dimensions that hold his corrupting body while rejuvenating his living being.

"I do not expect you to comprehend me, but you must believe me. I am only revealing my secret to you because I care for you, but I will probably have to leave you soon."

"Leave me? Why? I don't understand anything you're telling me!"

I love Wilhelm very much. The people only see this phenomenally gorgeous man, but I see him differently. He looks attractive, but he has a direful disposition. I thought Wilhelm was perfect, and I saw no flaw in him. Today he's so perfect that he looks flawed. I thought he possessed the most inviting dark deep eyes, but today his eyes are deep, dark, and menacing. In the past his eyes were enticing. They're now intimidating and frightening.

His conversation that wooed us and his intellect that used to stimulate us has turned. Now he rarely engages in conversation. If he does speak, it's more of a lecture than dialogue. Making love is now wearisome for him, and whenever I ask to see him, he's so cruel. Wilhelm was never froward toward me in the past, but now his new character often leaves me hurting.

"Clara, I am no longer physically attracted to you. Do not take it to heart. I am not attracted to anyone in that way anymore. I need women for other reasons, and I do not want you to be used to fulfill that desire. Believe me. My rejection is a kindness."

We were never lovers again. I would see him in town periodically with women, and it was killing me slowly. Although we weren't intimate anymore, I still desired to spend time with him.

He'll be returning to the States to tour for another ninety days or more. I beg him to please spend time with me before he leaves. He doesn't want to. Nor does he hide his feelings. Thankfully, he finds a glimpse of mercy in his heart. He comes to see me. We eat and converse, but I'm not there with Wilhelm. This heartless man I have spent this evening with is not my Wilhelm. Still, I love him so much. I need him to embrace me and show me affection.

After dinner, he moves to the couch. Seemingly, he's taking a nap. I walk over and begin to kiss him. He appears lifeless, but I continue kissing him. I kiss his cheek and then look up. His eyes have opened, but they're not Wilhelm's! I jump back and then call out his name.

"I own your soul," he softly and calmly says.

I feel paralyzed from shock as he keeps repeating, "I own your soul." He then begins speaking in an unknown language very softly. Still, he won't stop staring. I close my eyes and weep. I hear him moving, so I look up, and I realize he's standing over me. He lifts me up and then begins kissing me aggressively. My fear instantly leaves as I passionately kiss him back.

"No!" he yells as he shoves me away.

"Please, Wilhelm! I love you. Tell me what's wrong."

"Why won't you do what I tell you to do, Clara? I do not want to hurt you! I will be gone in a few days. Please leave me alone, and I will visit you once I return from my travels."

"No, Wilhelm! I won't endure your mistreatment. If you cannot respect me any better than you have in the past several months, it's best we part ways!"

"Thank you! That is what I have been trying to tell you for months! Finally, you are not behaving like a silly fanatic. Let me go! Find contentment without me! Maybe we will meet again in the future, but today's decision is for the best."

My heart is crushed. I stand there in disbelief, sobbing as Wilhelm simply shakes his head and gives me a disdainful look. He leaves.

I continued following Wilhelm's career, but he has put it on hold. I see him, but he doesn't see me. I secretly follow Wilhelm. I witnessed him court Mistress Constance. She went mad. Then Wilhelm was supposedly gone. It was rumored Mistress Constance's child was his. However, that rumor was quickly dispelled. Constance died after giving birth to her daughter. Lady Helena immediately annulled any plans of this child living with or ever seeing its biological father. Lady Helena seemed obsessed with this child. We thought it was due to her grief over losing Mistress Constance. Shortly after that, we heard rumors of how Lady Helena needed this child to return Wilhelm to the Berkley family. Of course, the latter story seems most logical.

Lady Helena is a unique breed. Although I'm devastated by losing Wilhelm, I'm sure my pain will never outweigh her misery. This was the only time I hoped Lady Helena's desire would be fulfilled.

Periodically, I'd see Wilhelm, but I never revealed to anyone I knew he was here in Britain. I didn't want anyone to know because he was in hiding. Despite our breakup, my heart was still very much with him. My faithfulness to him has not changed.

He was here for Earl Alistair's funeral. No one knew he attended, only me. I continued to see him for approximately ten years before he was gone forever.

I am now a fifty-year-old woman, but Wilhelm was still that young, handsome man who captivated all who encountered him. Once he became a legend, many stories circulated about Wilhelm. However, I'm the one to reveal our beloved Lord Wilhelm York never ages and that he's still seeking his one true love. I hope one day he'll find her. I see a vision of him in love, and it makes me happy. Wilhelm's happiness was all I ever truly wanted. Thus, I envision daily that he receives it, and it gives me peace.

In the Spirit of Wilhelm

I called Minister Antonio to hear where he's been and how he's been doing. After a brief conversation, he suggested dinner. I see him waving to get my attention as soon as I enter the room.

Hugging me, he says, "It's so good to see you, Regina. I really have been missing the fellowship."

"And we've been missing you. I'm not just being kind. We love and miss your presence."

We order our dinner. Then we share our hearts with each other. Antonio admits he was more committed to Peyton than his clerical duties, and I admit my infatuation for Maurice. He tells of his encounter with Wilhelm's lawyer. I tell him that same detective called, but I wasn't compelled to respond. I elaborate on how glad I am I ignored him. After we catch up on the past, we begin to speak of our experiences with Wilhelm.

"Regina I really don't know how to feel about everything that has happened. I try to make sense of what we've all experienced, not just Peyton. Although she's the one he's chosen, somehow I feel we were all affected."

I agree because Antonio's right. It wasn't until Wilhelm came into Peyton's life did we learn the deep-rooted truths about anyone. We'd fellowship or worked with one another, but we never allowed ourselves to build real relationships. Every relationship was conditional and restrained. Everyone missing is gone without any explanation or anyone close enough to ask.

Where are Casey and Maurice? Where are Attorney Pharris and Maureen? Why hasn't Tabitha come out of her home in months? Where are the Scotts? But most importantly, where is Wilhelm? They're missing persons, but the police have told us to accept all are probably deceased.

Antonio and I sit silently for a few minutes. The only sound is our forks touching our plates and the ice hitting the glass as we drink our beverages.

I think of all the concealed hatred, jealousy, and lies that were once among us. At that moment I decide to expose my secrets.

"Antonio, because we're building a real relationship, I have to tell you the truth."

He abruptly stops eating to give me all of his attention. I take a deep breath, and through a now shaking voice, I say, "I have known of Wilhelm."

"What do you mean?"

"I'm Wilhelm's real estate agent."

I have been Wilhelm's agent several years now. Vaughn approached me a few summers ago and asked if I could sell real estate in the luxury property market. He was a very attractive man in his late sixties to early seventies. He was average height. He still had all his hair. It was salt and pepper, but it is well-groomed and shiny. He always looked as if he had just come from vacationing on an island somewhere. Even during the winter months, he was nice and tan. He had gorgeous blue eyes that seemingly were always smiling. Initially, I thought he was attracted to me. Because of my faith, I wouldn't get romantically involved with a married man. However, his attraction was strictly business. He was very proud of his family. He had three sons and two daughters, and all were lawyers except his youngest son. However, they all worked at his law firm. And he absolutely gushed over his wife of fifty-two years. He seemed very wholesome and trustworthy.

I was a struggling agent. Vaughn not only helped me become a luxury property agent, but he also equipped and assisted me in selling a forty-three-million-dollar estate in California. Vaughn's client's commission changed my financial status forever. The money from that sale allowed me to start my own real estate office here in Burlington. I never met this client. Nor was I given the client's full name. All I knew was Vaughn called him Will. After that transaction I had no connection with Vaughn. Then a few weeks before Wilhelm moved from California to Vermont, Vaughn approached me. He informed me he had another client from out of the country who desired a secluded home in Vermont. I knew his people were extremely wealthy, so I saw Vaughn's return to my life as a blessing. I quickly found several multimillion-dollar estates to show Vaughn's client.

Vaughn informed me there was an abandoned estate near the mountains that Will wanted to purchase. He explained Will Yoorker would come to my office tomorrow. Then he and I could go from there. However,

Will never showed. I didn't know him, but I had seen him that very day, unaware of his identity.

Peyton and I were conversing on the phone. I saw her walk into the coffee shop, so I called to tease her for coming into my neighborhood without dropping by to say hello. I entered through the back of the same shop as she was leaving. I watched her get into her car as I joked with her. However, I noticed a black Maybach parked at my office. I was certain it was Will. I left my coffee on the counter and ran outside, trying to stop him from leaving. I ran across the street and called, "Mr. Will Yoorker!" But his eyes were fixed upon Peyton's car. In fact, he jumped into his car and followed her. Immediately, I called Vaughn to tell him my dilemma since I wasn't late. Vaughn called back the following day to inform me that Will wanted that estate in the mountains. Although that property had been empty for decades, it still sold for fifty-five and a half million, so I was content.

After seeing Wilhelm those few seconds, I couldn't get the vision of him out of my mind. I hated he left because I wanted so desperately to meet him once I saw him. I called Vaughn, hoping he'd insist we meet, but Vaughn had someone else fill out all of Wilhelm's paperwork. The home was purchased under Earl Alistair Estates, not even Wilhelm's name.

The night Wilhelm took Peyton from Tabitha's estate, I knew it was him. I gave a sigh of relief simply because I saw him again. I was so elated to walk over to him, although we had purposed to burn him. But then in a flash, he was gone again.

"Antonio, I wanted to tell you that night I thought I knew him. However, because of my connection with him, I didn't want to defame his name just to later learn I was incorrect."

"It's okay. Please finish!" he anxiously responds.

"I went home that night, distraught. I didn't know what to do. You, my parents, and our pastors were calling me, trying to figure out what was going on. For some reason, I just couldn't expose what I knew. I had to meet him before I turned him over to be persecuted. My miracle was seeing Peyton tell the authorities his name was Lee. I was so happy her demon wasn't my client. The reality is that Will Yoorker has sustained me these past few years.

Every time Peyton or Casey mentioned Wilhelm's name, I wanted to say something, but I just couldn't. Oddly, I was committed to his secrecy beyond reasoning. However, that miracle of Wilhelm's concealed association with me was short-lived. A few months later, Officer MacAleese called to inquire about Wilhelm Yoorker. I told Officer MacAleese that I never met him, hoping the officer would bring about a meeting between Wilhelm and me. Unfortunately, Vaughn stopped that from ever happening. Vaughn called and told me to shun Officer MacAleese, and if he ever returned, I was supposed to call Vaughn immediately.

Then Vaughn found out I knew Peyton. He was desperate to convince me to turn her over to him. He had all these unflattering stories about her and Wilhelm's lascivious lifestyle. Fortunately, she really was lost to me, which kept me innocent of any information regarding her whereabouts.

Vaughn revealed some disgusting things that I couldn't believe. However, what caused me to keep those secrets was my abhorrence for Casey. Also, Vaughn's accounts were too detailed. There was no way his accusations were true.

Vaughn told me about the first time he saw Peyton alone with Wilhelm. "I had no idea who she was. She and Wilhelm flew to Washington together. I had purchased him a very secluded estate, yet for some odd reason, he allowed the neighbors to still use his beach. I sent a car to bring him home, and this woman's with him. I know not to look at his kills, so I avoid looking her way."

"Is it to your liking, Will? I ask him.

He leans over, whispering into her ear. She nods. He then answers, "Yes. It's perfect."

"Excellent! Well, I need to go over some important information with you. May we have some privacy?" I ask, merely glancing her way.

She's wearing large shades and a lacy white sundress that's grazing her ankles. Her hair is combed back but beautiful and long. Wilhelm whispers to her again. She simply nods again. He then leans in and kisses her lips. She pecks his lips back. He stands, now gazing down at her. She then removes her shades, caresses his face, and then gives him a passionate kiss. Uncomfortable, I turn my back toward them. It's quiet, so I still can hear them kissing. I glance back and see Peyton heading upstairs. Wilhelm watches her as she walks away, still gazing his way. Intensely watching her, he says, "Pharris, we will finish this later."

I roll my eyes up to the top of the stairs where Peyton has stopped. Frowning, I say, "Wilhelm, this is very important."

Still gazing up at her, Wilhelm says, "Bye, Pharris." He then heads her way.

Hours later Wilhelm still hadn't contacted me. I needed more information on her to take to a pertinent psychiatric hospital and then back to Vermont before the end of the following business day. I'm attempting to ensure this abduction looks legitimate.

Nine that evening I return to the estate. I assumed by now Wilhelm would be alone, ready to discuss her death as well. I walk inside, and the house is totally dark. I then decide to go into the kitchen and call Wilhelm to inform him I'm here. As I head that way, I notice a light flickering in the great room. It's the fireplace. I enter to see if he's there, and he and Peyton are there having sex. There is a huge amount of open space in the room. The fireplace is to your right alongside the couch in the middle of the room. I can't see their nude bodies. I simply see the back of Wilhelm's head and shoulders. Peyton is on top. I guess she sensed my presence. She opens her eyes and looks directly into mine. My being there did not move her any. She watched me momentarily and then closed her eyes and proceeded with what she was doing. I quietly left, totally embarrassed.

The next morning I call from my hotel room. Wilhelm answers, "Good morning, Pharris."

"Will, I have to get back to Vermont ASAP! Do I need to send anyone out to clean?"

"I am well. How are you, Pharris?"

Sighing, I reply, "I'm good, Will, but I will be better once I have your affairs in order."

"I do not need anyone to clean. I can handle this one myself."

"Oh? Okay, well, I have two hospitals that are willing to cover for us—"

"The information we have already given the Vermont authorities should suffice. The Scotts' son is on the force, so relax. If anything starts brewing, he will let you know, right?"

"Yes," I say and huff.

Pharris gives a few more accounts that seemed as unbelievable as that one. I didn't know Wilhelm, but I knew Peyton! She would never be lewd and unrestrained in front of any of us, let alone a stranger! I could tell Vaughn had his own motives. Destroying Peyton's reputation was a scheme he conjured up to get me to talk."

Antonio is listening in amazement. I drop my head. Then I begin to cry.

"Why are you crying? It's not your fault. Don't take the blame for Wilhelm and Vaughn's wicked actions!"

Wiping my nose with a napkin, I look into Antonio's trusting eyes and then say, "Antonio, you haven't heard my secret yet, but please forgive me in advance."

Vaughn called me after I left Tabitha's the night Peyton permanently disappeared. Casey returned me to my car, so I was headed home alone when he called.

Nearly whispering, he says, "Regina, Will and Peyton are at his estate. Go there discreetly and see what they're doing."

I followed Vaughn's orders without hesitation. Vaughn informed me shortly after Wilhelm's purchase of his estate that Wilhelm had paid me double the commission of his property to keep his anonymity. I had involuntarily became his new employee.

I arrive at Wilhelm's estate. It still looks abandoned. I see his car parked up front and the door of his home is open. I sneak to the entrance. I see him kneeling in front of the fireplace. Peyton suddenly closes the door. I quietly hurry to the window. I see Peyton on the floor, and he's on top of her, aggressively doing something, but I'm not sure what. I see blood, so I cover my eyes and crouch down so he won't see me. I slowly rise to peek inside, and I see a black spirit hovering over Wilhelm and Peyton. This shadow begins to expand until it covers the entire room. What I'm witnessing is so frightening yet fascinating that I'm captivated. Wilhelm's now still as he and Peyton lie on the floor, lifeless, this darkness pulsating over their bodies. I'm unable to move. I watch Wilhelm interact with Peyton for two full days.

The last day I witnessed this darkness try to enter Peyton. The room was saturated with this shadow, and it was forcing its way inside her. Wilhelm yelled, stopping it. Instantly, this mega room covered in blackness merged with Wilhelm. Then it became a blinding light. He lay motionless next to Peyton for several hours.

Hours later Wilhelm rises, and his skin is glowing. He looks clean and refreshed. He walks to the full mirror and examines himself. Once he's done, he lifts Peyton's body and hurls it as hard as he can into the burning fireplace. He then squats in front of it, watching her body burn.

The smell is rancid, but I only run because now I'm horrified. I run to my car hidden in the trees and attempt to sneak off. As I go to back up, Wilhelm appears in my rearview mirror. I won't run him over. I stop, and he enters my car. As soon as he gets inside, Vaughn calls. Wilhelm motions for me to answer.

"Has he killed her yet?" Vaughn asks.

Gazing into his limpid eyes, I answer, "Yes, Vaughn. Peyton is dead."

I hang up the phone. I'm entranced, looking into Wilhelm's eyes. He gives me a warm smile. Then I wake up. It's now late in the evening. I notice Wilhelm's car is gone. I go inside his mansion, and it's clean and swept.

I return to my car to call Vaughn, but my phone's dead. I plug it up to charge and see I have sixty-six texts and voice messages in all. I look at my dates, and I realize I've been unconscious for six days. Now I don't know if what I saw really happened. Maybe I dreamed this. I calmly drove home, showered, and then slept soundly. Once I woke up in my bed, I concluded I wanted to meet Wilhelm so badly that I dreamed I had. Then I felt at peace responding to everyone's calls.

Dumbfounded, Antonio asks, "Why would you conceal this all this time?"

"I don't know, but I believe Vaughn's trust in me connected Wilhelm and me somehow. I believe Vaughn was secretly training me to be Wilhelm's covering. I knowingly embraced the call, and as a result, Wilhelm's spirit embraced me."

Antonio is speechless. We finish our dinner in silence. I pay for the bill. We hug and then quietly part ways.

I Feel Free

Wilhelm's home is darker on the inside than it is outside. The moon is our only light. Wilhelm appears somber as he escorts me inside, and then he leaves me by the door, unattended. I know he's daring me to try to run. He's now lighting the fireplace. I stay standing next to the front door, which has been left wide open. I don't close it or ask if he wants me to close it. I remain still as stone. Finally, he tells me to lock the door with his back still toward me. I gently shut it and move to the front of this massive foyer. After Wilhelm lights the fireplace, he kneels in front of the flames with his head hanging down. He then says, "Come to me."

There aren't any words to describe my fear. Terrified, I slowly walk toward him. "*Hurry up!*" he yells.

I collapse where I'm standing. He stands, turns, and then rushes me. I feel a sharp pain in my chest as I mentally drift away. I can't hear or feel anything except my thoughts. I begin to think upon my friends, my church, my life, my soul.

The first night Wilhelm took me from Tabitha's, I learned he owned the penthouse where the New Year's Eve party was given. Maurice's company had rented it for the occasion. It was stunning, but it didn't feel as if anyone lived there. The entire house was probably fifteen thousand square feet. The room of the party had royal blue damask walls with grand chandeliers. It looked very regal.

I remember waking up, lying on a purple velvet lounge chair with an ottoman, and looking up to a very high dark blue cathedral ceiling. I instantly sit up and see Wilhelm serenely sitting in a chair across the room, intensely watching me. I'm now in a frenzy. I jump up, knocking over the chair, flipping it on top of me. Again, I quickly jump up, almost kicking over this heavy mahogany table next to me. However, it's nearly unmovable. My knee is now bleeding, but my adrenaline is so high I feel no pain. I'm in a moment of madness as I cry, looking around. I feel as if I'm in another world!

Wilhelm slowly stands, and instantly, I fall to my knees, moaning in terror. I cry out, "Jesus!" and then start praying in tongues. As he drew closer, I stood and tried to run, but I slipped in my own blood. I fell, almost hitting my head on the edge of the door molding. Thankfully, I put out my arm, and it hit instead. Still I feel no pain. The closer he got I went into greater hysteria. I then faint from fright.

I wake up to him lifting me by my arms. I'm now hyperventilating as I choke on my saliva and mucus. He just blazingly watches me.

Frantic, I ask, "Where am I? Wilhelm, is that you? Am I alive? Oh God, I'm dead!"

He very calmly responds, "Yes, it is me. Why do you think you're dead?"

"If I'm going to turn into a demon, kill me?" I groan out.

"A demon? Why would you turn into a demon?"

I don't answer. I tightly shut my eyes and start shaking my head from side to side rapidly. I'm praying, hoping, and wishing that this is a nightmare and that once I reopen my eyes, it'll be over!

He then calmly says, "Peyton, you watch too much television. I am not a mythological creature. I'm real. If you want this to go well, act sane."

I look intently into his eyes as he gently sits me on the couch. Now sitting with a blank stare, I lose my ability to speak or even think. I fear I'm going insane. He runs me a bath and then tells me to undress. I do as I'm told, but I'm mentally gone. Now sitting in this marble Jacuzzi bath, I gaze into space trying to make logical sense of what's happening to me. The only visible signs of life in me are my heaves to breathe.

"Peyton? Do you need me to help you?" he asks.

I ignore him, but then he starts undressing. Instantly, I snap out of my trance and start slowly washing up. However, he still gets into the bath with me. I look up at him, eyes squinted, shaking my head.

"I don't understand what's happening to me. Why is this happening?" I mumble in a perplexing whimper as I keep searching my surroundings, unable to grasp that this is reality.

He then touches my face. I flinch. He caresses my arms and then pulls me close. I refuse to look at him. I'm trembling and crying as he gently kisses my lips.

After one peck I breathlessly pant out the words, "Why … are … you … doing … this?"

"Shhhh," he whispers.

He moves in between my thighs and then gently uses his body to push my body to the edge of the bath. He then starts making love to me. I had never seen a naked man in the flesh. Wilhelm's body was beautiful. His skin tone was a golden beige all over, not one blemish. I had to brace myself by holding on to him. His body was smooth and supple. I could feel every muscle and curve in his thighs, arms, and back as I held on. I wanted to hate it, but I felt so guilty and ashamed as I allowed myself to get lost in this passionate moment. Being in that penthouse with Wilhelm was unexplainable. Most moments I was scared senseless. Then in other moments it felt so right being there with him.

It seems as if all I had to do was confess my love. Maybe then Wilhelm and I would've come to an agreement. What would've happened? Would my friends and acquaintances still be alive? I really wanted to try my luck and see what may have been the outcome, but I already knew the outcome. Wilhelm killed anyone he found offensive and not submissive. My days were always numbered, and today confirms it.

Today he wants me dead because I never told him I loved him, but what would have tomorrow brought if I had told him my feelings? I believe Wilhelm truly wanted me. However, the history of his life reveals once he conquered anything, he was on to the next new thing. Wilhelm's problem wasn't solely my lack of love for him, but he wanted to rule over me. He wanted full control of everything and everyone in his world. He already had something ruling over him, and he hated it. He never acknowledged it, but tonight he exposed it to me. It was beyond dreadful. My only concern now is that I die speedily.

I'm awakened by Wilhelm violently shaking me. I hurt terribly all over. I barely open my eyes, and all I see is a blurred vision of red. I feel wetness all over my body. I'm sure it's my own blood. I let out a hearty sigh and then close my eyes. Again, I'm drifting into unconsciousness.

Faintly, I hear Wilhelm having a conversation. In desperation, he's begging for help. I hear whispers in some forsaken language. Then I feel totally submerged. I'm being brutally attacked all over my body. It feels as if I'm being smashed into a wall. I want to scream, but I haven't any strength in me to even whimper. I lie there, throbbing in pain, being crushed like a bug. Then I hear Wilhelm scream out, "No!"

The sound of his voice begins to echo throughout this large empty mansion. It sounds as if his voice is being bounced from wall to wall in different sounds, pitches, and voices. Then immediately, there's a calm. The pressure is lifted off me, and I can hear clearly. I feel Wilhelm sitting next to me. He's weeping. My heart's breaking because his cry sounds so genuine and innocent. I want to comfort him. I attempt to move, but that's the wrong course of action. As soon as I flinch, he attacks me.

I fell in love with Wilhelm, but wisdom surely constrained me from ever telling him. Wilhelm wanted my love, but he wanted control more. He wanted to control God! And he believed he could! So who was I in this fight? I was some weak female distraction he figured would eventually submit to his will in life or death. Imagine everyone you ever encountered easily submitted to your will during your entire existence. Then you meet me. In your mind I'm some scrawny, religious fanatic who has the audacity to boldly reject you! My will and servitude to his enemy was a spit in his face!

My love and submission would've taken him to another level! I don't know how he and his dark partner operate. Nor do I desire to know. I guess in his world it meant victory. I wholeheartedly thought it was my love he desperately needed, but I, too, was deceived. Although I wanted to give him all of me, that small, still voice hidden deep within me kept me from destroying myself. Today I am more than thankful.

The comprehension of life is complex. We see terrible people blissful and loving people suffering. We see wise people disrespected and fools being honored. We see children starving and dying but the greedy living and prospering. If we only believe what we see, then this life is surely horrible and meaningless.

I love Wilhelm because he's a believer beyond belief. I, too, am a believer. Wilhelm and I are so different, yet we are the same. He has a power living inside of him just as I do. And Wilhelm sees two worlds just as I do. We both possess two different sets of eyes. We can easily see the impossible as possible. We have both willed our beliefs. It's the war of the wills! And as life would have it, only one will wins.

I come back to consciousness, and tears begin to flow. Wilhelm leans in close to me. I sense his presence. I can smell his scent. I feel his warmth. I hear his heart beating. I feel my spirit departing. I know my life has come to its end, but I'm glad Wilhelm has come to see me leave. I can't open my eyes because that part of me has shut down. My body is dead. Only my brain is functioning in my last few moments of this life. I hoped I could see his face one last time. Thankfully, I can still envision it.

I see Wilhelm. He's standing at the counter of the bar at that exquisite gala. He has on the most elegant jet-black tuxedo ever created. He wore a deep, dark midnight blue bow tie. His tie matched his eyes. They were mysterious and overwhelmingly beautiful. He stood tall and majestic, and I knew from my first glance that his seraphic image wasn't simply a look.

I was content being single because I wasn't interested in your average, everyday romantic love. If I couldn't experience it in the way I fantasized and desired it, I didn't want it! Then I saw Wilhelm. His engaging stare revealed to me he was the only living being who understood my interpretation of love. My first kiss with Wilhelm in that crowded room gave me life. Hearing his enchanting voice call me beautiful and telling me how much he wanted to see me captivated my soul. In a matter of minutes, Wilhelm owned me. I loved Wilhelm the moment I saw him. But did he really love me?

I smile inside because I feel Wilhelm's breath against my ear. I hear him panting seemingly from exhaustion, and then he whispers, "I love you."

Those are the last words I hear. I exhale, and then I leave. Amazingly, I feel happy. I feel peace. I feel light. Then I feel … free.

I Remember: Me

I was every parent's dream. And if I needed one word to describe my childhood, it would be *joyful.* I was my parents' pride and joy. I was my uncles, aunts, and grandparents' delight as well. If I lacked anything, love definitely was not it.

I was the talk of our community and city since I was a child. I possessed a special gift everyone I encountered proclaimed. Throughout my school years, my teachers always spent a little more time with me. They sensed how special I was. I have always been brilliant, full of charisma and persuasion even as a very young child. I could equally persuade girls and boys … and then men and women to do whatever I asked.

At times I felt sorry for my parents because people were constantly telling them what they needed to do with me. Others always assured them these were merely suggestions. Truthfully, the people wanted to ensure my parents did not let my magnificence go to waste. Nevertheless, my parents gloried and gloated in pride. They were beyond proud I was their son.

In my adolescent years, I was just as awe-inspiring if not more. By the time I was thirteen, I had met the prime minister and the king. My gift of beauty and wit has gotten me much favor.

Young love was fairly easy and manageable. However, once I got into high school, my mother begged my father to have me homeschooled. Not only did I have problems with my female classmates, but often my female teachers would attempt to seduce me. I found it amusing, but my mother found it treacherous. Eventually, my mother got her way because the school had to diffuse too many scandals, but not because of me! I was a good boy. School was for learning. I was just as intimidated by women as the next teenager.

I did not defile myself with women until I got into show business. I was an adult on my own with no supervision. Hence, I ran wild. Still, I was no wilder than the next guy. I was a young man doing what the average young man does. My newfound fame may have attracted more women, but I was still only one man. My advantage was I had more women to choose.

After I became a superstar, it was rumored that I felt superior to my father and sought someone more dignified to raise me, but that was a blatant lie. I absolutely honored my father. He was the wisest man I ever met. However, because of my allure to the masses, my father chose Earl Alistair to groom me and make me into a gentleman.

He determined Earl Alistair had the wisdom to guide me and prepare me for my future status. I had excelled my father's status so young. Thus, he sought me out a worthy mentor to aid and lead me into the next phase of my life. My father chose wisely because Earl Alistair loved me unconditionally. Supposedly, his own son despised me, but Earl Alistair did not care. He had found his successor in me, and immediately, he started grooming me for greatness. He adopted me and engrafted me permanently into his lineage.

Earl Alistair hated I was an actor. He thought that career choice was beneath me. He feared I would be enticed into drugs, alcohol, and promiscuousness. Earl Alistair wholly convinced my father he was so stern because of his care for my well-being. However, I soon learned that was untrue.

As a child, he loved me as my father, but as I became a man, he seemed to have unnatural affections toward me. The few months I stayed under his protection before I was adopted into his family, he hated to see me with women. I assured him I was not intimate with the ones visiting his estate, and I constantly had to remind him I was never intimate with Clara under his roof. Seemingly, he despised Clara as the women despised her.

This particular day Clara comes over to visit. We decide to go out for lunch.

"Ms. Clara Derby again?" Earl Alistair says and huffs.

Clara looks at me from the corner of her eyes and then frowns.

"Earl Alistair, please respect Ms. Derby, or I will stop everything. I am only doing this out of respect for my father. I do not need you to be great. I am already great. In fact, remember, I am making you greater, not the other way around. So please remember why I am cooperating. This is only for my father, nothing more."

"Is she a worthy woman, Wilhelm? Does she even fear God? That's my sincere concern! I won't sit back and let some filthy, underprivileged woman defile you! Your father requires I do this! I must adhere to his wishes as well!"

"If Ms. Derby is defiled, it is solely due to me. I'm the only corrupt thing in her life. Are you satisfied?"

Earl Alistair stands vexed. He then replies, "If she were a decent woman, you wouldn't have to say that!"

I walk toward Earl Alistair. I'm now in his face, observing his mannerisms. He seems more nervous than Clara was the first night she and I became lovers. I lean in and softly say into his ear, "Your heart is showing, sir. Conceal it better, or I will never return here again."

I stand up taller with my eyes transfixed upon him. I can see the fear, humiliation, and desire in his eyes. I stand grimacing in anger and repulsion for a few seconds more. Then Clara and I leave. Earl Alistair made sure to keep his affections hidden from that day on.

I was not into drugs and alcohol, but I did get caught up in the women. Oh, the women! They would not leave me alone! It was a temptation that hunted me relentlessly. My parents and Earl Alistair hoped and prayed I would find a way to flee them. I comforted their concern by telling them I still upheld my moral standards. They had to holdfast, believing they had taught me well.

Once I was Earl Alistair's heir, my acting career changed. I was now a lord. My royal title gave me much more prestige and authority than my peers. Seemingly, I was considered highly above a mere man and slightly beneath God. Everywhere I went, people were in awe. My presence caused every other event of importance to cease. I was naturally intelligent, but now my words were worth more than any other that was present. If my philosophy or opinion was known, that became the new truth.

Initially, I was never haughty but extremely grateful for this wonderful life. I never despised the lot I had been granted. Every goal, dream, or desire I sought, I found and received to the fullest, and I was thankful.

My respect as a lord was excelling as my celebrity status began fading. Therefore, I purposed to take my talents to the States. Just as I started here and then became royalty, I had resolved to accomplish the same in America and abroad.

There are kings, queens, emperors, monarchies, prime ministers, presidents, powers in high places, and many more titles for every country's leaders. However, I knew I could become the first true world leader, period. My traveling the world and receiving the same honor and respect everywhere I visited allowed me to see I could be that tie that binds.

Being famous was a hall pass in every country. Thus, it was the vehicle I purposed to use. It seemed as if Britain was too small to contain me. It was time to break free, time to move into my destiny!

All was going as planned until I decided I needed to remain youthful in order to accomplish this goal and still be revered. How could I be the first to conquer this thing called life if I was old and dying? I would be the first and last to accomplish this goal. Frankly, there is only one me. I was certain there would not be another like me ever. The world easily could see what I have known my whole life. I was born to be immortal. I was one of a kind, a freak of nature, an anomaly! I would have failed everyone had

I allowed myself to become old and perish. Many people would have dreaded seeing that day, especially me. Many only saw me as their god.

I still give the illusion of beauty and godliness as I stroll along the beach in my linen island gear. Those observing will never notice I am a walking corpse. I'm slightly exhausted, so I sit down at a cafe in Tahiti, and I remember … me.

My full name is Lord Stratford Lee Wilhelm York. I was born October 17, 1882, in Quilliam Hill, and since my childhood, I've wanted to be equal to God Himself. Once out of my coma, the news, community, and even the church is ignorantly announcing that I miraculously recovered.

Berkshire Studios had gotten me movie deals in America, although I was unconscious. I thought I was loved by many before my coma, but now I was seemingly worshipped by all! I am basking in my glory!

I have been traveling the world with Berkshire Studios. I have been busy at least ninety days nonstop. I finally get a day of rest. It is a perfect day in spring. I go out and find an attractive lady of the evening. We drink to the fullest and commit every sin under the sun. After our full day, we are in a luxury suite, now asleep in bed.

Abruptly, I am awakened by a distinct smell. It is a scent I have never sensed before. It is a good smell, but it's not like a perfume, flower, or fruit. I simply cannot describe it, but it is very enticing.

I begin to sniff the air and then the bed. I then realize it is my date. I just begin to sniff her. The smell is stimulating my hunger. I begin to lick her. She tastes prickly but not sweet. As I am licking her neck, she awakes, giggling. I then start licking her chest, but I want to taste her flesh. Suddenly, I bite as hard as I can and rip a plug of flesh from under her breast. She is screaming for her life. I begin to lick and gulp the blood coming out of her. It is sweet yet intoxicating like wine. She continues to scream, so I rip a chunk of flesh out of her throat with my bare hand. I calmly watch as she drowns in her own blood.

I attempt to eat her flesh, but I am not fond of the taste. I spit it out. I savor the blood, but like alcohol. You only need a little to satisfy you. That's if you are not a drunk. However, it feels and smells great. It feels like silk and thick cream on my skin. It has a tantalizing smell that cannot be compared to anything that exists on earth.

I am fascinated with her decaying body. I begin tearing it apart and examining it as I admire her ripping flesh. I must have enjoyed her dead body for a few hours. Then my fascination leaves. Suddenly, I am compelled to go to the mirror. I examine my blood-covered body. I am more handsome and youthful than I can remember. My skin is glowing and every imperfection I had no longer exists. My eyes are different. As I try to decipher the color, someone says into my ear, "Now you are a god!"

Startled, I quickly turn to see him, but he is not there! I know the voice. It was the young man named Lee that I met at the New Year's Eve party. After looking over my surroundings, I return to the mirror to examine my eyes. I then realize these are not my eyes. These are Lee's eyes. Lee was no young man, and he now resided in me.

I Remember: Lee

Who was Lee? Where had he come from? How did he even know to find me?

The depths of my heart's secrets were truly only mine. The only person I vaguely exposed my desires to was Clara. Sadly, she did not take what I was attempting to reveal seriously. She saw my cry as a modest assessment of myself and thought I needed encouragement.

If we could only read minds, what vastness of darkness we would find! Nonetheless, unlike Clara, Lee had somehow heard my heart and mind.

I once believed only God could know our hearts and how desperately wicked it is, but not today. I now realize somewhere in time our finite minds were deceived into believing that whatever we choose to believe magically makes it true. How idiotic is that? There are many beliefs, but we all know there is only one truth to every fact-based question that exists.

This constant analysis of the mind—my mind, my intellect, my soul, and being—led me to this conclusion of needing more knowledge and power. And no matter how I tried to find justification in my desire, I knew wholeheartedly it was a wicked desire. I did not want to remain to make this place many call home and even some call their final resting place better but rather to make myself more.

When was youth ever a requirement to make things better for the world? Yet so many of us covet youth and sexual vitality, yet most intelligently choose to have no children. Or they claim they are wisely choosing less children so that their children will have better lives. Oh, I see! It's all about the children. How special! I watched as person after person proclaimed they simply did what they did or do what they do for the betterment of society. What a bunch of lies spewing out of the mouth of liars! I chose not to lie and simply embraced my truth.

I had no life-changing experience, and I rejected anyone who tried to indoctrinate me with a so-called better way of life. I was born this way. I happily accepted my natural state of being. However, like so many others I never spoke these words. These are thoughts and desires never to be spoken out loud. These were the words festering in my heart that daily looked for an outlet where they could escape. Clara was my only outlet, yet her finite mind could not comprehend my complexity.

Clara was an atheist. Thus, our realities were extreme opposites. Because of her desire to constantly please me, she never confessed her disdain for God, yet unbeknown to her, it was our bond. Sharing my heart with her became wearisome. Our very last conversation on God was about the soul.

"Wilhelm, I'll never doubt what you've experienced, but—"

"But?"

Hesitant and now cautious in choosing her words, Clara answers, "Well, not *but* as in dismissing what you've expressed, *but* as in introducing another theory."

"Clara, you have given me a lifetime of frivolous theories. If you want to impress me, find the soul. Then I will be impressed."

"Wilhelm, you do not perceive that this soul so many are intrigued with is merely our intellect and/or emotions?"

"Am I emotional, Clara?"

"Not often, but you do possess them."

"Do you comprehend what I am asking?"

Dropping her head, she nods yes. I lift it with my knuckle. Now staring into her eyes, I continue, "I agree with you. The soul is connected to our emotions. That is why I need the intellects and scholars as yourself to present it. Once found, I will be the first to rid myself of it."

"Now must we discuss your devil? Most people's emotions see the soulless as evil or wicked."

"How do you see me, Clara?"

"I find no wickedness in you."

"Please expound on why."

"Because …"

She pauses, sighing. Slowly shaking my head through squinted eyes, I ask, "Because what?"

"Because I know in my heart you're simply not. I could never love anyone wicked."

"Clara, that's an emotional response. What does your intellect tell you about me?"

Now gazing into my eyes, she answers, "My intellect sees a wise man who isn't moved by emotion but rather by rationale and logic. I see someone who is an exemplary example for many."

Now lightly chuckling, I say, "Clara, you are a perfect candidate for God and the devil. You allow your heart to lead you, even though your eyes are wide open seeing clearly what is before you. An open heart is God's playground while a blinded heart is Satan's. Either will be pleased to have you."

Confused by my words, Clara says in a docile tone, "Wilhelm, are you mocking me? I don't understand."

"I would never mock you, Clara. I am simply sharing my heart. Even if you cannot see me, I desire that you at least see yourself. Stop denying what your soul knows. Rejecting it does not make you right or wise. It classifies you as a fool."

Stunned by my true but harsh words, she nods in agreement. I gently kiss her lips and then continue our day. After that debate we never discussed our beliefs again. It is then I accepted Clara's emotional soul would never hear me, but Lee heard.

By some miracle, Lee heard my cry from the depths of my soul. Lee not only heard and knew me, but he understood me too. Lee knew the urgency of my need and that I had run out of time. He knew that evening I needed to be changed desperately, or I would no longer want to exist. Lee's timing was perfect.

I was amazed at how Lee was this outsider who could see deep within me. However, the truth is that Lee was on the inside then came out of me. I wanted him to be seen. I wanted him exposed. Thus, he granted my wish.

Lee was me. He was the black soul trapped inside that wanted to be acknowledged. The Lee everyone was intrigued with that night was simply me. Wooing and mesmerizing the people is what I have always done. Captivating those in my presence was second nature. It was so automatic and effortless I felt as though I was not there with my date and my peers. I imagined a more engaging version of me was present and controlling the room. When Lee approached me after I shunned Helena, it was really my desperate heart saying, "*Enough! Follow me!*" My soul spoke from within and made me confess out loud who I wanted to be. And then I was free.

Willful or abject servitude was the question. I thought I chose willful, but in reality, I chose abject servitude. I had chosen myself over some benevolent entity. I lacked and rejected love equally. I was not willing to change. Thus, I submitted to everything within me that promoted hate and self-indulgence. My existence was all about me, and I never deluded myself to appease the masses like the majority does. Once I fully embraced me, I was rewarded help—the help from the other side of existence.

Many of us dream of how awesome it is to only believe in oneself. Whether I win or fail is all predicated upon me. I do not believe in miracles, fate, prayer, luck, or blessings! Everything I am and hoped to be depends solely upon me, me, and *me*! Saying it out loud sounds narcissistic and idiotic, but that is how countless others and I think and believe. If you do not believe me, read a book.

I believed I could live as I am forever, and I received what I believed. However, I could not do it on my own, although I surely wanted to. The delusional, self-sustaining individual as me usually stops at a point. Still, there are a few of us who take it much further. Once we reach this point, our independence is now dependent on someone or something else. My something else hated the life within others. Thus, as a trade-off, I killed to pay for my eternal life. The barter was life for life, youth for youth, and wealth for wealth.

Did I sit and have a conversation with this something and sign a contract? Of course not! Who am I for him, it, or whatever to reveal his true identity?

I went from being everything in the natural world to nothing in this dark world. It owned me, and if ever I decided I no longer wanted to be who I was, I would instantly become nonexistent. If my master and I never conversed, how do I know this? How do I even know my end is torment? How do we know anything?

The truth is naturally within us. We know right from wrong, good from evil, dark from light from inception. Truth is visibly seen through something as simple as creation.

Moreover, the more I desired, the more I received. However, each time the cost was greater. Parents, friends, no one, and nothing became more valuable than receiving this power I was granted.

For 102 years, I sacrificed for this power only for it to be subverted by the love of a woman. Peyton truly was the only desire I wanted more than myself. I decided to introduce myself New Year's Eve and change her as I had been changed. I wanted her to start the new year with a new life just as I did. And instead of alone, she and I would be together.

I remember the night before I approached Peyton. I was with Pharris, getting the final fitting on my tuxedo for New Year's Eve.

"You seem anxious. Is everything okay? Should I be preparing for a massive cleaning?" Pharris chuckles.

I am examining myself in the full mirrors surrounding me. The tailor is gazing behind me, smiling. I nod, letting him know I approve of his work. He nods back and then exits the room. I then glance back at Pharris and ask, "Anxious? How so?"

"I don't know. Seemingly you're not yourself today. You act as if you're preparing for a big happening. And what's it been? Twelve years since you've celebrated a new year. Last thing I recall is you telling me, 'What's to celebrate?'" He chuckles again.

Unmoved by his supposed humor, I say, "Tell me about your wife. How did you know you loved her?"

"Ha-ha! Today, I'm not sure I do. But all jokes aside, it's hard to explain. It's like once I saw her, I just knew. No woman's smile seemed as bright as hers. No woman's scent was as enticing as hers. No woman's conversation seemed as interesting as hers. I wanted to spend time with her only."

"What has changed?"

"Time and circumstances. But she's still that woman to me. I know I've done my dirt, but I would die without that woman."

"Why would you die?"

"Not literally, although some people do die when the one they love so passionately dies. However, what I meant is we're one. It's the great mystery of God, as some call it.

In many ways love is unexplainable. You don't know why you have to have this person, but you just do."

"Do you enjoy this uncontrolled emotion?"

"Uh, I don't know. I guess most times you do, but other times you don't. You wished you could be rid of it, but it's too strong to just let go."

I was conversing with him through the mirror. I now slowly turn to face him. I ask, "As a man devoid of love, what advice would you give me? Should I seek love or forever shun it?"

Looking intently into my eyes, seeking the right words, Pharris hesitates. He exhales and then answers, "You're perfect as you are. As wonderful as it can be, it can frustrate things."

"What are you saying? Love is not worth it?"

"To be honest, I don't know what I'm saying, Wilhelm. I guess I'll leave you with this. If it finds you, embrace it. If not, keep living as you are," he says and shrugs.

As scattered as Pharris perceived his thoughts, I heard him. His words let me know I had found love, and against my own will, I had somehow embraced it.

Pharris talked of how alike he and his wife were, yet once Peyton and I met, I learned she was nothing like me. She was so pure and so superior to this forsaken state that I would not destroy her. I tried to convert her when we went out to dinner for the very first time, when I approached her at her car, and then after the bed-and-breakfast. Still, each time I would not. However, the unadulterated truth I learned in my quest for Peyton was that I could not!

The deception of absolute power! I had been in this state so long I truly had come to believe my power was my own.

Once I purposed to destroy Peyton, my love for her overwhelmed me. I realized I did not want to live without her. It is then I decided I would make her as I am, but this being only needed one body. If I chose Peyton, I was rejecting my own existence. My sustaining entity would have to abandon me and reside exclusively within her.

My dream of living happily ever after was a delusion. A delusion I had wholeheartedly bought into just as the other billions of clueless people in this make-believe world. I thought I was superior in my thinking. Tragically, I learned I was just as blinded as the next man. There is no life everlasting or attaining exceedingly and abundantly above all I could ever ask or think on this earth! This place is a world decaying daily and destined for destruction just as I am.

I once knew the truth, but it was not satisfactory to my standards. Thus, I searched relentlessly to obtain this lie.

As I begged my demons to accept Peyton, I saw life exiting my body and a sure death entering hers. I cried out from the depths of my belly, *No!* And then I returned to myself.

Peyton had not only despised me with her lie, but she had caused my dream to turn into a nightmare. My everlasting hope of immortality and unrealized power she had catapulted into a temporary illusion! Single-handedly, she revealed my life was controlled by a magnitude of abject servitude and weakness! The thing I dreaded most had become my reality.

Peyton was right. Our meeting did have purpose. The purpose was to destroy me.

My thoughts subside. I begin to observe my surroundings. I look to see if I am actually still on earth because the people around me seem lifeless. I then see why. They're watching Peyton. Mrs. Scott has made headlines. The world news is reporting this world-changing story. Finally, Peyton's words seem credible.

Suddenly all goes silent. Everything is frozen in time. I now feel as if Peyton is speaking directly to me. They are replaying every visual interview she has ever done. The part where she calls me *it* keeps replaying. The foul words from her published letters are parading across the screen. The world now knows and has willingly embraced the lie. Seemingly I alone now know the truth.

I now know that the he who lived in me tricked me into defeating myself. He came not to empower me but to destroy me. He came not to give me more but to steal what I already had. He came not to grant me life but to kill me.

Instantly I begin to feel tormented. I block my ears and begin to wail and gnash. Then I collapse. My spirit has departed. I see my dark alter ego fly off as a flash of light. I then begin to descend into darkness.

The thief does not come except to steal, and to kill, and to destroy. I have come that they may have life, and that they may have it more abundantly.

—John 10:10

F. Vawters McCloud earned a bachelor's degree from Michigan State University and is mother to a daughter, Meena. She and her husband, Robert, live in Michigan, where they are active in ministry. Wilhelm is her debut novel.

Printed in the United States
By Bookmasters